# Macleay's Swallowtail

Christopher Donald Blake

Cataloguing-in-Publication details are available from the National Library of Australia

ISBN : 9780994622587

ISBN-13: 978-0-9946225-8-7

Published by Myrtle Forest Press

Book One

of

The Broken Man

# Contents

# PART ONE:  Chrysalis

*The stage of the life cycle of the lepidopterous insect where the secondary metamorphosis begins.*

# Chapter 1. The House Call

The track wound up the side of the hill into the tree-line. It was getting steeper. Steep and slick with the dew and the damp. Mountain mists and the veil of trees skirting the mountain, wheels spinning in the dirt on the corners and a spray of stone and gravel firing into the undergrowth, rattling the leaves. The trees were sombre, heavy green and pressing, marching down to him from the ramparts of the mountain, hemming him in.

The call had come to the watch-house late in the evening, in the darkness. He had decided to wait for the morning, for the light. Some messages were better delivered in daylight. But some journeys were best travelled at night. Locked in the tunnel of your headlights you could not see outside your own projection; safe in the cocoon of your own beam, the outside shrouded in possibilities only revealed by the dawn. The trees were crowding him now, shutting out the sky. The track was winding like a snake. He liked open land. Here too much was hidden. Anything could be lurking in these woods; ambush country. What a tale to have to carry, what a sick sad note. At times like this he hated his job. Hated himself and the lost horizon.

Then the track flared into a sudden paddock and a house sat in a clearing in the trees; a small house, neat and trim; painted weatherboard, a single stack and a straight veranda; early settler's, that's what the realtors would call it, reproduction nostalgia, with wood smoke smudging the porcelain sky. Only the parked truck spoiled the idyll. A corralled horse and perhaps a buckboard would have been perfect.

He parked self-consciously in the paddock, pulled at the creases of his uniform, and marched up to the house. Some messages were best delivered in daylight. An old man they had said; a recluse living out his last years alone with the bush and the sounds of silence. What a thing to have to tell him. Perhaps he should have come at night? Then he could at least have hidden in the shadows. He suddenly wondered if anyone would answer. His four-wheel drive would have been heard ages ago as it growled up the side of the mountain. It would be too easy to slip away into the bush and wait for visitors to give up and go.

The door began to open before he could reach out for it. A woman stood framed in the doorway, red hair falling in waves, and green eyes dancing with amusement. A beautiful woman, in her early thirties he estimated, and much too full of life to be with an old recluse waiting to die. Clean and fresh, like mountain air. No taint of civilisation in those eyes.

He found himself stammering and she welcomed him in.
"I'm come to see a Mr. Smith," he managed to get out at last.
"Oh, da," she said, a hint of an accent that he couldn't quite place filtering through her words, "O he's up on the mountain, walking the dogs. He'll be back by 10. I hope. He usually is. Barring sidetracks."
"Sidetracks?" he queried.
"Yes," she laughed, "sometimes something catches his fancy and he gets carried away. He likes looking for the Macleay's Swallowtail. It's the time of year now that they emerge. Have you ever seen one? Beautiful green they are, rare for a

4

butterfly. Once he even thought he saw a thylacine. Probably a feral dog, but he tried to track it all day. Ruined his lunch."

He tried to smile back but his mouth could only crack with the strain.

"Serious is it?" she laughed, "don't tell me; he's forgotten to vote. It can't be anything else, he never goes anywhere."

When he didn't reply she chattered on, charming him with trivia. He forgot himself, and his mission, and began to relax. Later, much later when he looked back and tried to analyse what she'd said, he realised it had all been a lot of nothing: empty chatter to fill the vacant day.

Then a dog barked to break the spell, a door opened and cold air rushed in to chill the room. The man didn't look as old as expected. He was straight and lean with grey hair fading to white, and eyes as grey and bleak as a snow sky over the mountains: cold eyes, dead eyes. Did he know already? He said something to the girl in a foreign language: some soft tongue completely alien. The girl shrugged, flashed him a smile, and turned and left the room. The old man stared through him.

"So officer, it is the boy, I suppose?" the accent now was harsh and grating, a shovel on concrete.

The policeman relaxed slightly; so he was expected after all. That made it all the easier. "Senior Constable Jones, sir," he introduced himself formally, "I was to break the news," he said simply, "It was supposed you would not know."

"I do not know!" replied the recluse, "I guess it is the boy. What else is there to break the peace?"

So he did not know, the officer cursed inwardly. So he would have to begin after all.

"I'm afraid he's dead, sir," the policeman spoke the words bare and blunt, without preparation, without preamble. How could you ever adequately prepare a parent for that? Perhaps it was easier coming from a stranger: a bolt from the blue?

The old man stooped, and sank into a chair. "So perhaps it is finished, now," he said quietly. He seemed to collapse and shrink in on himself, fading into the contours of the seat.

Not really, thought the policeman; now it got harder. "I'm afraid there are some questions I have to ask you," he said.

The old man stared at him, eyes like ice.

"We need to know if your son had any distinguishing marks," continued the officer, "any scars, or moles, or birthmarks? Or whatever?"

"I do not understand," said the old man carefully, brittle words rasping the air.

"We have the body," stated the policeman. Keep it simple, keep it factual, get it over with. "Circumstances suggest it was your son. But the body has no hands, no head. We cannot I.D. for certain."

"I would know him," said the old man simply.

"How long has it been, sir?" asked the policeman.

"Years," said the old man, "but my son, my only surviving son?" he left the sentence hanging in the air, swinging on the gibbet of absolute certainty.

"We were hoping that if we could tally any distinguishing marks, we could avoid the necessity of a formal I.D.," said the officer. "I am also authorised to collect DNA samples," he continued, "cross-referencing could confirm without more intrusion."

"I have to see him," insisted the old man, completely ignoring the last and clinical suggestion.

"I am instructed to arrange a flight for you to the mainland," said the policeman, "what about your daughter?" he underlined the assumption with a gentle query.

6

"No!" the old man shook his head firmly, "I have to tell her of course, but there is no need for her to see. She idolised him, did not see what he had become."

The officer let that go, in truth he would not want her to see. But of course there was more. "You are sure there were no distinguishing marks?" he seemed to be repeating himself, "no tattoos or anything?"

"I have said that I wish to see him," the old man was quietly firm.

"Yes, of course you can," said the policeman. Then he took a breath. Might as well get it all out, get it over with. After all, he'd notice when he saw the body.

"Your son has been mutilated, sir," he explained.

"No head, no hands?" the old man laughed, a cold laugh, soft and brittle, like rotten ice. "Is that a joke?"

"No sir," said the policeman, forced to explain, "It looks as though he has possibly been tortured. Parts of his skin have been removed as well."

"How thorough," commented the old man, in control once more, "You are certain it is him though?"

"Circumstances and documentation do indicate that probability," affirmed the policeman, trying to distance himself in formality.

Now that it was over, he felt sick. He mumbled some triteness, and slipped towards the door and the clean air. On the edge of awareness he saw her face wilt and crumple as she heard the news. How much it was sanitised he would never know. The words were foreign, but pain was universal. He was halfway down the mountain before he remembered that they had no phone and he would have to go back physically to arrange the flight. He would give them a day; a day and a night. They deserved that at least. Then he would go back.

7

# Chapter 2.   The Reception

He eased to his feet gently, levering against the edge of the table for balance. Just slightly unsteady, but not enough to notice – he hoped. Not that it mattered really, this was hardly a state occasion, and he was supposedly among family and friends. Surprisingly, he did not feel that nervous, but of course the drink had taken care of that. He had judged that perfectly, he thought smugly; just enough to relax the inhibitions and loosen the tongue, not enough to stumble and make a fool of himself; a man in control, as always. He straightened his tie, squared his shoulders, and cleared his throat.

No one took any notice. The babble of gossip and good cheer continued unabated. He banged his glass on the table, rapping it sharply like a gavel.

"Order, order!" shouted one of the in-laws. The cry was taken up by a series of voices, and chorused round the room, to die suddenly into serious silence. They all stared at him, all those eyes watching, waiting. The silence was almost threatening.

"Perhaps at this point I should ask the bride if this is what is meant by a pregnant pause?" he tried nervously.

They stared back at him blankly. He had meant a light-fingered touch but it had turned to ham anyway. Some of the elder female in-laws glared at him with hostility and disdain.

"Over their heads!" he thought, "should have known."

He stared down at his script, momentarily tongue-tied.

"Speech, speech!" the chorus started up again, "Come on Jonesy, come on!"

"Have another drink!" a sharp voice cut through the chant.

He sipped nervously and glanced fondly at his foster brother, slumped down carelessly beside him, red-rimmed eyes glazed and vacant.

"It's usual for a groom to ask his best mate to be best man," he began, "but as my brother hasn't got any good mates, or at least none brave enough to face down a shotgun, he had to ask me!"

"Ha-ha, yeah good one, Jonesy!" heckled the buddies from the back.

"It's also usual for the best man to make a speech in praise of the groom, listing his many qualities and virtues, etc. But in Guzzer's case, as we all know, that's rather difficult, because he has always performed his best work after dark!"

Another crackle of laughter leapt around the room.

His foster-brother rocked forward in his seat, as if to rise to the applause, but his body slumped again and folded in on itself. Young Gus, the accident that should never have happened. That's what the doctors had said, that Ma could never have a baby. That's why they had fostered himself. Gus's forehead hit the table with a resounding thud.

"Empty barrel!" called out one of the in-laws.

The best man stared at the ceiling, and rolled his eyes in mock despair,

"As we can see," he improvised, "he can't even claim the saving grace of being able to hold his drink."

A chorus of tuts, clacking tongues and shaking heads rippled round the room.

"I have it on the best authority that he only had a few beers last night!" he declared solemnly.

9

"Yeah, that was in the car on the way to the pub!" a roar of laughter from the back again, "it was the two bottles of spirits that cured him!"

He held up his hand once more. "But to continue," he went on, "Guzzer and I go back a long way, for of course we shared the same roof." He lifted his glass and toasted Ma. She glared back with that searching look, as if uncertain of what he was going to say next, and certain that she wouldn't like it.

"We've been trading punches since he was knee high to a potoroo, and although I'm the oldest by a good few years, and the biggest and ugliest, that never fazed young Gus. The first time he kicked me, I was sitting on Mum's lap, and she was six months pregnant. He's always been a sneaky little scrubber. The doctors said he was an impossibility; I've always agreed. Looking back I don't know how Mum coped. I know we must have been a handful because I've seen her wedding photos, and there wasn't a wrinkle or a grey hair."

A polite ripple of laughter greeted this. Ma glared at him again.

"But of course she's still beautiful!" A rousing cheer now, and the old bastard looked as though he'd won the lottery.

"Anyway, that's all water under the bridge. Gus and I are now best of mates. We stopped fighting years ago, when I left home to go to the Academy. If he hit me now, I'd arrest the little beggar!" another crackle of laughter.

"Any rate, that's enough of that. Even though I'm best man I've said enough good things about the groom."

"You've said no good things!" interrupted a heckler from the back, one of the gang of Gus's many buddies.

"That's what they mean by best left unsaid," he parried, and carried on. "I'll just finish up by saying that I'm sure we all wish him well," a roaring cheer thundered from the back, "and before we toast the lucky couple, just a word of advice from an older brother," he paused and cleared his throat, glancing across at the bride. "As we all know, the bride comes from good farming stock, so I'll just pass on these well-known words of rural wisdom that I gathered at the local oracle, that fount of philosophy and tradition," the hecklers at the back started genuflecting solemnly, as though sat for a sermon.

"No, I didn't mean the church, I meant the pub," he persisted. "As you all know I'm a bachelor, so I've never actually had to put this into practice, but I'm assured on the best authority – only two are divorced, the rest are widowed, self-inflicted I am sure........ Tilly," he turned to the bride, "show us your feet!"

The bride blushed furiously, and stared at him confounded.

"Come on darling," he coaxed, "we know you haven't been able to see them yourself for the last few weeks, but you can show us."

She sat there stolidly, scarlet in confusion. He tried again, the wags at the back chanting in support; "Come on Tilly, show us your feet!" He offered his hand and she grasped it, rising gamely at last. She waddled out from behind the table, and stood on the edge of the dais. Lifting the hems of her wedding skirts she gave a delicate flick to a white satin shoe.

"More! More!" they shouted, "Can-can!"

"Can not!" she shouted defiantly, and sidled back to sit down abruptly.

He waved down the chorus once more. "Keep her barefoot and pregnant, and she won't stray the paddock. That's what the elders at the bar said. As you can see, Gus has already done his duty on the second, perhaps if he can remember to keep her away from the cobblers, she'll be right."

A series of catcalls and whistles erupted from the back. The huddle of in-laws in the middle of the hall glowered at him angrily. "But what?" he thought to himself, "did they expect, marrying into a working clan: silver service and fancy manners?"

He gazed down at his foster-brother fondly, young Gus, the good-natured larrikin, no-man's enemy and every girl's friend. Well he at least on the surface had done well for himself, marrying into a farming family that were not just small-holders, subsidising a few hundred acres of pasture and scrub with casual labour and seasonal work. The old bastard kind of ran a local business as a jobbing carpenter and undertaker, but it was dying, and Gus did not have the aptitude. Tilly's family were wealthy, measuring their land in four figure hectares. Perhaps when they had finally forgiven Gus's indiscretions, they'd make him a manager, maybe even give him some ground for his own. At least Gus wouldn't have to follow in his own footsteps, and leave this shrinking community in the lee of nowhere, the mines getting worked out, the timber mill cutting back, the inevitable slow decline and exodus. A sudden sadness washed through him, a flush of nostalgia for his own past. But of course he had never wanted to stay. The impulse to leave it all behind had driven him. He shrugged the feeling away.

"A toast!" he cried, raising his glass, "to the patter of tiny feet!"

"Tiny feet!" repeated the roar from the back.

"Annually!" added a lone voice, and the reception crumbled into anarchy again, groups and gaggles of people gossiping and laughing. All except for the in-laws; they formed a sullen phalanx isolated in the middle, glaring hostilely round the perimeter.

Mum strode over to him, towing the old bastard in her wake. "That was a bit strong!" she said accusingly.

12

"Lord, mum," he said, "everybody knows, you can hardly hide it. It's better to bring it out in the open, make light of it. Can't pretend it hasn't happened."

"You could have given her family some respect!" she continued.

He grinned wickedly. "They're stuffed shirts, Mum, up themselves. Why do you think Tilly fell so hard for Gus?" young Gus, mellow and easy, all fun and no worries. "Any rate," he continued, "look at the bright side. Soon I'll be able to ask Clement that question that's been bothering me since Grandpa died."

"What's that, son?" his foster-father asked warily.

"What's it like sleeping with a grandmother?" he chortled.

A charge from the back rescued him from the blaze in her eyes. The boys surrounded him in a huddle, separating him from her anger. He could never resist teasing her, he realised, and wondered why? But now was not the time. The press of young bucks, Gus's mates, the local team, swept him away towards the makeshift bar at the back.

"Duty done, officer!" one crowed, "time to get wet again."

"No drinking on duty!" shouted another, "so you'd best get out of uniform!"

"Strip, strip, get 'em off!" called another.

"I'll resign the jacket," he offered, "but I insist on the pants!"

"Spoilsport!" they groaned and skittled his hat, but they did allow him his trousers. Mum's fault, he acknowledged; she had wanted him to attend in full uniform. Which was contrary really, since she had never encouraged him to join the force in the first place. She'd been inordinately proud all those years ago when he'd managed to scrape into a Teacher Training course at the university, and annoyed in inverse proportion when he'd dropped out, as she called it, to join the Police. But now she insisted on showing him off in public. He had rather have not. The uniform always separated you, creating that thin blue divide, even here, in the hometown. His jacket sailed up into the air, and curved away to disappear somewhere in the throng.

"Jeez mate, you look almost human!" chortled one of the boys.

"He's almost good-looking!" said another, "perhaps he really is Guzzer's brother?"

"Are you getting any?" asked another, "what are the women like down there then? Hot for a shot?"

"I wouldn't know," he admitted, embarrassed. "I'm too busy."

"Ah bull!" one roared, "traffic offences and chook rustling!"

"Bald tyres and buggering the sheep!" shouted another.

"Where's your gumboots then, mate?" the wagging continued. "In the boot of the squad car? Is it true what they say about a good ewe? She might bleat a lot but at least she can't complain!"

The roar of laughter almost overwhelmed him. Traffic offences and trivia – that's what they all thought of the country cop's lot. And maybe it was, most of the time. But not when the traffic offence was a smash at a crossroads, and you were on the scene before the medics had arrived. And during the long wait you had all the time in the world to wonder why, and consider justice? Because of all the casualties in the wrecked car, the dead boy was so young. It seemed the least fair.

"You all right son?" the question rocked him out of his reverie. It was his foster-father, somehow at his side, that wary look in his eyes, belligerence tempered with caution. Was that the power of the uniform? "Happy couple's about to do the off, best we see them out." Mum's orders, more than likely.

14

"I was going to have a drink, Clement," Jones said obstinately. He could barely bring himself to call him dad, but forever took refuge in the distance of formality, even though he knew the true meaning of the appellation, merciful, a misnomer if ever there was one. He could not even allow himself the abbreviation of Clem that everyone else used habitually.

"Plenty of time for that later, son, all the time in the world," Clem was always insisting on the paternal. Perhaps the façade was more important than perpetuating the lie: after all he had been fostered for so many years that reality might finally have become apparent?

"Come on, duty calls," Clem was at least consistent, he had never been flexible enough to back down, "Best not miss this, you've annoyed your mother enough today."

Yes you old bastard, sure, that was life, the essential paradox. Duty calls, but there's all the time in the world: to remember, or to forget? Even with all the post-trauma counselling he had had, he could never answer that.

He went anyway. Tomorrow he was back on patrol. After all, who had he done this for, not for himself surely?

\*

# Chapter 3. The Deer Hunter

He caught a hint of movement at the edge of the paddock, but could not be sure. It was a long way, maybe 200 metres, maybe more. He concentrated on the spot. A few seconds passed and then a deer stepped out of the scrub line and ventured nervously into the spring wheat, sweet and green and beckoning, near two feet high now. He pulled the rifle into his shoulder and tried to find the deer in the field of the scope. It took a few more seconds of fiddling, and then he had the lenses focussed and the deer in the crosshairs. It was a doe. He lowered onto its shoulder, and just behind it, and then relaxed. He held the rifle for a while in the prone position and simply watched the doe. It too seemed to relax, and lowered its head to begin to graze. He continued watching, content to lie there in the setting sun. Some rays caught the stainless steel of the barrel, and flashed in his eye. He blinked in reflex, but did not move. The radio crackled by his side.

"Take the shot, take the shot!" Clem, impatient and angry over the ether. The doe raised its head briefly, and then stepped further out into the paddock and continued grazing. The radio crackled again with an expletive. The deer raised its head again, catching something, but too far away to be convinced of danger. Jones watched mesmerised, his finger nowhere near the trigger. A shot crashed out from somewhere right and behind him. The doe froze for split second, and then spun and bounded for the tree line. Jones watched it disappear into the

16

scrub. Silence returned, but hardly tranquillity. The light flared for a moment as the sun died in the west and the horizon burst into a riot of flame. Then the embers faded and the light began to fail. The cry of a currawong fractured the empty air. He lay there completely still and empty himself, devoid of feeling but waiting for the twilight to hide the remains of the day. Time passed at its own pace, and then Clem was upon him. His approach as always silent as death, expected somehow but with no warning.

"Christ old man!" Jones swore, a rare moment of blasphemy that the old girl would never have tolerated. His stomach twisted and the fear kicked in.

"Don't you 'old man' me, boy," cursed his foster-father, "I can still take you."

It was true of course; the old bastard always had that effect on him. He involuntarily clenched his buttocks and fell into paralysis, too scared to stand, too frightened to run.

"Why didn't you take the shot?" Clem complained. "You were nearer than me. I was out over 300."

"Eyes failing or the tremors of senility?" Jones mused hopefully on intimations of mortality, but he did not dare say it out loud. "It was a doe," he proffered an apology of sorts, if not an explanation.

"They're the best eating," said Clem, "your mother's favourite. You know she loves a roast. Now you've disappointed her again!" the voice icy with contempt.

She was not his mother of course; it was all a pretence. But it still hurt, all the same. Criticism did that to him, salt in an open wound, but he had learned long ago to hide.

"Don't know why you ever bothered to buy that thing?" Clem was on a roll now, relentless, "Stainless steel? Might as well flash a mirror on a hunt. Look at me, look at me!"

17

"I'll get you some camo tape," Gus had joined them now, "You can wrap the barrel."

Jones thanked his foster-brother out of politeness, but it did not matter. He had bought the lever-action because he liked western action shooting at the local club, but only at targets. He had got the Marlin .308 Express so that he could go long-range. It was more of a challenge for a shot of his calibre. The gun was not exactly authentic, but no one at the club complained. He had no intention of killing any animal. He never had had, but Clem once coerced him into shooting a rabbit when he was a boy. He had gut shot it and the rabbit had screamed like a baby. Then Clem had made him skin and eviscerate it. Inside were five or six kits, he was not sure of the exact number. He had been too upset to count properly.

"He's a good shot, Pa," said Gus, trying to reconcile the breach, but missing the point and inevitably making it worse. "He could have taken it if he'd wanted."

That was true actually. Jones was a very good shot. He had trained for the Special Operations Squad, and had passed, but declined at the last moment. The only thing he ever managed to despatch with any regularity was fish, but they did not scream. He knew he was incapable of killing a person in cold blood. His resignation, or rather lack of follow through, was another sore point with his foster-father, another failure to impress.

They trudged back to their ride empty-handed and in silence, even the usually irrepressible Gus. By the time they had got back to the vehicle twilight was darkening into the fullness of night. Their vehicle, or Clem's to be precise, was an old Landrover half cab.

"We'll get some wallaby," said Clem, "I'll not go back with nothing! You two get in the back, shoot over the cab. I'll drive."

Jones did not want to, and Gus looked as though the inevitable hangover was beginning to catch up with him, but neither dared say a thing. Clem drove them to one of the big open paddocks in pasture. He stopped at the gate and stared out into the gathering gloom.

"Don't see no sheep," he announced, "but I'm not sure about steers?"

Clement was losing it, reflected Jones, once he would have checked in daylight before the hunt began. Or maybe he had been relying on a deer? The danger of expectation was rejection. But steers were a real problem. Black Angus could be lethal in the dark, almost invisible, an accident waiting to happen. You would be upon them before you could see them. If you hit one the sheer bulk of it would demolish your vehicle, and woe betide the occupants. Clem passed out the shotguns, one pump and one auto, both illegal unless you had a special permit for pest control. Jones had never dared to check it out.

"I'll drive out to the ridge of the hill, before I turn on the lights," said Clem.

Then they were off, hammering into the dark. Fear washed over Jones in waves; lack of control terrified him. Gus yodelled like a banshee waking and the old bastard pounded on the roof of the cab from inside to shut him up. Funnily enough though, Clem was a safe driver, if anything about driving a paddock in the dark with no lights could be safe. A rock or a wombat could flip them, just like that. But nothing ever had, in all the years of killing. Then the rover bucked over the crown and main beam flicked on and they were roaring down a tunnel of light in the outer darkness. Red pinpoints glowed briefly as eyes lit up in the beam.

"Sheep!" shouted Clem out the cab window, "Hold your fire!"

Once a drunken Gus had shot up a donkey for a stag, some hobby farmer's escaped pet going where the grass looked greener. Grey shapes ghosted through the dark.

"Wallaby!" yippeed Gus as he opened fire. The roar of the 12 gauge thundered through the night. Jones just clung on for dear life as the half cab bucked and reared through the darkness.

"Just reload for me!" Gus swapped guns and continued the barrage. Bodies buckled and writhed in the beam. The noise seemed relentless, deafening.

"Hare!" shouted Gus and Clem gunned after the weaving animal. Gus blazed away but the hare jinked and twisted, hardly slowing.

"Out of ammo!" shouted Gus pounding on the cab roof. "Let me down, let me out!"

The cab screeched to a shuddering halt and Gus tossed Jones the gun and leapt out and continued the chase on foot, empty handed. Clem accelerated off again, Jones once more clinging on like a leech. Gus was sprinting in the beam now, legs pumping, arms akimbo. He was gaining on the hare. It was insane, a mad nightmare out of an impossible dream.

"That's my boy!" screamed Clem, then Gus suddenly threw up his hands and collapsed in mid-flight and crashed to earth, the drink finally winning the race.

"Your turn!" screamed Clem, "Relay, take the baton." He braked again and Jones leapt down, too surprised to argue. He sprinted after the hare, nearly out of the range of the beam now, but his foster-father was accelerating again.

"Go, go!" he heard over the roar of the engine, and he was flying through the night, his feet barely touching the ground. He too was gaining, and he got caught up in the madness. At the end of the paddock the hare hit the fence and fell back stunned. Jones was upon it before it could scramble upright. He caught it by one hind leg and held it up, not knowing what to do. It kicked and clawed at his arm desperately, and began that terrible tearing scream. Jones froze. Somehow Clem was with him, and he grabbed the hare with both hands, head in one, hind leg in the other. Then he stretched the body and broke its neck. The screaming died.

"Skin it out!" Clem handed him a folding knife, opened out the blade.

Jones nicked and ripped off the skin, too numb to argue. Then Clem took the carcase out of his hands and turned it slowly to inspect it closely in the light of the beams.

"One pellet through one lung, apart from that, not a scratch," he pronounced finally, "Miracles don't happen. There's always a reason. I knew you could never be that fast." No mention of Gus, no implied criticism of his real and favourite son, the eternal profligate.

They walked back to the Landrover and turned back to pick up the boy. Gus was still gasping on his back, a beached fish out of water. They picked him up and tossed him in the back. Then they went searching for bodies in the dark.

"How many did you hit?" Clem asked.

Jones shrugged, he had not fired a shot, but could hardly admit to that.

"Maybe a dozen?" he hazarded a guess at Gus's total.

"Two boxes of shells?" complained the old bastard.

He always expected a kill for every shot; no thought of excess, he would freeze everything down for the dogs. Gus had blown Jones out of the water again.

They gathered up the carcases and hung them from the side-rails. Then they motored towards the perimeter nearest the trees, but slowly this time, a sedate hearse, bloated with death. At the edge of the paddock they skun out the bodies, left the hides, heads, feet and guts for the devils to clean up. Once upon a time his foster-father would have kept the hides and cured them, but the market was gone, and in any case these skins would be too full of holes. But at least Jones did not get the blame for that, unvoiced anyway.

"Let's hit the pub," said Clem, "I could do with a wet."

It was more of an order than a suggestion. Jones did not want to go, but somehow the words permeated Gus's consciousness and revived him.

\*

Jones tried to wash up a bit in the toilets, but the old bastard went into the bar as he was, bloodstained and indifferent. Gus of course was pristine apart from grass stains. At the bar old Wally was regaling the audience with war stories, of a sort. He was eighty if he was a day, but had been too young to catch any real action. His basic training had been in the dying days of the war.

"Silly old fart won't lay down and die," that's what Clement said, but behind his back. He was always polite to veterans in public, even wannabees.

"I went hunting once at the end of the war," Wally said, "in India, on some rajah's private preserve."

"We weren't in India," said Gus, looking to his father for confirmation, and getting nothing but a slight shake of the head.

"The Brits were," said Jones quietly. Wally was an ex-pat. He hoped Gus would not stir the pot.

"A group of us NCOs" (Wally had been a Lance-jack) "wanted to go on a hunting trip, so we applied to the C.O for some recreation leave, and he teed it up with the local maharajah. Let us loose in his private park for a week: just a small place, about the size of Tasmania, mainly jungle, but with a few villages. C.O fixed us up with a couple of cooks, privates they were, to tend camp and fix the nosh. We went out on our own for a few days. Shot a few chital. It was jungle country mainly: hard work, no visibility. Then near the end we came back to camp one night and the cooks had gone on strike. Said it wasn't right that we had all the fun. So we agreed to let them go for a shoot on their own the next day, and we'd swap duties."

"Never knew the Imperial Army was egalitarian," interrupted Clement solemnly.

"We were NCOs, Clem," said Wally, "all rank and file together, not bloody officers."

Clement nodded his head and withdrew once more into silence.

"Anyhow, the next day the two clowns had a lie-in, and finally set off about ten in the morning. We could hear them shouting and calling to each other as they crashed about in the jungle. Hopeless. They would have frightened off anything within ten miles. Then about midday there's silence for a bit. Then all of a sudden there's a flurry of shots. .303s, you get to recognise them. Two full mags. We couldn't believe it, talk about amateurs and dumb luck! Anyhow, eventually they staggered

23

back into camp, totally whacked. They'd shot some wild buffalo and wanted us to go back and butcher it for them. Some cooks, couldn't even prepare their own meat! Anyhow we did a route march back through the jungle over their trail, and at the end of it there's a horde of angry natives. The bloody idiots had only shot the local village's sacred cow. It was nearly the Indian Mutiny all over again. We had to put all our spare cash together to buy off the headman to replace the cow. Most expensive shoot I ever bloody well went on."

A ripple of amusement rustled round the bar. "You ever hunt in Vietnam, Clem?" Wally shot the old bastard a loaded question if ever there was one.

Clement shook his head. He never spoke about the war.

"I saw a documentary once about Vietnam," Wally was in his stride now, "Some Yank base, somewhere in the jungle. A Vietcong sniper was up a tree shooting across the perimeter at them. So the Yanks put a plan together to get him. Called it Operation Batman or something. They got up the next day at 7a.m., had a big sit-down breakfast in the canteen, and then fell in. First of all they called in the artillery to shell this tree, and then a tank led the column into the jungle. The tank had to turn back because of the trees, so they continued on foot. When they got to the tree, surprise, surprise, the sniper was gone. So they dynamited the tree, so it couldn't be used again. This is in the middle of the jungle mind. Then the tree comes down on the head of one of the grunts. The last shot of the doco was of this fellow with a crease down his helmet, holding his head in his hands going, 'O my head, my aching head!' I knew then they'd lost the war. What did you think of them, Clem?"

Clement considered him in stony silence. The bar held its breath.

24

"Sounds more like a comedy show," Gus tried to clear the air.

"The septics were amateurs," Clement said quietly, "We never lost control of our patch."

"How's that?" asked Gus, game to the last.

"Tactics," said Clement simply. "The septics would always patrol to a routine. Armoured columns, radios blaring; same track, same timetable, same bloody stupid routine. If they weren't always stoned, you could have set your watch by them."

"And you?" asked Wally.

"Full kit, field rations, camo and face paint. Before we'd set out we'd jump up and down for five minutes to make sure nothing worked loose and rattled. Then we'd go out on wide patrol on foot, always a different route, always a new destination. No talking, full radio silence. No noise. We'd stay out 3 to 5 days, field bivouac at night. No talking at all, not ever, just sign language. We brought everything back out, wrappers, rubbish, even our shit in bags. We left no sign. No routine, no pattern. The Cong never knew where we'd be. They called us ghosts."

The bar was completely silent.

"No shit!" Gus at last breached the impasse.

"No talking!" emphasised the old bastard, "You'd have been well fucked, son."

A ripple of laughter broke the tension.

"Was that an attempt at a joke?" thought Jones to himself; his foster-father did not make them. But then, neither did he swear?

\*

That night he didn't sleep well, but kept slipping in and out of sweaty dreams.

Once in the small hours he woke to find his foster-father sitting on the edge of his bed in camo fatigues and backpack, his face smeared with grease paint. He looked impossibly young somehow, his hair thick and brown, no wrinkles lining the foundation of his face. But the eyes were old, aged beyond endurance. He reached behind and produced a package and unwrapped it slowly. Inside under layers of tissue and rubbish was a rotting wallaby skull. It smelled of faeces. The stink jolted Jones awake and he squirmed uncomfortably. He had soiled himself. He had not done that in a long while; not since childhood. He went to clean himself up and strip the bed. He finished up lying on the couch, waiting for the dawn. Sleep was a lost cause.

\*

# Chapter 4. The Collection

The sun was on his back warming the creases of his uniform as he walked round the side of the vehicle. It was one of those clear days with the light so fine that it cut the edge off distance and walked the mountains down to the paddocks. For a moment he breathed deep and savoured the view. The farmstead nestled in the valley bottom with the hills ranging behind, and the mountains a distinct blue against the green of the pasture. A line of willow and alder followed the course of the winding creek in front of the house. Relics of the European invasion, he wondered what natives they had replaced; paper-bark, swamp gum? He did not know and suddenly wondered why? A tractor stood orange rust and idle at the side of the house. Too stalled to ride off into the sunrise, or too tired? Wood smoke tainted the air above the chimneystack. That was a positive sign, he reflected. Meant they had kept the fire in. People on the edge of dissolution did not bother with trivia, did they?

The bailiff grunted at him in cursory acknowledgement. A large coarse man, well padded, armoured in the flesh against the emptiness of his soul. His companion, his employer, the representative of the bank, twitched nervously in the still air, the sheaf of papers clutched in his hand trembling ever so slightly. He looked like a rabbit, ready to bolt. So perhaps there was hope for him, a man who had mortgaged his decency beyond redemption surely would have the assurance of a predator.

"The bastard took a shot at me!" he whined, dispelling the illusion. He was merely terrified after all.

Jones stared at him without sympathy. "I doubt it," he said shortly, "Charlie's a good shot. He wouldn't have missed."

One of the farm kelpies barked uncertainly from the porch. The bank man glanced at Jones and flinched away. Could not even look him in the eye, let alone hold his gaze. The policeman sighed inwardly; there seemed to be too many sad days lately. A pair of black cockatoos swooped down in the line of gums shading the back of the house, their strident cries shredding the tranquillity of the valley.

"So what's the plot?" asked the bailiff. He yawned lazily into his fist.

"Dunno, lost it, I suppose," muttered Jones. The sky was so blue you could see forever. Tonight would be a good one to lie on your back in a dewy paddock and count stars and ponder the gateway to infinity. Eternity could wait until tomorrow; if tomorrow ever came.

He walked out into the open, in the middle of the driveway down to the house. He unbuckled his belt slowly, deliberately.

"Headquarters said to wait for the tactical unit!" squealed the bank man. His voice trembled on the octave of hysteria. "They'll send a trained negotiator!"

Jones swung out his belt by the tongue of the strap and held it with outstretched arm. The gun hung limp and heavy in its holster near the buckle. The weight of it pulled on his shoulder, dragging down his arm. It seemed to lower itself of its own accord, slowly and steadily into the dust of the track. Sunshine caught the back strap, and it glinted gunmetal blue in the light. Jones let go and the belt followed like a snake coiling down into itself. His arm floated up with the release of the pressure.

"Wait for the specialists!" the falsetto voice insisted, "I won't be responsible!"

Neither will I, thought Jones. Chaz was hardly a mate; he did not have any. But he did know him, and Steph, and the kids. Why should some dead shot outsider, trained to kill and over-armed have an invite to jeopardise that? This was his patch. He carried on walking, and raised his other arm, hands turned outward, empty. The sun behind him cast his shadow on the road. He realised that no matter how fast he walked he could never overtake it. Not unless he turned around.

"If you come any closer I'll shoot!" the voice echoed up from the house startling the cockies into flight once again. Jones shrugged and carried on. The sun was hot on his back; he could feel the sweat under his arms. Charlie shouted a tirade of abuse at him.

"Don't be stupid, Chazza!" Jones called, "shoot me and you'll lose everything; the wife, your family, maybe your life. The tactical boys are on their way. You know their reputation."

"You arsewipe!" screamed Charlie, "you frigging stiff-necked up yourself arsewipe. I've already lost everything. The bastards are taking the farm. I'm gutted, there's nothing else!"

Jones kept on walking. There was no shade. The sweat was trickling down his back now. "You can start again," he argued, "you've got back-up, you've got Steph, you've got each other, you've got the boys!"

"You come any closer and I'll shoot the boys!" He was on the edge, not up against the wall, but on top, and crumbling. Jones stopped. The farm kelpie found its courage and rushed at him, the hair across its back and shoulders standing up like a bristled comb. It circled Jones on sprung legs, taut as a bow with mad eyes and an incessant bark that grated on the nerves like galahs and a hangover. The shot whip lashed the air and smashed the dog in the gut. It turned wounded eyes on Jones and hauled itself away on its front legs confused and whimpering, its back legs dragging behind like broken wands. A woman's scream cut through the shock and Jones flung himself forward bursting into a sprint. One hundred and fifty metres and he tried to count the seconds but his feet were lead and time hung on the gibbet of uncertainty. One hundred metres and it was too long and he forced himself on, waiting for the bullet to finish the countdown. His lungs were bursting but the shot never came and he made the porch and shoulder-charged the door. The sound of a struggle drew him on and he smashed through the clutter and into the living room. Steph had Chaz pinned on his back on the floor by the window. She was astride his chest flailing at his face. The rifle was out of reach, flung across the floor near the sobbing kids in the corner. Jones bent down and removed the bolt. Then he went over and hauled her off him. She was spitting like a wildcat. He spun her round and caught her fists.

"It's over, Steph," he soothed, "it's all over. It's O.K. now. Go and sort the boys."

He pointed her in the direction of her offspring and turned back to Chaz. He was curled up on his side, sobbing like a baby. Steph returned and kicked him viciously in the back. "You bastard!" she hissed, "you didn't have to do that to Bonnie."

Jones removed her firmly. The boys came over and clung to her legs. Their eyes haunted Jones, wide and wounded, the death of innocence. He knelt down beside Charlie. "Jeez mate?" he asked, "have you just gone and shot the family pet?"

Charlie groaned and pulled his knees up to his chin. Jones coaxed him up. The farmer hung onto him and cried into his shoulder. Jones did not know what to do, what to say. So he patted him on the back and eased him to his feet.

"Come on mate," he said, "let's go to the kitchen, get Steph to make us a nice cup of tea."

An hour or so later Jones walked them out. He hoped the team had had the sense to move the dog. A boy swung on each arm, clinging to his fingers. They chattered excitedly; he had promised them a ride in his patrol wagon. Jones wished their parents were so easy to please. The bailiff stopped them at the drive's exit.

"I'll have to check the inventory," he tapped his clipboard.

Jones glared at him.

"Just doing my job, officer," the bailiff pouted like a mullet rising. Steph walked by with regal disdain, Charlie shambling alongside, a jerky automaton. The bank rep stuttered forward and flashed a sickly smile.

"I'm so glad it's turned out alright," he spluttered.

Bad publicity for the bank if it hadn't, thought Jones.

"Do you sleep well nights?" he asked quietly.

The bank rep flinched and looked away. Jones walked the boys up to his wagon. They scrambled in.

"Can we put the siren on?" said one little one.

"And the flashing lights?" said the other.

"All the way to grandma's," said Jones. He ruffled the nearest tousled head. Sometimes you win one, he thought; sort of. But where there's life there's hope. The tactical squad still had not arrived, one of the joys of rural isolation, the freedom from city sharpshooters.

No one had mentioned the dog. She must have crawled off into the scrub to die.

# Chapter 5.   The Proposal.

The call from headquarters did not say much. It was simply
an order to drive down to the city and present himself for an
appointment with senior officers in the afternoon.
Unspecified, just be there. It was a two-hour drive; they had
given him plenty of time. Plenty of time to worry over his
career, like a dog chewing on an old bone. What he might have
done, what he might yet do? Perhaps there had been a
complaint from that episode at the farm: unprofessional
remarks to a bank employee, or conduct unbecoming to an
officer? More likely it was reckless endangerment of police
property, namely his uniform. Or to attempt the positive,
perhaps he had been put forward for a commendation? But it
was an informal appointment. It was not promotional
procedure. Not disciplinary either, for he had the right to have
a police representative present. In any case he could not think
of anything else he might have stuffed up. He had a wide
patrol, but what was there to miss: small-scale rustling, traffic
offences, some drunk and disorderly, the odd battering? Only
once a case of incest erupting like a boil in the community.
And then there was that suicide, the sad man's perennial
choice, the bullet in the brain. No chance of second thoughts
there.  Only in this case it was a shotgun in the mouth. And
there was no one to clean it up. Certainly not the wife who had
deserted for the city, and bright lights and short nights. So it
had been left to him. Shotguns were very messy. All in a day's
work for a country cop. But mostly it was just out on patrol,

showing the uniform, being seen; the thin blue line winding through the paddocks, over the back tracks, and along the highways and byways; reminding the righteous of the safety of their slumber.

He tried to concentrate on the scenery to clear his mind. Usually the landscape invigorated or soothed him. But by now he was out of the high country and down in the valleys. Bare paddocks began to roll by in dreary monotony. The drought was still biting hard. Near to the river, or at least access to irrigation, the poppy fields waved gentle puce and soft purples in the breeze. The irony of it never failed to amuse him; outside the wide world rocked to the war on drugs and the war on terror, but here in Tasmania they grew opium for the pharmaceutical industry. Out in the open no less, paddocks and paddocks of it, no security apart from indifference; just hop over the fence and you could be into it. In the valley bottoms the air seemed to be holding its breath, another northerly building, getting ready to blow in from the mainland.

The interview room in the city station was functional and featureless, packed with stainless armrests and vinyl recliners, and seating faceless men in drab suits and tired uniforms. The walls were neutral in shades of grey. He thought he ought to recognise more than one of them. The island was small and the force had long since been rationalised. He had been out in the sticks too long. They said it was informal, but no introductions were made, and he could not relax. He sat on the edge of his seat like a store mannequin locked into place.

"Do you remember Mr. Smith, Senior Constable?" the interrogation began.

"It was some weeks ago," he declared, stalling for time. How could he forget that? How often in your career would one have the burden of informing a man that his only son had been dismembered, parts missing, whereabouts unknown? He could not understand their interest. What was going down? He had played it by the book. The old man had refused to fly, and said that he would only travel on the boat. Jones had even offered to call round on the daughter to check if she was all right while the old man was away. But she had asked him not to. She had said that she would make all the necessary arrangements for her father, and seemed more than competent, so Jones had put it out of his mind; no longer his problem.

"What do you know about Mr. Smith?" the questioning continued.

Not much, as it turned out. Of course the name had to be a giveaway, but then his own was hardly any better. In small communities folk mostly knew everybody else's business as well as their own. If not better, cause what they do not know they make up. He had sort of asked around after his visit, mainly to satisfy his curiosity about the daughter. He had not known of her. Had not known of the son either, for that matter. They had left before his time. All he knew of was the old man on the mountain. When he asked, people remembered the girl going to school, to the district high. But not the son, he was older. Very good-looking, so handsome it was almost embarrassing, and a devil with the girls, and older women. He was wild, they said, always a truant, always in trouble. He did not stay long after grade ten, ended up leaving for the big island, as some of the locals called the mainland. The girl was very bright, and went on to university somewhere on the mainland too and trained as a teacher. She was very quiet, and made no friends. The local kids used to call her the 'Spacegirl', because all of a sudden she would appear out of nowhere, and then disappear again, only turning up occasionally in the holidays. Story was she got a teaching job in the ACT. No one knew where the family was from; somewhere foreign in Europe because of the funny accent; refoes probably, from some war or foreign tragedy? Who knew, the tales grew exponentially in the country mill of gossip and rumour? The truth was buried in the past, and never talked about by the family, some private grief no doubt. There was no mother to the girl, so that encouraged suggestions of a martyred wife, and the old man still faithful to her, hanging on to her memories in the mists of the mountain. And he had to be rich too, of independent means, never having to work. Never having to farm either, nor till nor sell stock.

"So how many people knew him well?" was the next question.

Where was this leading?

"Seems like no-one, sir," Jones replied, and the truth of it hit him like a gust of wind off the mountain, cold and sharp.

"So where did he shop?" another interlocutor, another piece.

"He doesn't, sir," Jones explained. "He has a standing monthly order with the local store, arranged by the girl. They drop it at the end of the track. Pick up the cash from the mailbox. He probably shoots his own meat, a lot of the locals do, wallaby, rabbits, the odd deer? Unless he's a vegetarian? He does tend his own vegetable garden. Apparently he doesn't get much in the way of post either There's a regular monthly letter postmarked Canberra, with a typewritten address. It's assumed it's from his daughter, though on some occasions she writes by hand – they recognise her own handwriting. Mind there was a letter to him from the mainland a couple of days before he sailed. It was so unusual the postman mentioned it to me when I was asking around. Express delivery too."

"So this man shoots?"

"Yes sir, shots are heard up there occasionally, when the wind's blowing off the mountain."

"Make a note of that. Run a check through the Firearms Registry," this in an aside to a colleague. "So this man has been in the area for how long, about thirty years? And no one knows him? He's just become part of the scenery?"

"You do realise that we have a lot of vets up there," said Jones, feeling somehow that he was being accused of something, and wanting to defend himself, "on bush blocks round the lakes. Everyone respects their privacy." The community did in fact have a lot of tolerance for ex-servicemen; it was the continuation of a long and proud tradition. And of course trespassing could risk unnecessary confrontation, but he said nothing out loud.

" So this man has become an island sufficient unto himself? And survives? Does he talk to no-one?" the interrogation would not be diverted.

"I think not, sir, apart from the minister occasionally. The minister used to make a point of calling on him once in a while. Apparently he used to say that the man on the mountain lives closest to God."

"Used to?"

"Yes sir, gone north, to the mainland, a new mission."

"So it seems as though you are the only person who has had any recent contact with this man?" another question, another full stop.

"Yes sir, only briefly of course."

"But you have a clear recollection of him. You carry a clear picture of him in your mind?"

"Yes sir, of course," memorising the faces of strangers, overtly suspicious or just passing through, was one of a country cop's instinctive reactions. That was how you policed your district.

That and sticky-beaking into everybody's business, so you knew what was going down before it had happened, or occasionally, before it had even been thought of.

"So you could work with a police artist, and get together a good Identikit of this man?"

"Yes sir, certainly. Could I ask where this is leading, sir?"

"If you could just wait outside a moment, Senior Constable, we'll call you in a moment."

He paced outside, relentlessly grinding the passing of time beneath his heels, a bare corridor outside a closed room, the past behind him, and the future going nowhere. What was going on about that old man? A sad old man on the edge of existence, waiting to die. An old man who had buried his past, and now lost his future? And what of his own future? Where was he going? He had to face the thoughts he had had when he got that call to come here to the city. He had been in his district for six years and more now. It was time and past to move him on. Where would they send him? What did he want to do?

They called him back in, and this time they tried harder to get him to relax. His commander called him Jonesy, pressed him into his seat, and smothered him with bonhomie.

"You're not married, Jonesy?" he asked, as if they didn't have a file on him, on everyone who worked in or for the department, "you don't mind if I call you Jonesy do you?"

Jones shook his head and cracked a weak smile. What the hell was going on?

"Nothing in the wings either?" asked the commander, "nothing pending, no girlfriends getting serious?"

"No sir, kind of gets in the way of the job. You know, choices, career moves," he felt obliged to explain.

"That's good," nodded the commander, "very good. So there's nothing to stop you then. The thing is," he went on to explain, "I can't make this an order. It's in the way of a request. These gentlemen here," he indicated the two suits at the back, "are from the mainland. Inspector Andrews is from the Federal Police." The smaller and leaner of the two officers nodded bleakly at Jones, an expressionless face, with not the hint of a smile, pointed features, like a ferret. "They'd like you transferred over there for a while, all expenses paid. Indefinitely actually, until this business is cleared up. But it could be seen as a very positive career move. When you come back, it would look very good on your record for your chances of promotion."

Jones was stunned. "I don't understand, sir."

"It is quite simple, officer," the lean suit from the back enlightened him, "an elderly gentleman with no I.D has disappeared in our city. It seems you are the only person who can identify or recognise him." His enunciation was clipped and precise. A fastidious man, thought Jones, or was officious little prick the more apt description?

"I can work you a good Identikit, sir," he countered, "we've already discussed this. A missing person hardly warrants my removal to the mainland. I'm sorry for the old bloke and all that, but…?" he appealed to his commander.

"It's not that simple," said the suit, "this old gentleman, this recluse as you call him, has no records. No bank accounts, no passport, no record of entry into the country. No Medicare card. Nothing. On paper he does not exist. And now he has gone missing. This is very serious. On one level it is a question of national security. It undermines our whole system of government. We have to find this man to discover who he is, how he got into the country, and how he covered his tracks.

38

No mean feat in a modern democracy. It is a very disturbing scenario to a federal police officer. We must have someone on hand who can recognise him."

"He can hardly be a terrorist. He's an old man, almost a hermit!" Jones felt almost on the point of insubordination. "You want me to look at every face in the city, sir? So I might just recognise the one in three million that you want to catch up with?"

"We were expecting that you could work in our Missing Persons Bureau. It is a specialist department. I am assured that there are in fact fairly limited locations where a visitor could be expected to go. So we think we do know where to begin to look. But how can we look out for a man who doesn't exist? You are a trained observer. You saw this man in his own environment. You have a clear impression of his posture, his body shape and his face. That might just give us the edge we need to locate him."

"What about the daughter?" tried Jones? There must be other leads, another way that did not involve a personal upheaval of such dimensions.

"She's disappeared as well," said the other man.

Jones looked across at his boss. The commander confirmed, said he had sent a team to the homestead to check her out.

Behind my back, thought Jones.

"It is the middle of the holiday season," shrugged a suit.

"Contact her school," said Jones, "the one where she teaches."

"We don't know where it is?" said a suit. "Even which state. She could be anywhere on the mainland."

"The gossip says she teaches in the ACT," said Jones.

The suit took a note of that.

"Bank accounts, credit cards?" Jones stated the obvious.

"Maiden name of Smith," the suit commented quietly.

"Medicare card?" Jones tried to redeem himself.

"Disgustingly healthy, apparently," responded the suit. "Must have been all that mountain air?" A hint of sarcasm, did he think they were amateurs?

The commander asked him to go away and think about it. The suits pressed for a quick decision but they were overruled. Even if he said yes Jones would need time to pack.

He drove back to his station, whiling away the miles with speculation and questions. Something didn't ring quite true. They were expending a lot of energy for one old man. It was the age of terrorism, and a lack of identity might terrify a contemporary bureaucrat, but the old man had been around for so long. Whatever tricks he had used to bury himself were too far in the past to be of present concern, surely? And then he had another thought. They knew that the daughter had disappeared, and they had had the house checked without his knowing. That would have been easy to do when he was on patrol in the opposite direction. But did they know about the dogs? The old man had dogs and there was no one left to look after them. Which meant that the daughter must have taken them. Two, wasn't it? Two dogs on a plane manifest or on the ferry shouldn't be too hard to trace. It might give him a destination or at least a direction, a trail to follow.

It was late when he got back so he decided to chase it up in the morning. He was too unsettled to do nothing though, so he decided to utilise the evening to visit the retired postmistress, who still lived locally. She had been renowned as a gossip with all her fingers on the pulse of the community. He was wondering about that regular letter from the mainland. The current postmaster had told him that it never missed. Jones wondered how far back the delivery went?

The retired postmistress remembered it right from the very beginning, from when the family turned up on the mountain. So it could not have been coming from the daughter? When he pressed her memory, she brought up something else that was odd. Apparently in the early years the old man used to walk in once a month to cash a money order. It was always the same amount, $200, issued in Canberra by Smith to Smith. The postmistress surmised it was from an ex-wife or a relative. In later years the boy would come to cash it, and later still, after the boy had left, it was the girl who was the carrier. Nothing had been mentioned by the present postmaster, so Jones had to assume that whatever it was had run its course? But he was at a loss to understand anything. The postmistress had one more peculiar observation. She said she clearly remembered the girl doing very well at Business Studies at college, and was sure that she was going on to train as an accountant, so was very surprised to hear she had gone into teaching. The old postmistress could not shed any more light, and began to descend into rambling gossip about a past well before his time and interest, so he made excuses about another appointment, late as it was, thanked her and managed to extricate himself

In the morning, when he tried to track down the old man's dogs, he got nowhere. No pair of dogs had left the island in the relevant timeslot. Several singles but all booked out to different passengers. And none named Smith. There were many unaccompanied travellers going under the name, but none with the relevant home address. Then Jones reflected that she was probably travelling on a return ticket, which would have been booked out to her mainland address. Which of course he did not know, and certainly did not have the resources to find out if the feds could not. She at least would

41

have had a school and a university record. Would not that be enough for a start, for a computer search? He did not know; it was not his area of expertise. But he was thrown about the dogs. So he decided to drive out to the mountain just to check out something.

He did not really expect to, but he found the grave in a glade just inside the tree line at the top of the back paddock. It was at the side of the trail leading up from the house, and was ringed with stones, and planted with a cross and a bunch of withered blooms. Then he had to go back for a shovel. And then dig it up. They had been buried deep when he finally got to them, to keep them safe from devils probably. Two bodies, partly decomposed, but he controlled the urge to vomit. One black and white pied, and one brown, both shot in the back of the skull. Small calibre it looked, .22 rimfire? He wondered which one went first, and how the old man had contrived to keep the second quiet? Then he put them back and filled in the grave. There was little point in reporting it; who but the R.S.P.C.A would care? But it was then that he decided he would go to the mainland. He had to find out what manner of man would shoot his own dogs, and then lay them out tenderly in a well-executed grave?

*

42

# Chapter 6. The Acceptance

They gave him two days to settle in before he reported to the station. It was at least a day too long. He was not there as a tourist and he had no wish to see the sights. And cities could be so lonely if you knew no one, so full of strangers. So he occupied himself by finding reasonable lodgings within range of the station, and checked out of the hotel. He had an expense allowance but he liked the idea of meals and ironing being provided. It meant he could concentrate on his work. Get it over, get it done with, and get home.

And then he was left with time on his hands, so he hit the streets to try and get a feel for the place. The first thing he'd noticed on arrival was the smell. The air was full of traffic fumes and industrial pollution. The noise he could learn to switch off to, though sleep had been long in coming that first night. But that smell was offensive. It and the pressure of people wore him down, and he retreated into a café with a pounding headache, and sat at a window watching the world march by. So he decided to call in at the station a day early. He needed to be occupied.

Not only were they not expecting him, but also they did not even seem to want him when he had finally convinced them of his identity. He was shunted off to a side-room and left to stare at the walls. And he thought his presence had been deemed essential? Perhaps things had changed, perhaps the old man had come in or been found? Perhaps no one had got round to informing his superiors? The arrangements had taken time to organise. A lot could happen in a few days. He had just about persuaded himself that it was over, he was not needed and he could go home. Then a suit walked in, a tired suit with a grey face and lined eyes and hands that hung on slumped shoulders: hands with palms that faced to the back, closed hands in hiding. Jones introduced himself.

"What are you doing here? You're not supposed to arrive till tomorrow!" the voice sounded pained, like a hinge that needed oil.

"I'm all set, sir. Like to get into it. Thought maybe you'd want me on board as soon as possible," Jones tried to appear keen without sounding over-eager.

"Well I don't! Not today. Haven't you heard of timetables? Do you think we can just drop everything and fit you in? Take a tour. See the sights. Go sit and have a drink. Just….." the suit was waving him off, having none of it.

A braided head in uniform poked round the door and told the grey suit that he was needed at the desk. The suit swore, told her to sort out Jones, and was gone. Jones felt overlooked and discarded, like unwanted baggage.

"So what were your instructions, sir?" she asked, her tone querying the honorific, testing his rank. Actually it was irrelevant, him being from out of state, but he didn't let on: one advantage to being out of uniform. She looked bored and disinterested, as though she'd dismissed him already.

"The boss mentioned a tour," said Jones, "so you'd best show me round the station. And a drink, so we could maybe end up at the canteen."

"Ah, a V.I.P. are we, sir?" she asked sweetly, her nose in the air.

"Evidently," said Jones, feeling the need to be treated like one.

The station seemed a maze of claustrophobic corridors in a bunker without windows. The air was stale and recycled. He was looking through the cells after he had spoken to the watch, when he bumped into the suit again.

"What the hell are you still doing here, Constable?" hissed the suit, "Tying up my staff. I told you to piss off out of it!"

"Constable?" queried the female uniform with icy contempt.

"I was just about to get that drink, sir," said Jones, "I believe you recommended the canteen?"

"Smart-ass!" swore the suit, "you know damn well what I meant!"

Jones smiled blandly, "I was hoping to meet the team I'll be working with, sir."

"My team's too busy to be baby-sitting a country hick. Now get!" rasped the suit.

He got. Found a cinema, and buried himself in it for the remainder of the day. Tomorrow could be a fresh start. He hoped.

\*

He felt awkward going to work out of uniform. Yesterday was just an unplanned visit, casual clothes for a casual call. His reception in the morning was actually little better than the previous day. There were uniforms everywhere, but few plainclothes. Apparently the morning briefing had been and gone before he had even arrived. The day team had already hit the streets. Yet he had been on time, as always. Perhaps the shifts were different here? But they certainly had not had the courtesy to inform him. The duty sergeant tracked down a desk-bound detective, and dumped Jones on him. The detective stared grimly at Jones over a mountain of paperwork, his brow creased in concentration. He was a big man run to fat, now grossly overweight with a puffy face and piggy eyes almost buried in folds of flesh.

"I'll hand you over to Grabelli," he decided, "she'll take you under her wing." The fat man relaxed slightly and allowed himself a smile. "She'll like a bit of fresh," he grinned, "she's a honey actually, likes to swing and move. Do yourself a bit of good, and front her up. She likes a man to be direct."

"I'm sorry, sir?" said Jones, playing dumb, playing safe, "I don't know what you mean?"

The big detective sighed. "What I mean Apples," he said, "is that Grabelli is cock-happy and you've got a chance to get laid. Get off to a flying start. Score 1 in the big city. And it's a freebie! Use a condom though, you don't know where she might have been or what she's been up to, or down!"

Jones didn't know what to say? Did the fat man think him a fool? "Apples?" he managed to ask at last.

"You've turned bright red, and you're fresh off the island. Mind you look a bit sheepish. What else do you want me to call you? Ram?" the big detective laughed derisively, before choking off in a coughing fit.

Jones found Grabelli in an interview room running through the tape of a deposition. She was casually draped over a plastic chair in an ensemble that looked to be straight out of the pages of a magazine. She was not amused to see him either; especially when he called her by the name he had been given. She was fairly good-looking, he supposed, but hard round the edges: not at all easy on the gaze. Her eyes looked right through him.

"My name's Garelli," she said. "I suppose some slob back there fed you a line. So I'll make this quite clear. If you ever make any sexist cracks to my face I'll slap a harassment suit on you faster than you can blink. If you ever touch me I'll break your fingers. If you ever seriously piss me off you'll walk into my line of fire in the next situation we're at. That's if I'm ever unlucky enough to be teamed up with you. I trust I make myself clear?"

Jones nodded, she was clear all right. She obviously liked to exaggerate, but the message was clear: clearly a seriously uptight lady. But she need not have worried. "I never mix business with pleasure," he said. "Besides, you're not my type."

"So picky are we?" she backed off slightly. "Well you're not mine either. So who are you, and what do you want?" all brass and no protocol.

Jones told her.

"And you're a uniform?" she asked. "Sounds like a complete waste of time to me."

"The D.I who I met yesterday seems to think so," agreed Jones, "but upstairs has insisted, said it might give the team an edge. Could be crucial if anything breaks?" he shrugged. He certainly didn't feel particularly crucial, relevant, or even wanted at that moment.

Garelli stared him. "I almost feel sorry for you," she said, "you're like a sore thumb. A neat clean redneck! Even your casuals are ironed and creased. You got expenses?"

Jones nodded, hesitant. He wasn't sure how far they stretched.

"Not open slather," he said.

She appraised him critically. "Not open slather," she mimicked his seriousness. "You do realise you're now working for one of the most corrupt forces in Australia?" she shook her head hopelessly. "You'll have to learn to dress. If you're going to be on my team, you'll have to blend. I need a break. Come on, I'll take you round the boutiques."

Jones locked up, felt himself go red again.

"Humour me," she said, "Appeal to my feminine side. I love shopping. Come on, I'll sign us out."

He trailed behind her through the station like a lost dog.

"Good one Apples," said the desk slob, the fat detective, "First boundary to the country look."

"I see you're sitting on your brains again, Mulligan," she said, "Just remember not to flush when you go visit the little boy's room."

The fat man swore at her. She turned and wagged a finger at him.

"You got something to say, big boy?" she asked, "come on, let it all hang out. I've got a witness. I'll get that harassment suit yet."

Mulligan glared at her. "Apples wouldn't back you," he said.

"So you're a gambling man," she continued. "He's already told me what you said about me," she lied. "We're going upstairs to make a statement."

"His word against mine," blustered Mulligan, glaring angrily at Jones.

"If he had any balls," Garelli said to Jones, "he'd say it to my face."

She led the way out.

"Apples?" she queried at the door.

"I suppose it's meant as a joke?" Jones mumbled.

"I remember reading about apples in the Bible," said Garelli. "Eve picked one. That wasn't so funny!" She laughed hilariously

.

*

The D.I winced as a spasm seemed to flicker across his face. He bent forward and pressed a fist into his side.

"So what's with the fashion statement?" he asked. His throat sounded as dry as a saltpan in summer, the wind whispering with the heat. Jones wondered if he ever smiled.

"It was Detective Garelli's idea, sir," Jones felt guilty, all that money spent and gone, "so I don't look conspicuous, like a policeman."

"Jones," the D.I stared at him without expression and spoke very slowly and clearly, "this is Missing Persons. We check hotel registers, go knocking on doors, and circulate descriptions. We're high profile. We depend on the public's co-operation. People need to recognise us so they can talk to us. We try to look like police officers."

"Yes sir," Jones felt like a fool.

"Did you expect to go undercover and lie in wait? We're not after suspects, Jones. We are looking for victims."

"Yes sir," Jones repeated dumbly.

"What are you doing here, Jones?" asked the D.I tiredly.

Jones did not know exactly how to respond without further dropping himself in it. "I was invited, sir," he tried a safe option.

The D.I stared through him. "By who precisely?"

Jones shrugged noncommittally. Only Andrews had been introduced by name, and a mere inspector probably would not have had the clout to organise his transfer. Surely the D.I knew who was giving the orders? "Upstairs, sir," Jones suggested casually, "someone terrified at the prospect of a citizen with no papers. The Feds are involved."

"Bloody bureaucrats!" swore the D.I. He winced again and belched. The smell of rot and vomit drifted under Jones' nose.

"Acid stomach," the D.T excused himself. "It's all pointless. You realise he's dead, Jones. We're just waiting for the body to turn up. You're officially on morgue duty. Let's just hope you can still recognise him. A lot of stiffs get weighted and slipped into the bay. The channel's a favourite cause of its depth. You'll need a good imagination after the sea-lice and crabs have been to work."

"Imagination, sir?" queried Jones. He felt sick already, imagination was the last thing he could wish for in such a scenario.

"To reconstruct the features," nodded the D.I. He turned to go.

Jones called after him. "Does that mean I'm assigned to the mortuary, sir?" he asked nervously.

The D.I turned back. "No, Jones," he said, "we're not that overrun with bodies. All I meant was that if one turns up with no I.D., one that we can't fit, you go and have a look-see. You're assigned to Garelli, restricted to the station. Paperwork and computer search only. Garelli's grounded. You can hold her hand."

"Grounded, sir?" queried Jones, totally lost.

"Desk-duty only. She's off the streets pending the outcome of the investigation."

Jones tried to look blank. When in doubt, always take refuge in stupidity. He wondered if the shopping spree would be classed as a disciplinary matter, if discovered.

"Officer Garelli was involved in an incident," clarified the D.I. "Ethical Standards is looking into it." He headed for the door again. At the last moment he turned with some advice. "Be careful what you say around Garelli, officer," he said, "don't embarrass the force."

Jones nodded, and mumbled his thanks. The advice was doubtless well-intentioned, if a day late. He went in search of his new partner.

Garelli was parked decorously in front of her terminal, stabbing at the keys with one finger of each hand. Jones almost cracked a comment, but bit it back.

"Can I help?" he asked.

"Only if you can cross-reference a man who doesn't exist with current Medicare, Centrelink and tax records," said Garelli.

"I meant with the typing," said Jones.

"Don't tell me," said Garelli, "While I was doing metalwork and automotive engineering, you were into keyboarding and home economics?"

"I did a TAFE course evenings before I went to police college," said Jones. "I was told typing was fairly essential for the modern officer." Actually he had learned to type at school. It was regarded as essential for university entrants. The TAFE course had only been a refresher to increase his speed. But now did not seem the time or place to mention any of that.

"This is a waste of time," Garelli did not buy into it. She spun away from the console and told him, "We should be out on the streets."

"So how's the investigation going?" Jones asked as he checked over the computer.

"Are you deaf?" snapped Garelli, "or are you just making polite conversation? I just said it's a waste of time."

"No, no," said Jones, "Not this, your investigation. The D.I said you were grounded pending a clearance." The D.I had not exactly said or even implied that, but Jones thought it sounded less threatening if he assumed the likelihood of a reprieve.

"My investigation?" queried Garelli. "My business!" she snapped.

"As we're working together I figure you might want to tell me about it," he said.

Garelli stared at him coldly. "I already have. Accidental discharge of my weapon at a bust."

"At a bust? In Missing Persons?" Jones risked the query.

"I was with the Criminal Investigation Bureau," said Garelli.

"So this is a lateral career move?" commented Jones.

"Clever!" said Garelli, "think of that all on your own or do you carry a thesaurus?"

Jones looked down at his feet, then up at the ceiling. "Some team, eh, what a pair of experts," he muttered.

"Hey, at least I know what I'm doing here," said Garelli, "but you, what's your excuse?"

"I can recognise him," said Jones.

"In this city?" Garelli laughed. "You don't even know it. Be realistic Jones. You're a slopping wet fish right out of water. What can you do here but get in the way?"

\*

# Chapter 7.  Nightrider

The question kept running through his mind. He lay on his
bed in his room with nothing else to do but think. He had
spent all day going nowhere in circles. How could you go
anywhere if you had no starting point? They were right of
course, Garelli and the D.I. What could he do but get in the
way, and clutter up the corner of some side office? He knew
nobody, had no contacts, and very little knowledge or
experience of investigative searches. Not many people went
missing on the island; the communities were too small for
anyone to escape attention. Walkers got lost more in the
wilderness than the bush, but that required different
procedures. A physical beating of the bounds, tracking, and
helicopter overflights. In any case most sensible walkers left a
route and an estimated time of arrival with someone reliable or
official. Jones was suddenly reminded of the old man. He had
been around for so long that he was simply accepted as part of
the scenery, the eccentric in the mists: but what of his arrival?
What had the locals thought when this stranger had arrived
out of nowhere? How had the property been bought? How
had he originally established himself? Jones wished that he
were back on the island, where at least he could be doing
something useful, like carrying out property searches and
asking pertinent questions in the community. He resolved to
contact his own force on the morrow and ask if someone
could at least check with the Titles Office. It would be

something; even if the old man had never attempted to be active since his arrival, there would have been a beginning somewhere. But his was a passive mystery, grown with the passing years, the recluse on the edge of awareness. Not a disappearing act, not a missing person, not even a person in hiding, just a person who liked his own company, and avoided that of others.

How could such a man cope with the city? Jones himself knew almost nothing of the city, almost less than nothing. He was like a grain of sand blown by the wind to a distant shore. The more he thought about it, the more ridiculous it seemed that he had been called in the first place. It had seemed plausible at the time, had it not: but in hindsight? If all he was expected to do were to recognise a body, would not a photograph have sufficed?

What a waste of his time. He felt like pulling the pin and heading back for the island. Thing was, back home he would have been replaced. Someone else would be covering his patrol, indefinitely. That was the arrangement. If he went back early he would be surplus, a spare part. He did not know what they would do to him. They might even have to transfer him down to headquarters in the city. Shunt him off somewhere with a pile of paperwork, a repeat of today indefinitely into the future, a circular paper chase going nowhere. It did not seem fair, one moment his life was on track, rolling along sweet and true, then a call out of nowhere, a chance meeting, and he was sidelined. Now he was in limbo. He lay there thinking about that meeting, reviewing it in his mind. He wondered for the hundredth time what had happened to the old man. The old bloke had refused to fly, insisted on going by boat. Said he was afraid of flying. Funny thing was, he had not looked the sort of man who would be frightened by much. But you could never tell with old people, different values, and different frame of reference. Actually it made very little difference, except in time of arrival. It would have delayed the I.D of the body by a few days: the additional time taken by the overnight ferry across the strait, and then what? Jones suddenly wondered at what point the old man had been deemed to have disappeared. They must have known he had arrived in the city, but how? So someone else must have seen the old man; and clearly enough to recognise a description? So where did that leave himself? Where did the trail go cold? He would ask tomorrow: two strangers in a strange city, where could either of them go?

Twilight faded and he lay there in the darkness, his mind turning in tightening circles. Lights from the city fluttered through his blinds. Street lights, neon lights and headlights sliding across his walls, shadows gliding as the traffic flowed past and fast. He could not settle and he could not sleep. In the end he got up, got dressed and went out into the darkness, to wander the walkways of the night. The shadows seduced him, soft and subtle they blurred the edges of the urban day. Lights flickered and sparkled across the skyline. The city built fairy castles in the air, and grew almost beautiful. A flock of gulls wove white hauntings through the searching beams that lit up a skyscraper, and moths lived and died as they flickered in and out of the light. He was drawn inexorably onward, to the play of light in the shadowed sky. Then a shopping strip cut across his path, and the horizon was lost in the neon blare. He flitted from shopfront to shopfront, mesmerised by electric dreams. In the end he hailed a cab. He could not give a destination because he did not have one, but he remembered he had a full docket of cab-charge vouchers so he just told the cabbie to drive. The cabbie wanted to take Jones to where the action was, but Jones did not know what action he wanted.

The driver told him that all nocturnal fares were stoned butterflies going nowhere, either circling or escaping the light. Jones stared at his long hair and ponytail and paid him off. He kept switching cabs till he found a driver that would give him peace. One that would not hassle him about pubs and clubs and brothels and whores, one that would not whinge about wives and maintenance and bills and taxes, one that would simply sit there silently and drive away the night. He lost himself in a neon dream as they drove for hours, riding the lines of light circling the centre, always turning back on the edge of the outer darkness. Red lights, green lights, stoplights and headlights, and the lights of the plazas glowing and the bistros pulsing, and the pubs throbbing and the pavements thronging gaudy butterflies preening under the beams of artificial suns. Then the doors shuttering and the windows winking out and the dance dying and the nightlife finally fading with the false dawn. Only the cabs flitting through the dead streets like blowflies feeding on the carcase of the night.

In the end he discovered that his cabbie could not speak or read English, so Jones had to study the cab's street directory to get himself home. He paid his fare in the early hours and stood on the doorstep watching the cab drive away, wondering if the driver knew the way back to the depot. Then he tried his latchkey and unlocked the front door. But he could not get in because the landlady must have dropped the chain. So he slumped in the doorway and half-dozed through the dawn. The land breeze kept him warm and he hovered in and out of sleep till the rattle of locks and chains snapped him awake. He explained to the dubious landlady that he had been out on night surveillance. It was 7a.m. He fled to his room, pulled the blinds and crashed in comfort. He would give the station the flick. They would hardly miss him.

The sun streaming in through a break in the blinds played on his face and woke him in the afternoon. He called in sick and was put through to Garelli. She called him a bum and demanded his address. After he had put the phone down he wondered why. Surely she was not intending to make a social call? Later he was so bored he almost wished she would drop in. In the evening he sat moping in his room, full of energy and worried whether he would manage to get back to sleep that night, after such a late lie-in.

Finally he decided on an old remedy, and went out once more.

*

# Chapter 8.  Blue Morning

The landlady woke him up in the morning, hammering on his door like a chippie on piecework. Obviously he had not remembered to set the alarm.

"There's a young lady at the door for you," she said. She looked slightly disgusted, as though she had walked into a bad smell. At least it was daylight. She looked as if a nocturnal visit might be terminal.

Jones stood on the step in his t-shirt and boxers, feeling a trifle exposed.

"Don't tell me," said Garelli, "you forgot to pack your rooster?"

Jones shrugged. "Dawn has lost its mystery," he said.

Garelli stared at him. "How did you get that eye?" she asked.

Jones touched the side of his face. He had not looked in the mirror yet. The swelling did not feel so bad.

"Walked into a door," he muttered.

"Well you'd better wear some shades," said Garelli, "can't have you showing at the station like some small-time bruiser. Well move it, are you going to invite me in or not? Or do I have to stand on the doorstep like a debt collector?"

"I think that would be best," said Jones. He closed the door in her face and cut away to pull on some clothes. The landlady looked slightly mollified.

"You've got some neck," said Garelli as she marched him to her car, "pulling a sickie on your first day on the job. Are they that casual on the island?"

Jones stopped in his tracks, reached out to catch her by the arm, and remembered himself just in time. "I thought I was the fish out of water?" he recalled, "don't tell me you've discovered a use for me?"

"Don't go all coy on me," snapped Garelli, "there's a body in the morgue. It's time to strut your stuff."

"So how come you're here?" asked Jones. "I thought you weren't allowed out?"

"The D.I's in hospital with a perforated ulcer," said Garelli. "I'm a free agent. Let's go. I've made an appointment, and I'm never late. I make a point of it."

"So you follow some rules," commented Jones as he climbed in beside her.

"In this job," said Garelli, "a woman has to be better at everything. So I'm more than punctual."

Jones thought about it. "I understood it was considered O.K for a woman to be late? Expected almost?"

"You really are from a time warp," said Garelli. "Just don't try to be smart, Jones. Leave the thinking to me. That's what I'm here for."

"So what am I exactly?" asked Jones, "a bodyguard?"

"I don't need one," said Garelli, "no, you're my partner."

"Well thanks for looking out for me," said Jones.

"Don't take it personally," said Garelli, "it's regulations we work in pairs. The team's a member short."

Jones thought carefully about that. "You mean no-one else will work with you?" he hazarded.

At the next lights she turned in her seat and looked him in the eye.

"So what's the truth about this door?" she demanded. "I like to know where my partner's coming from."

Jones considered this. "I got into a blue down the pub," he admitted: went out looking for a scrap if the truth were told. He had been that depressed, that frustrated, it had seemed the only way to let off steam. He had not done it for years: could not in a small community, and obviously not as the community policeman. But once there had been a time, before he had been sent out to the sticks.

The lights turned to green. Garelli ignored them. "That was pretty reckless," she said, "not a sound career move. You don't seem the reckless type to me?"

Jones shrugged. "I was off-duty."

Horns started blaring in the queue backed up behind.

"Bull!" she said, "we're supposed to set an example." She wound down her window and spat a stream of abuse at the cars behind.

"You ever get the urge again," she said as she pulled out and drove away, "you come and see me. I'll give you a workout."

Jones laughed.

"What was that supposed to mean?" she asked.

"You're a woman!" said Jones.

Garelli hit the brakes. They skidded to a stop in the middle of the road. Cars screeched to a halt behind them.

"I'm Aikido First Dan, and Shoto-kan Black Belt," she stated. "Let me tell you something about women. We're faster, sharper and we've got a much higher threshold of pain. And most important of all, we've got no balls to get kicked in. I can disable any man in two seconds flat."

Cars swerved around them horns blasting.

"You're crazy!" said Jones.

"It helps!" admitted Garelli.

60

Jones did not say a word the rest of the way to the mortuary.

*

He wondered if he would ever get used to death. Morticians obviously did, but him? He had seen a few bodies, but evidently not enough. Until they started to smell you could almost expect them to get up and walk away, if they were not too broken. He remembered that road accident, the one that always returned to haunt him, impossible to delete. When he had arrived on the scene one of the fire crew, he looked to be the newest recruit, had the skull of a child cupped in his hands. The boy had been flung from the back seat through the windscreen. No seat belt. Its skull was split. The young fireman was trying to hold it together. He was stretched across the concertinaed bonnet, locked rigid, barely breathing, not daring to move. The tears were streaming down his face, falling like rain. He stayed there for over an hour, while the rest of the crew cut the car apart around him, to get the boy out. When the paramedics could finally take over, they had to pry apart the young fireman's fingers to release the head. It did not seem fair, they were both so young: the young fireman starting his career, the young boy his life.

Scenes like that were indelible. Like the shotgun suicide you could never quite escape them. But at least you were sure it was death you looked at. This one now, was quite unexceptional, lying on his tray as if in sleep, composed and relaxed. Unbroken. Someone's husband possibly? Someone's son? Once, definitely. A lover, a friend? Probably. And they were all there, locked in eternity. Only the key was lost. The mechanics were present, but the spark was missing.

"How and when?" Garelli was all business.

"Last night, about 2 a.m.," said the assistant.

Last night, reflected Jones, when he was cruising in circles, this man's lights went out, perhaps as he passed by.

"As for the how," said the assistant, "you'll have to help me turn the body, rigor is beginning to set in."

Garelli leant a hand to turn the body on its side. It rocked stiffly, like a store mannequin. The assistant parted the hair at the back of the head. A small neat round hole winked out at them through the thicket of greying hair.

". 22 rimfire. Point-blank," said the attendant. "We've taken X-rays. It was a hollow point. Shredded the cortex. We think low velocity from the powder burns."

"You got the bullet?" asked Garelli.

"Still in there," the attendant tapped the side of the head. "We thought we'd leave the surgery till the I.D was over. Saves on cosmetics."

"So is it him?" asked Garelli.

Jones shook his head, "Nothing like."

Too young, too flabby, and too bald; he had written up a detailed description back home, and worked with a police artist. Had they not circulated it?

"Perhaps they just want to make you feel useful?" suggested Garelli.

Jones grunted. The method of execution was bothering him. "When will the lab get the bullet?" he asked.

The attendant shrugged, "Later, maybe tomorrow. Depends how busy we get. It's not like pulling a tooth." He grinned, "I'll have to sharpen the saw."

Jones turned away, felling sick again.

"Odds on it's the same as the others anyway," continued the attendant. "The M.O's similar. The identities of the others were known though."

62

"What others?" asked Garelli.

"There's been two in the last three weeks or so," said the attendant, "that we know of."

Garelli looked angry. "The murder squad could have told me," she hissed.

"Why?" asked Jones, "You're in Missing Persons, different department, different frame of reference." He bit back his revulsion and bent forward to inspect the bullet wound again. It was so clean it was almost clinical.

"Because I used to work with them!" snapped Garelli. She struck out for the door, "I'm only sidelined till I'm cleared. Then I'm back where the action is, where it matters. And it's going down without me!"

Jones wondered at that, at Garelli's hierarchy of priorities? Murder was after all simply about death, a condition too absolute, too finite to reverse in any way. How could it be more important than looking after the living? But now was hardly the time to debate it.

"Hey!" called the attendant, "You finished or what? The meat's turning!"

"Yeah," said Jones, "Thanks, put him back."

In the car Jones's mind was turning restlessly. "I've been meaning to ask," he said to Garelli, "So when was the old man last seen? How do they know he arrived in the city?"

"The hire car," Garelli muttered wearily, "was checked in at the airport depot."

"So he hired a car?" Jones had not known.

"They say it's a long walk, and apparently an even longer swim," said Garelli, "But then you'd know more than me. I've never had the inclination to visit."

"But the airport?" queried Jones, not to be put off by mere sarcasm.

"It's the biggest depot. Maybe he couldn't handle the thought of driving in the city," Garelli explained patiently, "caught a cab in, or an airport bus."

"He could have flown out!" said Jones, "Gone anywhere."

"Now that would make sense, wouldn't it," said Garelli, "after taking all the trouble to catch the boat across."

Jones felt a fool, and fell silent. But none of it made sense. The airport was in the city. He himself had flown in to it. The old man would have had to cope with city traffic to get to there from the ferry terminal. And how would a bush recluse handle city driving? Maybe he came in at night? If he caught the Saturday overnight ferry, it would have docked at the terminal early Sunday morning. That might be early enough to beat the traffic, which might be late and fairly light on a rest day anyway. Perhaps he thought the airport was the easiest place to drop the car? He did not know the city well enough to be sure, but he assumed access to the airport was clearly signposted and relatively easy? But why had he not simply caught a coach to and from the ferry terminals? Why bother with a hire car? If he really had made the decision to drive, why not go in the personal utility, or perhaps that was simply deemed too old and unreliable? But why indeed decide on a car at all? Jones thought he could at least answer that. A bus would be too crowded, too public for a man who had cut himself off from the world for so many years. At least a car would afford some measure of privacy, a steel cocoon on wheels.

Something else occurred to Jones, the question that had been bothering him on a previous night of lost sleep and little hope. "How did they know it was him?" he asked.

Garelli shrugged, "That came from upstairs. Airport's security's pretty tight nowadays; the Feds gave us the tip-off."

"CCTV?" asked Jones.

"Now that would make even more sense, wouldn't it?" said Garelli, "with you being sent here and all!"

But to Jones it made absolutely no sense at all. How did the feds know it was him? How could a man with no I.D have a driving licence, and how could he hire a car without showing one? Which they knew he did not have? He thought back to the truck parked outside the refuge on the mountain, and wondered whom it had been registered to? He himself had never known or heard of the old man driving it. In any case, would a man that cautious risk discovery by driving without a valid licence? He made a mental note to ring headquarters back home and get some answers to his questions. They could at least check the registration of the vehicle.

In the meantime it was assumed a proven fact that the old man had got to the city, and of course they knew his intended destination. He was to go to the mortuary. Jones himself had supplied him with a contact number for when he arrived.

"So he never made it to the morgue?" asked Jones.

"If he had he would have been in the company of police officers," said Garelli, "trained observers, and your presence here now would hardly be necessary, now would it?"

"So he disappeared between the depot and the morgue," said Jones.

"Very perceptive!" sneered Garelli.

So where would a stranger go in a strange city, thought Jones?

"Did you check the hotels?" he asked.

"O for God's sake!" snapped Garelli.

Or there was another way of looking at it, if he had been killed, who had done it and why? When and how had the contact been made? Who could possibly know the old man was coming, and arrange to kill him? And why had three bodies turned up in the period since the old man's disappearance, and as the pathologist had informed them, all with the same M.O?

"Have you still got contacts at Murder?" Jones asked and Garelli nodded wearily, "Could you get them to pull the files on the other two killings?"

She glanced across at him, "What for? We're in Missing Persons, remember?"

"Just a hunch," said Jones. He fell silent again. It was the method of killing, that bullet hole. It felt too much of a coincidence. "Can you get the ballistics reports too?" he persisted.

Garelli groaned, "What T.V. cop show you been watching?"

"Bear with me," said Jones, "It might be nothing, but it might be a link. Wouldn't you like an excuse to check out those killings?"

Garelli hissed between her teeth. "Very good, Jones," she said, "I almost begin to think you might have some intelligence after all."

*

# Chapter 9. The Ideal Man

Back at the station Jones got on the phone to home. It seemed to take ages, as he kept being passed on to the next link in the chain. Finally he got hold of one of the senior officers who had authorised his transfer to the mainland. He lied a little, hinted at a lot, and exaggerated even more. He ended up convincing his old boss that crucial evidence might be buried at the recluse's homestead in the mountains, and got a commitment to have the dogs dug up and the bullets removed and run by Ballistics. He was told it might take a week or so, but the sense of urgency was never the same on the island. He also asked for the truck's plates to be noted and run through the Motor Registry. He was told that was more of a possibility.

While he was waiting for Garelli to get back from her visit to her old squad, Jones started going through the files on the search for the old man. All hospitals and emergency services had been contacted first up, and then all the major city hotels had been contacted. Next came all the smaller ones, and then guesthouses, motels and flophouses, followed by the Salvos and the hostels. Then all the outlying places had been targeted; anything or anybody remotely commercial that might possibly be able to put up a single man had been contacted. As the circle widened a full description and identikit picture manufactured from his own-recorded observations had been left at every counter and with every landlady. Even estate agencies with rental services had been approached. Jones did not know the city at all well enough to know if there were any gaps, but he suspected there was nothing obvious; just the fact that the enterprise was so massive that something somewhere could easily have been overlooked or passed over. But the investigation did appear impressively thorough. It really looked on the surface as though the D.I was right; they were just waiting for the body to turn up. After all the old man would have had to book in at a hotel of some kind, because he could not possibly know anyone in the city to stay with, or could he? What about his son's place of residence?

Garelli came back with the files from Murder and Ballistics. They sat and worked through them together. Both the victims were younger than the John Doe in the morgue and were known drug-dealers. One was Asian. On the photographs of one corpse the track marks up his arm were clearly visible. Both had been killed with a .22 rimfire, fired point-blank, one in the back of the head, one in the centre of the forehead. That was chilling.

"The murderer must have fronted him up, and looked him right in the eye," said Jones, "That would take some neck!"

"So he was pissed!" said Garelli, "There's some hard men out there."

The murder squad's attitude was that there was a drugs war going down, brewing over control of certain districts of the city. They did not know jack all really, because Asians were involved, and the Asian community kept to itself, a closed shop, with no way in, for outsiders or informers. Only one side appeared to be losing heavily, since Ballistics said the same gun killed both victims, a gun firing either low-velocity shorts or long rifle subsonics.

"They don't crack the sound barrier," said Jones authoratively.

68

"What a mine of information," said Garelli, "So what?"

"So with a silencer there's absolutely no sound," said Jones.

"Ballistics says there's no rifling, no identifying marks on the bullets," Garelli said next, skimming through the report, "That's not possible, is it?" For once she was not sounding so sure of herself.

"Yes it is," said Jones thoughtfully, "You can get .22 smoothbores, designed for dust shot."

".22 shotguns?" exclaimed Garelli, "What on earth could they be good for?"

"They're used for protecting orchards in Europe," said Jones, "don't damage the fruit too much. And butterfly hunters used to use them, especially in rainforest canopies."

"Butterfly hunters!" repeated Garelli. "Jones, you're a worry. You keep surprising me. Am I supposed to believe this?"

"I'm a gun buff," he said, "Comes of growing up on a farm I suppose; all that boundary riding."

As if their few acres could support a horse. But at least he'd had the State Forest to roam in, and all those second-hand shooting magazines to bone up on.

"Hell!" swore Garelli, "We're looking for a butterfly hunter. I'll tell Murder. They'll love it!"

"A professional," qualified Jones, "No sound, no rifling, no means of identification, no calling card; a hit man."

"And no accuracy," Garelli surprised him, "So how does this help us with the old man? Genius!"

Jones would not answer her, not yet. It was too bizarre.

"I was wondering about the son," he countered.

"Very cute, Jones," said Garelli, "Now how did you pick that?"

Jones was lost. "I don't know what you mean?" he queried.

"They all shared the same morgue," sneered Garelli, "So there must be a connection."

"All I meant was," said Jones, "was that where the son lived ought to be checked out. In case the old man went there."

"Jones!" snapped Garelli, "I can't make out if you're being arrogant or stupid. The son lived in a rented flat. His last address was in the Eastern Suburbs. Of course we checked. Murder put together a file. We had it sent over. A copy's around here somewhere."

"I'd like to see it," he said simply.

"You're pushing your luck," said Garelli, "It's been scrutinised by experts."

Jones changed tack again. "At what point does Missing Persons hand over to another department?"

Garelli stared at him. "You've already tried that once. Now it's past its used by date."

"There's obviously a connection between the son and these latest killings," said Jones, "look at the timing."

"The M.O is totally different," said Garelli. "In case you don't know, Boysie Smith had his head and hands missing," she suddenly laughed.

"That's funny?" asked Jones.

"It just reminded me of something," said Garelli, "almost the ideal man." She sobered and stared Jones in the eye. "Do you have any idea of the annual tally of suspicious deaths in this city? How many do you get over on the island? One? None?"

Jones ignored that. "Missing Persons only has to hand over to another department if and when a crime is known to have occurred. If his body turns up, and it's suspicious circumstances, then we have to hand over to homicide. Until we find the old man any lead is relevant."

Garelli stood up and shuffled the files together. "These have got to go back," she said, "unless you can show a connection, these are in Murder's jurisdiction. I'm not crossing boundaries. I want my career back."

She walked out and left him.

Jones spent the rest of the day going over the search files again and again, trying to find a flaw. He did not really expect to be able to find anything, but at least it kept him occupied. In the dying minutes of the shift he got a personal call from the island, his old commander.

"Thought you'd be interested to know, Jones," the brisk disembodied voice echoed in his ear, "sent a team out this arvo. Nice day for a drive. The dogs have been disinterred. They are in the lab. Forensics should be on it tomorrow."

"Thank-you, sir," said Jones. "I wasn't expecting anything so prompt." He was sweating now; this was more than a long shot. He must have overdone the urgency bit. If it proved to be nothing, it would be very hard to justify the expense, and impossible to explain his logic. Garelli's tongue would be nothing in comparison.

"Well," continued the commander, "we put out a call to the local man, you know, your replacement, and he ran out to the place of residence a.s.a.p. Seems like the place has been burned to the ground. Nothing left, very thorough. So we made your request a priority."

"Thank-you sir," Jones could only repeat himself. What the hell was going on?

"We'll keep you informed of developments," said the brisk voice. "We've got the arson squad on it as well. By the way the truck was torched too. The plates are registered to the daughter. Same address. Keep up the good work Jones,

71

remember you are representing us. Don't let us down." The phone went dead.

Do not let them down, thought Jones. Do not show them up in front of the big brothers on the mainland, he meant. Arson squad! They did not even have one, just borrowed a specialist from the fire service if and when, which was not very often.

So the old man's place had been torched? And by the sound of it had not even been reported. That was the downside of being a recluse: no one to notice. A fire lit in misty weather would hardly be seen. Had it been local kids out for sport? Was anything missing? Would they ever know?

Jones sat in the office thinking and trying to make sense of it all. It gave him a headache. He suddenly realised how late it was, and rang his landlady to apologise. He told her he would skip the evening meal because he would be working late. He would eat out, grab a counter meal. He could not face an evening in at any rate. He needed to centre himself, touch base somehow. But he had nowhere to go, nothing to do. He could only try to lose himself in the night, hide from the light. How could places so full of people feel so empty?

\*

The butterflies were thronging the pavements again, flitting and fluttering from pub to club, mascara and silk, spangles and glitter, long hair wafting like wings in the evening breeze, and clothes splashing all the bright colours of the rainbow: painted ladies, drawn to the lights. The men were drab denim by comparison.

He wandered from pub to pub, sipping slowly, a pot in each, trying to hang out the evening and retain an impression of sobriety. It seemed to be impossible to strike up casual conversations. The feeling of isolation deepened as the night dragged by. Then he found himself in a bar where the butterflies were men, and one touched him and mouthed obscenities into the smoke and fumes. Jones's rage exploded red and vicious, an animal unchained. The leering face in front of him crumpled in a mess of blood and gristle. His fists and feet smashed holes in the thrusting crowd as he drove for the door. They squealed like wounded rabbits, and collapsed like broken dolls. Then two bouncers blocked him, big and brutal in lipstick, eye shadow and chains. His anger was bright and controlled now, hard as a knife. He took one out, kicked in his kneecap. But the second blind-sided him and battered at him with a barstool. Jones went down in a sea of boots and stabbing pain, and in the end, mercifully, passed out.

He came to in the back of a police wagon, covered in vomit. A drooling drunk slumped in the corner by his head. Jones wondered if it was the drunk's vomit, or his own. The wagon squealed to a halt in a babble of shrieks and shouts. The back doors opened and two tarts were thrown in screeching and protesting. They were all flesh and make-up and clothes so brief they could have been beachwear: so much for gender equity. Time was when a man could rely on meeting only his own in a paddy wagon. They would be having mixed jails next. One whore complained about the smell of the drunk. The other propositioned Jones. Twenty bucks for a quickie in the back of the wagon. He decided she was either blind or flying kites. He stank worse than the drunk.

At the lockup the cops threw him out on the pavement, and batonned him when he tried to protest. The whores laughed madly; shrilling cries of encouragement. One cop silenced them with a flourish of his nightstick and an icy stare. They

73

made Jones crawl to the cells on his hands and knees. When someone finally came for him to get his particulars he showed them his warrant card.

"Wrong state son," shrugged the duty sergeant, "won't wash here."

Jones tried to explain and finally got them to phone Garelli for confirmation. They made her come down to the nick to formally identify him. It was past three in the morning when she arrived. She spat a stream of abuse at him and got the sergeant to bury the paperwork. Then she hauled him out of there. He tried to babble a drivel of apology and thanks but she cut him short.

"You owe me!" was all she would say.

She ended up taking him back to her flat because it was much too late to go back to his digs. After she had made him shower he sat at her kitchen counter in her bathrobe and she poured coffee down him. A cat wound itself round his leg, purring happily. Another stared at him suspiciously from the safety of the doorway.

"You're lucky you've got no cracked ribs," Garelli said finally, "The patrol said that was some kicking you took."

"They stood and watched?" asked Jones incredulously.

"It's a trouble spot," shrugged Garelli, "Maybe they get paid to look the other way? Maybe they don't care? You mind telling me what you were doing in a gay bar?"

"I didn't know," Jones said simply.

"You naïve hopeless hick!" cursed Garelli. "There's the couch. Mind the cat. I'm going back to bed."

*

# Chapter 10. The Weekend

She barely spoke to him in the morning: just enough to order him into her car, still in the bathrobe. She dropped him off at his lodgings to pick up fresh clothes. He scuttled in stiff and bruised, still in her robe. Mercifully he did not meet the landlady in the hall. When he got outside again, shaved and fully clothed, Garelli was gone. He had to catch a taxi into work.

"It's the weekend," said Mulligan when Jones finally arrived. Mulligan seemed to have taken on the mantle of acting D.I.

"I didn't realise, sir," said Jones.

Actually he hadn't. He'd lost all track of the days somewhere, somehow.

"So what are you doing here?" asked Mulligan.

"I've nowhere else to go, sir," said Jones.

"Get a life Jones," said Mulligan, "and in future get here on time. You're late."

"Sorry sir," apologised Jones.

He did not really see how he could be late if he was not supposed to be there, but decided to play safe; diplomacy in the daylight. He was suddenly grateful that the kicking had been directed at his body, not his face. He would not have liked to explain last night to a superior.

"What's with the shades, Jones?" asked Mulligan, "Our northern sun too bright for you?"

"Yessir," agreed Jones.

Mulligan snorted. "Better not go out to play in it then."

Jones nodded and excused himself to find Garelli.

"And Jones," Mulligan called after him. Jones stopped in his tracks and looked back over his shoulder. "Keep that bitch away from me. Keep her occupied, you understand what I mean?"

"Yessir," repeated Jones; he thought he did.

*

Garelli stared at him strangely when he found her at her desk. It made him feel guilty about the previous night all over again.

"Jones?' she quizzed him quietly after he had sat awkwardly at his own desk, "Who exactly knew you were staying at that hotel?"

Jones was nonplussed. "Hotel?" he queried.

"I thought you were booked in at a hotel when you arrived," she said patiently.

"That's right," said Jones, "all set up by the department. But I decided to move. At my digs I get my washing and evening meals. And it's more of a family atmosphere."

He noticed Garelli's eyebrows lift. "The landlady's not so bad," he muttered weakly. "Besides," he added the real reason, "I can cut back on my expenses, save out of my allowance." He felt himself grow red.

"And spend it on drink?" commented Garelli.

"I'm not usually like that," blustered Jones.

"No?" queried Garelli, "two out of three looks good to me."

"I don't have a drink problem," said Jones, "if that is what this is all about."

"No it's not that," said Garelli, "though I am beginning to wonder. No, it's just that we've had a call from your hotel, your ex-hotel. A message was left for you last night. It was on my desk this morning, from the night clerk. Missing Persons left photokits at every reception in the city. The clerk seems to think that someone answering the old man's description was asking for you last night. They're off duty now, but I've got the home address off the day-manager. It's probably nothing but it will get us out of the office."

\*

The city seemed still, somnolent. He wondered why he had not noticed it before on the cab ride in to work. Perhaps the windows had been tinted, or maybe it had merely been his bleary eyes. It was too early for the Saturday shopping traffic. Only desultory cars limped through the littered streets, probably ferrying tired shop assistants and parking meter attendants, too poor to expose their resentment to the scrutiny of the unemployment queues? Friday night was only for the privileged, those who could afford to lie in of a morning, or those who simply did not care? Lone street cleaners were out in the plazas, mopping round the derelicts with casual disdain. Garelli swept out into the suburbs and the concrete landscape changed to lawns and picket fences and the palisade brick boxes shuttered and curtained against the morning sun. Only newspaper boys and bored dogs broke the sanctity and the peace.

The desk clerk lived in a bed-sit near the river, in a purpose built barrack block of rectangular concrete, barely softened by a screen of trees. Jones thought he remembered her, bright and bubbly with a flashing smile. Now she was hard to rouse, and half-asleep when she finally responded and let them in. Garelli smoothed her ruffled feathers by complimenting her on her powers of observation and her sense of public responsibility. Soon they were sitting comfortably on the edge of the bed and chatting like sisters. Jones stood awkwardly, feeling totally out of place in the feminine clutter of the cramped room. She remembered him from the hotel, which he was surprised at, after a stay of only one night.

"It's those baby blue eyes," grinned Garelli and Jones felt himself flush bright red and did not know where to put himself. Apparently the receptionist only recollected his visitor because the man drew attention to himself. He asked her if Officer Jones was in his room, and seemed surprised when she said he had checked out. When she said there was no forwarding address the visitor appeared annoyed. He did not hang around but left immediately.

Garelli went over the visitor's description with the girl. He had brown hair, a moustache and a beard. But she thought it was a disguise. The height and the build were right, and the eyes were unmistakeable. 'Bleak grey' was the description she gave, Jones's own words. The face was old and lined, belying the colour of the hair.

"He looked right through me," said the receptionist.

"What about his voice?" asked Jones, "Did he have an accent?"

"European, I think?" the girl was apologetic, "but good grammar, like he'd been here a long time. He was coughing a lot into a handkerchief. Said he had a summer cold. But he was very well dressed: Italian suit and silk shirt. Nice tie, subtle, not flash."

"You're very observant," commented Garelli.

"Thanks, I make a point of it," said the girl. "I want to join the force; I'm studying up for the next entrance exam. I'm going to train in the academy, then once I've done my time in patrol I'm going to be a detective."

Nothing like conviction, thought Jones. He wondered what was driving her? There was a difference between ambition and passion. He wondered why Garelli had not picked up on it?

Back at the car Garelli told him he should have asked the girl for a date, or at least left a card. Jones changed the subject.

"So what do you think?" he asked Garelli, "dyed hair and make-up?"

"I think it's bizarre," she said, "Part of me would like to think that a lonely girl with an over-active imagination wants your number. You never did answer me about who knew you at that hotel?"

"No-one, outside of the department," said Jones, "it was all set up for me on arrival." "No-one back at home?" asked Garelli, "didn't you inform family or friends? Don't you have a wife or a girl-friend?"

"There's no-one," Jones insisted abruptly.

"Who knows your current address?" asked Garelli.

"Only you," said Jones.

"Keep it that way," said Garelli.

As they drove back through the suburbs life was beginning to stir. Occasional men stood in manicured driveways washing and polishing gleaming cars. Grass cuttings sprayed into the air, weeds died and the broken dream buzzed and grated with spluttering noise: just a late start to another suburban Saturday.

In the station Jones hung around like a lost dog with nothing to do and nowhere to go but get underfoot. The investigation had died a slow death, if indeed it ever had life. It felt there was nothing to do but wait around for something to break.

The ballistics report from home could take days, and realistically, Jones admitted to himself, it was unlikely to help. Twenty-twos were as common as kitchen sinks in the country. Virtually every home had one.

Garelli slumped at her console staring at her screen. Eventually she went round to Mulligan to harass him about the I.D of yesterday's John Doe in the morgue. Mulligan told her they were running searches interstate, it was not her assignment, and to keep her nose out of it. She picked at him casually like a hovering fly, irritating him to the point that he finally ordered her to assist on the youth file, and go out on a street check for missing kids.

"Outside?" she queried, "Put it in writing."

"Do you think I'm blind?" grunted Mulligan, "So where've you been all morning? Powdering your nose? And yesterday?"

"That was official," shrugged Garelli.

"So's this!" insisted Mulligan, "And take Jones. He can hold your hand."

"What's with the playing hard to get?" asked Jones as they headed for the car pool, "I thought you wanted out to play?"

"Reverse psychology," muttered Garelli, "Make it too obvious and that slob will throw away the key."

*

**PART TWO: Imago**
> *The complete and final transformation of the lepidopterous adult that emerges from the chrysalis.*

# Chapter 11. A Leap in the Dark

The crumpled girl collapsed against the kerb like a wilted flower. Tears wept gullies through layered mascara and dribbled salt stains on the asphalt ground. He had never noticed these brittle blooms before in the evening dance of the butterflies. How could he have been so blind?

Garelli was as patient as a stalking snake. She worked through the ranks of the unwanted, gently coaxing, soothing panic, checking stories, filing faces, listening to the lies of a society that let its children prostitute themselves in public. Some of them even propositioned him. He turned away embarrassed, appalled at how cheaply they valued themselves.

They checked the train stations, the bus depots and the tourist strips. Then in the end they ran out of street: so much tarmac, so short a day. And the sun fell out of the sky and the nightlights brought out a fresh parade, and they toured the strips again: moths to the flame. Then finally the butterflies were bedded down for the night and the candle guttered and the streets died.

Jones and Garelli sat in a café through the small hours, too strung out to sleep, talking the dregs of the night away. He said she was so good at talking to these kids that he was surprised she wanted to go back to the crime squad. She said they were victims and she wanted to catch the perpetrators. He said he felt so useless out there. They shied away from him, distaste and hurt shining in their eyes. She said it was because he was a man, and did he not know that most abuse came from men?

He stared at the set of her jaw and the curve of her neck and wondered at her own story, but did not dare ask. She was never so coy.

"So what about you Jonesy?" she smiled with her mouth but her eyes were hard, "What happened to the woman in your life? Divorced?"

"No," denied Jones. He always felt slightly awkward fending off enquiries like that. It was if society expected you to be married and pigeon-holed and distrusted you if you were not.

"And no girl-friend either, I seem to remember?" Garelli was persistent to the point of rudeness.

"In between," lied Jones, "She'll have to wait till I get back home."

"So I'm out of luck then?" Garelli jibed mercilessly.

Jones felt himself go bright red. He seemed to be doing that a lot lately.

"You never try to hit on me?" mused Garelli, "Most men do. I suppose it means you're safe. But it's hardly reassuring. Don't you find me attractive?"

"Sure!" blurted Jones, his face now burning. He had to look away. "It's just that you don't seem to be available," trying to mask his disinterest.

"How very perceptive of you," Garelli's teeth flashed in a crocodile grin, "We'll make a detective of you yet."

He felt irritated to the point of walking out on her. Just when he was finally beginning to feel comfortable with her, she twisted the knife. He was too tired, the night was too old, and his patience too brittle. But in truth he was too fragile to fight, so he changed the subject back to safer ground.

"So where do we go next?" he asked, "We've run out of street, or have we?"

She stared at him quietly, stirring her coffee, taking her time, "Surely not to bed? That would be too mundane!"

He did not bite, but tried again. "We've spent half the day and half the night and achieved nothing," he insisted.

She shrugged wearily, "Maybe no news is good news. Maybe we can reassure those parents that at least their kids aren't on these streets? Isn't that something?"

"I'm too tired," Jones muttered. The inside of his eyelids felt layered with grit. "How am I going to face the day?"

"We'll go in to the station to clock on in the morning, then we'll sign ourselves out," said Garelli.

"To do what?" asked Jones.

"To go home," said Garelli, "and sleep. In the afternoon we'll start checking out the squats. I'll get a printout of all known locations. Plus there are some safety houses. Then we'll tour the strips again in the evening. It's easy to miss these kids when they're active."

"How thorough!" Jones remarked wearily.

"Is there any other way?" asked Garelli, "Come on, we can catch a couple of hours sleep before the clock chimes."

"My landlady!" muttered Jones anxiously.

"My couch," said Garelli, "but don't get too comfortable."

*

Part way through the afternoon Jones came to a profound realisation about the nature of squats. By definition they were illegal, so by probability were unknown to the authorities. Most of Garelli's addresses were already obsolete and deserted as well as derelict. Only those of the streets could know the current sanctuaries from them, and there could be dozens, if not hundreds hidden in the huddles of a large city: closed factories, warehouses and homes with absentee, dead or bankrupt owners; shuttered by day, breached by the night. It made him wonder how many could hide in the underground of a sub-culture. It made him wonder about the old man. What if he had taken another way? What if he had avoided the bright lights and lost himself in the shadows, gone underground? Jones mentioned it to Garelli.

"Somewhere to hang his suit, and put on his make-up? I thought we were waiting for the body to show? It's a lot easier on the imagination, and common sense!" Garelli was cynical.

But Jones persuaded her to hand out the posters on the old man when they hit the strips that evening. They gave them to the street kids, told them it was someone's grandfather gone missing on a futile search for a missing grandchild. Some of the kids seemed happy to help, perhaps touched by the shadows of a vanished past. Jones almost felt embarrassed by his lies.

Garelli followed the trail of glitter into a sequin night. Bright bodies postured on the crowded pavements, setting snares for the crawling cars. Faith leapt blindly as they got in, left the light and drove into the dark. Garelli thought she saw a face she recognised from the files: shoulder-length hair framing the white face and the shadowed eyes. Stencilled brows and fluttering lashes, blush on the cheekbones and lipstick so purple the mouth was almost bruised in the neon light: poised over a tank-top baring the belly and the hand on hip pouting.

"Very pretty," said Garelli, "O.K Jones, time to do your man thing."

"What do you mean?" he was nonplussed.

"Go over and check it out," Garelli pretended patience, "Act cool, find out what's on offer, and look interested. I'll get round behind."

"I can't do that! It's a boy!" spluttered Jones, "Let's just walk up and collar him."

"If he makes us as we close in," hissed Garelli, "he's gone. And there's no way I can out sprint a 14-year-old boy in a crowd with these shoes. How about you?"

Jones shrugged indifferently. Garelli was always a fashion statement. He didn't want to buy into this at all.

"We do the job," insisted Garelli, "as best we can. Obviously I can't proposition a rent-boy, but you can. Just flash some dollars, get him onside, and we've got him. Now get over there," she gave him a shove in the small of his back.

Jones stumbled forward woodenly, feeling trapped by Garelli behind and the crowd in front. His eyes locked onto the boy, and the crowd seemed to part to let him through. Then suddenly he stood before him, and the boy smiled and wiggled his hips provocatively. His eyes were as old as the earth.

"How much?" croaked Jones, his throat uncomfortably dry.

"The usual," grinned the boy, quietly confident.

"Where?" Jones struggled to make conversation.

"Your car would be good," said the boy, "unless you want to pay for a room."

Jones bit his lip, trying to hold himself together. Where in the hell was Garelli? Suddenly she materialised out of the crowd, and seized the boy's wrist. She twisted it up behind his back in a vicious hammerlock.

"Bitch!" screamed the boy, "get off my arm."

"Christ Garelli!" exclaimed Jones, "ease off, he's hardly criminal, just a missing kid."

"Help me cuff him!" ordered Garelli, "and watch his teeth, you don't know where he's been. Some of these little darlings have got HIV. Look at his arms."

Jones stared at the track marks, mesmerised. The crowd suddenly surged around them, confronting and feral. Garelli pulled out her I.D and ordered them to back off. The press hardly slackened.

"He's got AIDS!" she shouted, and the crowd melted away like smoke in the wind.

"Let's get him to the car," she said to Jones.

"What do we do with him?" he asked.

"Lock him up for the night," said Garelli.

"He's a minor," said Jones.

"Underage street prostitution is still technically an offence in this city," said Garelli, "It's enough to hold him. Community Services can sort him in the morning."

The boy was writhing helplessly and weeping with frustration.

"Your folks are worried about you," said Garelli gently.

"Get real!" sobbed the boy, "what would you know? At least here I get paid!"

"Oh you'd be surprised," said Garelli quietly. She remained silent the rest of the way to the station, concentrating on her driving, seemingly lost in the focus of her own headlights.

They left the boy in the cells, sullen and withdrawn, and went upstairs to the office. On Garelli's desk was another message, concerning the identity of the John Doe from the morgue. She passed it over to Jones. The body was a drug dealer from interstate.

"So drugs are the connection," stated Jones.

Garelli did not even bother to reply. They called it a night and Garelli dropped Jones off at his place. He had eaten out already so he went straight to his room and bed. He figured his landlady would have given up on him by now in any case. In the night he had this feeling that someone was outside his room trying to get in, but when he woke up sweating he realised it was only a dream.

*

In the morning Garelli sat in on the boy's interview with Community Services. She came out after an hour looking tired and drawn. Jones wandered over to her.

"So how did it go?" he asked.

"Nowhere," she muttered, "Back into care until he runs again, but I got some addresses of some current squats."

"I thought his folks want him back?" queried Jones.

"His mum does," admitted Garelli, "but he claims his stepfather abuses him."

Jones was appalled. "Does she know?"

"I believe the question should be: does she wish to believe?" sated Garelli.

Jones shook his head. "The addresses sound good," he decided at last, "we could go and check them out."

"Go out and get some fresh air?" questioned Garelli.

Jones nodded and tried to smile.

"It's one hour past the morning peak hour," she said, "and you want fresh air? Don't you know anything?"

A uniform came into the corridor and rescued him. "Constable Jones?" he queried, "There's a fax just come in for you."

It was from home, the ballistics reports on the dogs. Jones skimmed through it avidly. Despite himself he found he was trembling. He had not realised just how much interest he had invested in the findings.

89

"No rifling indentations found to be present. Bullets compacted through close impact, but weapon surmised to be smooth-bore," he summarised.

"Well, well, Jonesy," considered Garelli, "you are full of surprises aren't you? Let's talk as we take some of that air." She went over and picked up a folder off her desk.

They headed for the car pool.

*

# Chapter 12. The Squats

The path through the shrubbery was like an overgrown tunnel of twisted trees. Sunlight leaked through the canopy overhead, and sprayed patterns of lace that shifted with the breeze. It was hot and oppressive. Sweat dribbled into Jones's eyes. A sidetrack veered to the right. It looked newly forged through the undergrowth, bushes kicked apart and plants trampled. They followed it to the side of the house, and finished up underneath a small sash window with one broken pane. He reached across and pushed up at the bottom sash. It jarred upward awkwardly and shuddered to an obstinate halt part way up. "Too small for me," Jones muttered. He tried to contemplate the contorted gymnastics required to negotiate the opening.

"I'll give you a leg up," offered Garelli. Actually it sounded like an order. He stretched up on tiptoe and kind of wedged his head and shoulders through. Garelli threw the rest in after, and then wriggled through behind him.

"Don't we need a search warrant or something?" wondered Jones.

"As usual your timing is impeccable," whispered Garelli, "We're already inside, now be quiet."

He followed her into the bowels of the house. It was not derelict, or even neglected, just seemed very old-fashioned, with faded embossed flock wallpaper, picture rails and cornices, and even dado rails in some rooms. The kitchen was filthy with recent dirt and rubbish: crumpled wrappings, discarded bags and cartons, and empty pizza boxes. Paper and polystyrene cups cluttered the sink. Jones tried the cold tap. The pipes started to knock and rattle back through the house.

"Water's on!" he declared, "Perhaps they found the stopcock. You'd think they'd clean up after themselves?"

"Shush!" hissed Garelli, "if the squatters are here I don't want them to bolt!"

But as it turned out the occupiers were not at home. It was hard to work out how many were using the squat, but three of the rooms were set up to sleep in: huddles of dirty blankets in corners, some crumpled sleeping bags and pieces of foam; nothing much in the way of possessions anywhere.

"See what I mean," said Garelli, "there's no security in a squat. A lot of these places are discovered through burglaries. Any place you can break into, anybody else can do the same. So anything of value you have to carry with you. A lot of these kids carry their worldly goods in a carrier bag. Anything they can't carry they have to hide in the daytime. And then they run the risk of someone watching them, or just stumbling on to it."

"I still think he's out there," said Jones, "Somehow, somewhere. I've got this feeling."

"It's implausible," said Garelli, "An old hermit living rough in a strange city, and sneaking out nights to bump off drug dealers? It's more far-fetched than Superman."

"The ballistics reports match," insisted Jones.

"We've discussed this," said Garelli, "It's not a match. There's no rifling. You cannot match shotguns. It's circumstantial."

"You're splitting hairs," argued Jones, "This has to be more than a coincidence. It's too unlikely."

They moved back into the hallway. Sunlight spilled a rainbowed reflection through the stain glass panels beside the front door.

"We've no motive, no logic, no sense, nothing!" said Garelli.

"There has to be a reason," said Jones, "We just have to find it. I'm sure the old man is capable of killing. You should have seen his eyes. They were dead. And so is his son. It could be revenge?"

"I agree it could piss a parent off," said Garelli, "but we keep coming back to the same thing; and old man alone in a strange city. No contacts! I've read your report a dozen times. Hardly any post to speak of, no phone, no known contact with anybody apart from the daughter: a recluse for years. Now how can he function here?"

Jones stirred at the pools of colour with the toe of his shoe. Dust motes played a kaleidoscope in the air.

"We don't know about contact," said Jones, "we don't know what contact the daughter had with her brother. She could have been a go-between. She disappeared from the island too, but no one is bothering about her. She could have a flat in this city. Has anyone checked?"

"I tried to locate her," said Garelli, "but without much luck."

"You ran a check on her?" asked Jones. He took a punt at a dog-end, tried to kick it back down the hall into the kitchen.

"I tried," repeated Garelli, "She has a history; school record and university and according to you a bona fide teaching job. She sounds solid to me, a career girl. But I haven't been able to trace her yet."

"I did hear she worked in the ACT," said Jones. He thought he had already passed that on, but could not remember for sure. Perhaps the wires had got crossed somewhere in the departmental overlap? "How come she's got papers, and not her father?" he asked.

"Schools don't interrogate kids," said Garelli, "They just enrol them. A school record is a good foundation for an I.D."

"Can we get out through this front door?" asked Jones, focussing on the present once more. The past seemed too contrary. He decided he did not want to wriggle through the window again. He rattled the latch. "Someone burned the old man's house down," he continued, "gutted it." He undid the chain.

"When?" asked Garelli, "I didn't know."

"Recently," muttered Jones, "It could have been vandals."

"Try turning the knob," said Garelli. "There could be another way of looking at this," she mused, "Someone from the mainland might have killed the dogs, and the drug dealers, and the old man, and presumably the son?"

"Why would a hit man shoot two dogs?" asked Jones. He managed to open the door. Sunlight streamed in.

"To silence them?" suggested Garelli, "Perhaps he was looking for something?"

"And buries them afterwards, and leaves flowers on their grave?" Jones looked up at the sky. It was clear blue with a hint of smog round the edges. "Besides the timing's all wrong. It doesn't make sense!"

"What does about this case?" snapped Garelli, "Perhaps the killer likes animals."

"The son must be the key," said Jones, "How did the police know where to contact his father when the son's body was found?" He walked out onto the porch.

"That's a little complicated," said Garelli, "The body was found in the back of a skip at a demolition site in the suburbs. There was a trash bag alongside with some clothes in it. Blood

94

on the clothes matched the body's. In a back pocket of the jeans was an account balance slip from an automatic teller. Murder Squad took the print out to the bank to get the I.D and address. At the son's flat they found the father's address."

"So what about the head and hands?" asked Jones.

"Never turned up," said Garelli.

"Doesn't make sense," said Jones.

"You're repeating yourself," said Garelli. "But I'll look out the son's file when we get back. Just to shut you up. But I can't remember anything of significance in it."

"That's funny," said Jones, "I distinctly remember the old man implying the boy was trouble. It was almost as if he were expecting the worst." He tried to recall the exact words, "Something about breaking the peace?"

Garelli shrugged. "To a hermit a visitor would be breaking the peace. Are you going to close that door or what?"

*

The other addresses yielded little more. A scattering of discarded syringes in one, and a couple of bodies dead to the world in another, but still breathing gave Jones some worries about overdoses. Until Garelli pointed out that the bodies were surrounded by bottles, not needles. The final port of call was some waste ground cluttered with massive unlaid pipes at the back of the urban freeway. The pre-cast concrete sections were almost wide enough to walk into. They were bare and empty.

"I suppose these should only be checked at night," said Garelli, "No one would lay up here in daylight."

"What are we doing here?" muttered Jones, "today's been a waste of time."

"I seem to remember someone wanting to get some air?" commented Garelli, "Besides, now we've checked out all the locations and exits. Have you ever tried to find your way into a strange house in the dark?"

"What are these pipes?" Jones changed the subject, "they're monstrous."

Garelli shrugged, "Storm drains I think, or sewers? Does it matter?"

"Suppose not," he muttered, "I dare say they keep the rain off."

"We'll come back in the early hours," said Garelli, "see what the cat brings."

"I wouldn't mind a decent night's sleep for once," said Jones.

"I expect these kids feel the same," she said, tapping the folder against her leg, "You could take an afternoon nap."

"I'd like to see that file," insisted Jones.

\*

Jones was feeling irritable by the time they got back to the station. It was the clash of priorities. His was the old man. It was why he was here. Garelli's now seemed to be the youth file. He could not get her to see his point. And then Mulligan got into them about unwarranted overtime, said he could not authorise night work when the day shift had eight hours unproductivity to go begging. Garelli commented on the tightness of his rear-end, and said she was prepared to help missing kids for free. Jones left them to it. Out in the corridor he bumped into the suit from the Feds, the silent partner of the outraged bureaucrat who had set up his transfer.

"Officer Jones," said the suit, "So how are you? Are you settling in O.K? Are your expenses enough? How's that hotel we arranged for you? Is it O.K?"

Jones was embarrassed. He supposed they were checking up on him. He suddenly wondered whether his wheelings and dealings on his expenses were allowable after all.

"Well actually," he admitted, "I found the hotel a little sterile. So I moved into lodgings. More homely."

Jones told him the name of the road. The suit nodded reassuringly. He did not question Jones's savings. Jones felt a mixture of guilt and relief.

"So how's the investigation going?" the suit continued pleasantly.

Jones wondered for a moment at the use of language; it was more of a search than an investigation, or was at least supposed to be? Force of habit, he presumed automatically. He decided to seize the opportunity anyway.

"I'm beginning to suspect there's a drugs connection, sir," he proffered. But this was not his city; he needed perspective, somebody to give him the low-down. Impulsively he decided to bypass Garelli. She was obstinate most of the time, all of the time? She did not even attempt to see things his way, but then, after all, he was the rank outsider. He tried for humility.

"I could do with some expert advice, sir. I'm totally at sea, out of my depth," up the creek actually, and no paddle in sight.

The suit nodded again, self-importantly this time. "I've got some contacts in the Drugs Squad," he said, "I'll get someone to call you. What number can I reach you on?"

Jones gave him Garelli's desk extension. The suit indulged in a couple more platitudes, then thankfully got lost.

"So what did he want?" asked Garelli from the doorway to Mulligan's office.

97

"Oh, he was just passing the time of day, seeing how I was doing," said Jones.

Garelli looked cynical somehow.

"He's one of the Feds who asked for my transfer," explained Jones.

Garelli shook her head, "He's State Police. That's Superintendent Campbell from the C.I.B."

"Are you sure?" asked Jones.

"He was my boss for the last five years," said Garelli, "the jock that got me placed here. If he had anything to do with your transfer, it was to wind me up."

"That's paranoid," exclaimed Jones.

Garelli raised an eyebrow. "No," she said, "that's sexual politics."

"Garelli?" asked Jones, "what did you really do to get transferred?"

"I told you already," she said.

"Your gun went off," said Jones, he knew there had been a problem of accidental discharge with some of the newly issued automatics, "that was all."

"It was where the bullet ended up," admitted Garelli.

"So where was that?" asked Jones.

"In someone's butt," said Garelli.

"Whose?" insisted Jones.

"A man's," said Garelli. She crumpled a sheet of paper into a ball and turned and launched at the waste bin by Mulligan's desk. It sailed through the air in a perfect curve.

"Goal," cried Garelli and gave a mock squeal.

\*

They could not find the file on the son.

98

"I think the D.I had it last," said Garelli, "Maybe it went back to Murder. It's in their court really. The D.I said it didn't help at all."

Jones rang up homicide. They said they would get back to him. Towards the end of the shift they phoned back. They could not find it anywhere.

"You lot have lost it!" they accused.

"The D.I said it was innocuous anyway," said Garelli, "A few minor misdemeanours years ago. You know, public drunkenness, fighting, nothing out of the ordinary for a young bloke. It shed no light on anything. Murder even surmised the death might have been a random thrill killing? Some pervert? A psycho-sadist?"

"In which case there'd be another," suggested Jones.

"We're all waiting with baited breath," said Garelli.

"So what sort of work did he do?" asked Jones.

"Don't know," said Garelli, "The D.I didn't say, but it couldn't have been important. I don't think he was a butcher." She yawned lazily and arched and flexed her back, like a cat stretching. "I'm going home to crash for a few hours. How about you?"

Jones shrugged noncommittally. "I'm going to hang around for a while," he decided. "I might run that fax from home across to Forensics, see what they say about the ballistics."

"Sure," said Garelli, "I'll pick you up about 10p.m, there's no point going out any earlier."

Jones groaned at her departing back. He really did not want to hit the streets again, but he did not have the neck to tell Garelli to her face. He wondered if he could think up some excuse to get out of it. Then while it was on his mind he decided to run a computer check on the son's work. But he could not find a tax file number, or a Medicare or social security number in the system. That was most likely a mistake on his part, so he would have to ask Garelli to crosscheck his procedures. He decided to give it away until he saw her again, and wandered over to Forensics.

Everybody was too tied up, too busy, or too plain parochial to bother with him. In the end he got a clerk to pull the files on the recent shootings, and then he harassed a young female technician about to go for a break into comparing them with his fax. The technician relented just to get away, and invited Jones and the files to the canteen with him. Over a coffee she studied the reports.

"It's a possible match," she nodded finally, "but that's all. The ammo's the same. All the bullets were definitely fired from a smoothbore: probably from the same gun, because I have never heard of one used in Australia before. It is too much of a coincidence, but I suppose that technically it could be two different firearms. You would have to ask the Prosecutor's Office to ascertain whether it could be entered as evidence. I suppose it could be circumstantial, if you could prove a connection between the bodies. Who got shot in this?" she held up Jones's fax.

"A couple of dogs," said Jones. He felt embarrassed again.

"Dogs" queried the technician, "if you are referring to human females of a less than glamorous outlook and a bitchy disposition I would remind you that we take verbal harassment very seriously in this State."

Jones nodded. Garelli certainly took it very seriously. "No, canine," he admitted weakly.

"I'm on my break," said the technician wearily, "and you have got me doing veterinary work?"

Jones muttered his thanks, and left hastily.

*

The call to Garelli's phone gave Jones instructions how to find the squad's main base of operations. The disembodied voice had more than a sense of flatness to it; Jones felt the caller was just going through the motions. He made an appointment anyway, a.s.a.p despite the caller's reluctance. Jones wanted to take advantage of Garelli's absence.

The Drugs Squad was in the same building, but almost in the basement.

"To be near the sewers as possible," grinned the young bloke who met him at the squad room door, "Our section's like a toilet, it's always full of shit." He laughed crazily.

Jones wondered if his guide had been sampling the wares.

The young bloke introduced Jones to a sergeant, who looked over Jones wearily. He told him clearly to pass on any relevant information, and threatened Jones if he should stuff up any ongoing investigation. Jones said he could not determine relevance without context, and that was what he had come for. The sergeant told Jones he was too busy and handballed him back to the young bloke.

"Acro," he said to the youngster, "Take Apples here and take him on a tour of our orchard. Don't let him pick any rotten ones. All in the spirit of inter-force co-operation," he glared at Jones balefully, and stomped back to his desk and a mess of paperwork.

Jones was getting fed up with all the fruit jokes.

"Acro?" he asked hopefully in retaliation.

"Theo Xanakaredapopoulis. Greek," replied the young bloke, "but thick-skinned, like an olive."

"Didn't know they were?" commented Jones.

101

"Stick to your area of expertise, Apples?" Acro won that round hands down.

Actually he turned out to be not too bad a lad under all the swagger, and he took Jones up to the canteen to feed him all the grisly details.

"There's no clear lines," said Theo sitting down with a half-dried sandwich and a weak coffee. "The city's awash with cash. It's what we call high liquidity," he laughed again but Jones didn't get the joke. "All the local sopranos want a piece of it. It's a free market. Everything's up for grabs if you've got the balls to take it. But there are generalisations. Generally speaking the bikers control the amphetamines, the Asians control the hardcore like heroin, and the bangers run the ecstasy."

"Bangers?" queried Jones.

"Shoot anything, especially themselves," grinned Theo. "Bang, bang, you're dead."

"What about marijuana?" asked Jones?

"Amateurs," dismissed Theo, "Grow your owners. Hydroponics in the roof. Bush blocks, hobby farmers. Strictly small potatoes. Es are where the volume is. There are at least a dozen raves going down every weekend. It's the party drug of choice. Dance the night away and kiss your hangover goodbye."

"I think I'm looking at Chinese?" said Jones.

"Heroin probably," said Theo, "it comes out of Asia."

"They all had track marks," said Jones, thinking back over the sequence of bodies.

"Sounds like you've been looking at bottom-feeders," said Theo, "Just remember that administration doesn't do the product, only foot soldiers."

"Any word on the street?" asked Jones.

102

"Their community's a fairly closed shop," said Theo. "We don't often get informants. There's usually some maggot who'd squeal out anybody, especially their own mother, but not there. There were some rumours about triads a coupla years back: some business people from the Shenzhen Special Economic Region seeing an opportunity for export. Or perhaps it was the Hong Kong Administrative Zone? It's all Chinese to me!" he laughed uproariously.

Jones did not know what specifically he was talking about, but figured the young bloke had to be showing off, so he purposefully ignored the fine detail, and the ethnic joke.

"So how did you hear?" asked Jones of the contradiction?

"From the opposition," said Theo. "We had to process the bodies."

Jones nodded. Like now, he thought, it had come full circle. But where was the beginning, and how did the old man fit in? He thanked the young bloke for his time and got up to leave.

"No probs!" said Theo, "If anything mushrooms I'll give you the heads up."

\*

# Chapter 13. 666

The girl was waiting for him in the seat at Garelli's desk. She was twitchy and strained, turning in the chair and drumming her fingers on the top. He always found shaved heads in women very threatening, let alone repulsive, and this one also had 666 tattooed into her scalp.

"Where's the lady cop then?" she snapped, "They told me to wait for her here." Her voice was strained and abrupt, on the edge of rudeness. She was dressed in black, like a mourner, and she wore a plain earring pierced through one eyebrow, and a stud through one nostril. She almost fascinated him, like a snake.

"Officer Garelli's out for a while," apologised Jones. "I'm her partner. Can I help?" he wondered if an earring was still an earring when it hung from an eyebrow?

She pouted and looked aggressively sullen. "You're a man!" she stated and went silent.

Jones hardly felt reassured by that. It did not sound intended as a compliment. He too regarded her silently. He wondered what would happen if she blew her nose. Would the stud pop out like the plug of a volcano? Would snot spray all over her face like erupting magma? She started to pace up and down on the carpet, her shoulders slumped and her head pulled in, her feet kicking at the pile in angry stabs.

"You've got guts!" said Jones, flying by instinct; "Marching into a cop shop must take a lot of bottle for someone like you."

"And what's someone like me?" snapped the girl.

Jones cursed himself inwardly; how did he turn that around? He had to be positive. She was young, but he could not say how. She was probably a street kid by her attitude, and possibly an addict by her behaviour, but he could not place her, could not remember her from his nocturnal forays.

"Well!" he cleared his throat, "You look like a survivor to me, a real survivor in an alternative world. Part of the underground!"

She stared at him closely. "Yeah!" she said at last, "I'm an outlaw."

Jones felt himself relax. He had got her onside.

"You're that redneck prick Garry was towing around the other night," the kid shattered his delusion, "You gave me this poster," she produced the flyer with a flourish, held it out at arm's length. "What's it worth?" she demanded suddenly.

Jones was nonplussed, "What do you mean?"

"You said you wanted info on the old fart," she spat, "on the lost grandpops. What's it worth?"

Jones stared at her. "I....I've no idea?" he stammered. He was totally at a loss. "I'd have to refer to Officer Garelli," he prevaricated.

"Shit!" swore the girl. She spun and stamped angrily to the door. "When you make up your mind, I'll be at the usual place," she shouted over her shoulder.

"Wh...wh...where's that?" called Jones, but she was gone. He stared after her mesmerised, rooted to the spot. When he snapped out of it, it was too late even to run after her.

Jones thought about it for a while. He was caught between desire verging on desperation to discover exactly what the girl was offering, and fear of arousing Garelli's possible derision and undoubted temper if he should have the gall to go and

105

immediately wake her up. In the end desperation got the better of discretion, and he decided to contact her. He persuaded himself that he only had to stand up to her and she would see it his way and give him credit for this latest break. So he elected to avoid the phone but to go in person; at least that way he might be able to insist on a hearing. He ventured down to the car pool, but they would not sign out a car to him, not without Garelli. That instantly reinforced his sense of ambivalence about his role and the confusion of his official identity. So he decided to walk regardless, and strode out in to the street with head held high, determined to strike out for the nearest cab rank or passing flow of traffic.

But it was the sort of day when the ranks were bare and the fares relentless so he was constrained to keep walking, hoping against hope that eventually he would manage to flag down an empty taxi. As he walked a sense of unease began to build within him, and he began to feel a sense of foreboding, a premonition almost. He did not know if it was the crush of the crowds, or the heat of the day, or the traffic fumes, or just the simple edge of exhaustion. Maybe it was paranoia developing with his increasing isolation and alienation from his surroundings. But he began to feel he was being followed. Someone somewhere behind and to the side that seemed to slide into shadow or slip into doorways if he turned. But nothing certain, an elusive blur too far back in the crowd to be distinctive. Eventually he did manage to catch a cab, and once cocooned in the cut and thrust of the traffic he was able to shrug the feeling aside.

Garelli withered him with a prolonged icy stare. He felt himself shrinking into the floor, could not hold her gaze and ended up mumbling into his boots.

"It's.s.s.s a g.g.good break," he heard himself stammer, "Shows I was right with the posters."

"Why on earth?" Garelli was flat and controlled, "didn't you give her some money?"

"I…I didn't know the procedure," said Jones. He had never had a paid informant before.

"The procedure," declared Garelli, "is that you dip into your back pocket and come out with a century. It's called an on the spot decision. You concentrate on the opportunity, worry about the paperwork later, and the money. You are a tightwad Jones. You're a single man. What are you doing with all the money you earn?"

"I'm saving," explained Jones, "for my retirement. I want to buy a farm."

"Jones," exclaimed Garelli, "you're barely thirty, and already you're planning for death?"

Jones tried to change the subject. "What do you think she knew?" he tried to sound eager.

"How the hell should I know?" swore Garelli, "I wasn't the deadhead who let her go!" She started storming around her flat, picking random pieces of clothing off various pieces of furniture. Then she slammed into the bedroom.

"She was probably desperate to score," said Garelli on the way out, "If we move fast maybe we can still catch her."

"If she's got no money what's the rush?" asked Jones. "She'll have to wait."

Garelli stopped at the car and turned to face him. "If she needs a fix bad enough to walk into a station to score, she'll be headed to the Strip to try to turn a trick. That could take her anywhere."

Jones had a little difficulty with the idiom. "She's too ugly to be a prostitute," he hazarded, "and she looks like a lesbian."

"And you're too naïve to be true," stated Garelli, "That's a market place out there, and demand exceeds supply. She owns a commodity; it's just a question of money. And as for being gay, what has that to do with the price of meat? Why do you think these kids take drugs?"

"To get high!" grunted Jones as they headed down town; he was not that naïve.

"Wrong!" denied Garelli, "It's to get lost. To hide the pain."

Jones thought about that, and then let it go. "Do you really think she might know something?" he turned the arrow back.

"Like I said," Garelli sounded tired, "she fronted up at the station. To do that as a scam would take more than balls."

Garelli parked up in a side street, hit Jones for his spare change and loaded up the meter. They began to tour the central strip, but there was no sign of the girl.

"Maybe she meant somewhere else," implied Jones.

"Not this time of day," stated Garelli, "this is where the action is."

They shuffled through the packs of tourists wandering the sidewalks. Chairs and tables from the street cafes spilled over the pavements. The sightseers strolled aimlessly in the sun, slowing the pace of the hustling natives. Gusts of hot wind funnelled in from the skyscrapers and stirred the litter and debris in the gutters. Crumpled papers bowled along in the breeze. Garelli started checking the arcades and pinny-parlours. Jones was feeling cramped and claustrophobic. The air was hot and fouled with dust and fumes. It was hard to breathe. He stayed outside on the pavement, feeling lost and alien. A street kid came over and hassled him. "Can you spare a couple of dollars mister? So I can buy some food?"

Jones shook his head in disgust, totally affronted. Most likely the kid only wanted smokes. Beggars on the street in his country, it was offensive? The kid should be in school, getting a future. He told Garelli when she emerged into the light. She laughed at him, harsh and cynical. Her eyes were mirthless.

"Try talking to them," she sneered, "about their past. These kids have no future. They're all trying to commit suicide, but slowly. But they won't admit to it. Life's like that. It fools you into carrying on, when every minute you're only dying. Some of us just take longer than others. But we all come to the same place in the end. Who's the more honest?"

Jones did not want to attempt to answer that. In fact he did not think it was even worth thinking about. He just wanted to find the old man and then he could escape this urban dream. He could go back to a frame of reference he could comprehend.

"Let's make some enquiries about the girl," he decided, "She's quite outstanding. She must be known round here. She knew you."

Garelli bit her lip. "What do you think I've been doing here, Jones?" she asked, "Just stay here propped up in the sun and leave me to my thing. You frighten the children."

"No I don't!" he felt compelled to remonstrate, tiredness and irritation overcoming sense. "I've had a lot of professional guidance on how to deal with children: I'm good with them, I've done Teacher Training."

Garelli stared back at him, silent for a moment. "You've done Teacher Training?" she repeated, "So are you qualified and registered, or was this some Adult Ed bullshit?"

"I did two years of a B.Ed," Jones felt himself flushing, and wished he'd never broached the subject.

"So you flunked out on the practicum," stated Garelli, as if it were obvious.

"The opportunity to join the Police came up," Jones tried to justify himself.

"Good with children?" sneered Garelli, "You're a woodentop, Jones. So uptight it's a wonder you can shit. Frighten the children? Don't you remember me telling you you're a man? Or haven't you looked in the mirror lately? On reflection you probably terrify them!"

She strode off into the crowd without a backward glance. Jones sighed and tried to follow her. She lost him in moments. So he gave up and slumped in a chair against the wall of a sidewalk café.

Garelli woke him up from his doze. He was still nursing the dregs of his cappuccino. The flecks of chocolate clung to the bottom of his cup like sediment. Garelli looked tired and drawn, like the frayed end of a bad day. She pulled up a chair and joined him.

"You were right," she admitted, "She's not a hooker."

Jones nodded solemnly. "I've been thinking about that. There are alternatives; shop-lifting, house-breaking, stealing cars and so forth."

Garelli nodded wearily. "Don't get smug Jones. All that requires planning and time to organise sales from the thefts. Only prostitution provides instant cash. Addicts don't always have the luxury of time. Street kids by definition don't have the luxury of somewhere to store stolen goods."

Jones felt undermined again. "So what have you got?" he asked.

"She's got a girlfriend," said Garelli. "She's the hooker. Our girl looks after her. But she's crook. Crook as a dog. Crashed in the squat unable to trade. Hence the glitch." Garelli sighed and stretched. "I've got an address," she muttered, "another across town squat. But I need to recharge. I'm stuffed."

She sprawled in the late afternoon sun, her arms hung loose and her head thrown back. The light played over the taut skin of her face, accentuating the planes and contours of her skull. Somehow, for the first time since he had met her, she seemed strangely vulnerable.

"By the way Jones," she murmured quietly, "I had to pay for that address. You owe me 50. Partner."

*

The music led them through to the back of the house and helped mask the sound of their coming. It was throbbing relentlessly, some sort of heavy metal painfully vibrating the musty air. Jones was surprised that they risked any noise at all, but supposed it was not really turned up that loud, it was just the oscillation of the low notes that hammered in his gut. Besides, it was a noisy neighbourhood: trains and boats and planes, between the docks and the airport. Maybe it was party time.

As Garelli opened the back room door Jones could see one girl huddled in a sleeping bag in the corner. The shaven-headed girl, their quarry, was kneeling beside her. "Is that you, Mouse?" she called without looking up as the door swung open. She was concentrating intently on her arm. "Give us a hand, I can't find a vein." Her own hand was shaking and her whole body shivered like a pine in the wind.

So she had scored somehow. Jones supposed the how was not particularly relevant, but he would still have liked to know. Garelli walked quickly over, and gently took the syringe off her. Only then did the girl look up and acknowledge her.

"Oh shit!" she moaned, "oh sweet shit!" Her trembling exaggerated into a convulsive shake. She was on her knees

111

before Garelli, the tears rolling down her cheeks. "Please," she pleaded, "I've got to have it."

Garelli held the syringe up to the light and flicked at the barrel with a finger. "Is this gear O.K?" she asked.

The girl nodded eagerly. "I've just fixed up Emmy, she's off with the clouds."

Jones realised she could not have been back long. He looked at the other girl. She was lying there, breathing softly, her eyes glazed and staring out of a pasty grey face. Ulcerated sores covered her lips and the edges of her nostrils were rimed with a yellowing crust. A tangled bundle of dirty clothes were a pillow for her head.

"You share needles?" Garelli asked the shaven girl.

The girl nodded indifferently. "I can't get the tourniquet tight," she complained, her free hand fumbling with the cord lashed around her other arm. Garelli bent down and fiddled with the binding. Jones suddenly realised what she was doing and stepped forward to intervene.

"Don't fuck with me," pleaded the girl. Garelli looked up and stopped Jones dead in his tracks.

"I wouldn't dream of it," she said to the girl.

She got the girl to pump her arm a few times and handed back the syringe. The girl bent over her arm squinting intently. "There's one," she said at last.

Garelli steadied her other hand as she slid the needle in. The lines of tension seemed to leach away and the girl's body relaxed and folded in on itself like a flower closing. She knelt there for a moment rocking gently, and then crawled carefully in with the other girl.

Jones turned away, utterly appalled. He stumbled out the door, almost crushed with the feelings of disgust and distaste.

112

Garelli wandered out after him. He turned on her savagely, gripping her shoulders and shaking her violently.

"What the hell have you done?" he demanded, "What the hell did you do that for?"

Garelli pried his fingers loose. Her eyes were unblinking. "I've helped her to a few hours peace," she said. She looked straight into his eyes. He saw a depth of sadness there he would not have thought possible.

"I thought for a moment you'd helped the silly cow kill herself," he said.

"I told you before they don't want the quick way out," she said, "just the easy one."

Jones shook his head hopelessly. "You're an officer, you can't behave like this. Supposing it got out. You'd be finished."

"How?" asked Garelli, "Are you going to dob me in? They aren't."

Jones shook his head. "What now?" he asked helplessly, "We're still none the wiser."

"Now we wait," said Garelli, "till they come down. Then we'll have a talk."

She leaned against the wall and slid down it to sit on the floor. Jones hunkered down beside her.

"How come you seem to know so much about all this?" he asked her, "You haven't been in Missing Persons that long."

"I worked in C.I.B for years," she said, "It seems like nowadays most crime is drug related. On the street level at least." She yawned hugely and made faces at Jones. "I'm so tired," she declared, "Promise me when it's over you'll take me away from all this. We could do a river cruise; take a walk in a forest. Try and find some of this fresh air you're always on about." She sniggered softly and Jones realised she was taking the piss. For a moment he had thought she was serious. Then she closed her eyes and appeared to doze.

Jones tried to relax but could not. He sat down beside her and decided to maintain guard as the evening drew in. Her head began to sag and lolled across to rest on his shoulder, and her hair tickled his nose. He sat there stiff as a dummy fighting the urge to sneeze. It was the nearest he had been to a woman in years.

Jones woke up to the soft murmur of voices. A guttering candle flickered gross shadows through the doorway. He stretched and rolled to his feet and peered in. Garelli was hovering over the bedding on her knees, her hands fluttering like wings. The candlelight made a halo of her hair. Then she eased up slowly like a sapling released from the wind. Her hand pulled something from her purse. The note fluttered to the ground like a falling leaf.

"I'll see you tomorrow," she said. "I'll be in all day. I'll take you out to lunch."

As she turned towards the door the light was behind her, and her features fell into shadow. Her face advanced on Jones like a black mask.

"What are you doing?" he hissed, "Why aren't we bringing them in?"

She put a finger to his lips, took him by the elbow and led him out.

"What's the score then?" he asked as they broached the night. The neon glow of the electric constellation warmed the edges of the dark. It was hard to see the stars.

"Garelli 2, Jones 0," she said, "That's a century you owe me now."

Jones tried hard to maintain his cool. "Jesus Garelli, you're so...."

"Exasperating? Or expensive?" she finished for him, "Isn't that a woman's prerogative?"

Her eyes flashed in the lamplight.

Jones shrugged helplessly.

"What we've got," Garelli took pity on him, "is another face. They've got a friend who's been staying with an older man in an expensive flat by the beach. The man is looking for his son."

"You paid $100 for that?" gasped Jones, "That's lamer than a three-legged milking cow!"

"$200, actually," corrected Garelli, "$100 each. You still owe me. But this is genuine. I told you one of these kids wouldn't front at the station on a scam."

"So it's a coincidence," snapped Jones, "but it can't be our man. His son is dead, remember?" He was angry; many more wild goose chases like this and he would be bled dry. "So how do we go about claiming this on expenses?" he asked.

"Lighten up, Jones," groaned Garelli, "this really is serious. The man had designer stubble and a moustache. And eyes like a fish, unquote. Our girl met him. Let me explain as we drive back to the station. I want to check up on something."

*

# Chapter 14. The Stalker

"There's this girl working the Strip, about fourteen, a real looker; honey-blonde and grey sparklers. Wears her hair in a pony-tail, dresses her age down, you know the lollipop look. Goes for the school-girl image."

"Surely she is one," interrupted Jones.

"Shut up and listen," continued Garelli. "This man is touring the kerbs one night. He's got this old photo of this young bloke, looks school age, but really cute. Wavy blonde hair, baby-blue eyes, sexy smile. The girls don't know if it's really his son or a runaway rent-boy, but the old man is flashing big bucks, so honey-bunch says she thinks she recognises the boy. They talk and she goes off with the old feller. Couple of days later the girls see her again. She's flush and flying high. She treats them all to a fix, so they adjourn early to the squat. She tells our girl the old bloke has taken a fancy to her, but is treating her like a daughter, won't touch her. Insists that she stays at his flat, gives her money and a latchkey. She spins him a line about the son, but she gets the feeling that he's not that interested. What he keeps asking her about is drugs, how available they are, and from who. She offers to score for him but he doesn't want that, doesn't want her to do drugs any more either. She's thinking he's weird, that maybe his son died from an overdose or something. Any rate he wants her to point out her dealer to him. Not introduce, just point him out.

Anyhow the girls all get smoked and that's that till the following week, which is the next time Honey turns up. She's quiet and withdrawn, says she's left the old bloke's place and wants to catch up on the squat scene. She won't talk much, but our girl says she was running scared. Something about photographs."

"Pornography," muttered Jones, "the filthy old bastard."

"No!" said Garelli, "That wouldn't bother these girls. No, the old man's out and she's searching the place, looking for some extra pocket money and she finds these photos. Really sick. Mutilated bodies. So she bales out."

"So where's this address?" Jones took a deep breath.

"Don't know," admitted Garelli, "somewhere near the beach."

"And this Honey girl?" queried Jones.

"Hasn't been around for a while," said Garelli. "Our girl's going to come in tomorrow and help us with a photofit. We might want to put out an all points bulletin? We'll need to think about it."

"Why?" asked Jones, "Surely we have to find this girl?"

"It seems to me," Garelli said carefully, "that this latest description matches with that of the hotel receptionist beyond the bounds of coincidence. If it is, as probability suggests, one and the same person, what you have to ask yourself is why should the old man want to see you? Sweet as you are Jones, I don't think that a man who deliberately drops out of sight would simply want to spend the time of day with you? So do we want to draw attention to the importance we place on this girl by publicising it? It might put her in harm's way."

"What choice do we have?" asked Jones, "What other way can we go?"

"We could attempt to be discreet," suggested Garelli. "In the meantime there are a couple of things I want to check up on."

She fell silent, staring intently out through the windscreen.

"Such as?" prompted Jones. He wondered what she saw: taillights in the dark?

"These kids aren't too good on time frames," said Garelli, "it's all the drugs. But I'd like to check up on the dates of those dead dealers. And I think you're right, we really need to pull the son's file."

"But it's gone AWOL," said Jones, "remember?"

"We'll just have to rebuild it," said Garelli.

Jones nodded self-consciously, insignificant again. He did not want to admit that he had tried that and failed. He suddenly felt overwhelmingly depressed by his own inability and her competence. He was also exhausted and hungry. By the look of the streetscape outside they were getting near his digs.

"Garelli?" he suggested tentatively, "I'm whacked, let's call it a night. We can run the checks tomorrow. While we wait for your girl to come in."

"What's the matter?" snorted Garelli, "I thought you were keen, is our pollution tiring you?"

"Don't go out of your way," insisted Jones, "just drop me on the corner at the lights. I'll walk down. Over there, then you won't get routed into the one-way system."

He bade her a curt goodbye and strode off into the night. The lights hummed, the air smelled and his head ached. His street seemed pleasantly quiet after the throb of the clearway, and almost deserted. As he walked down the avenue of trees planted in the paving a leaning figure detached itself from a trunk and fell in behind him. Jones felt uneasy and as he entered the periphery of light cast by the next lamppost he turned uncertainly to face this shadow. A man was following him. A tall spare man carrying a walking stick strolled out of the darkness. The light from the overhead lamp left no illusions. The eyes were unmistakeable, cold and glowing like ice in the moonlight. Jones watched the hand swing the stick up slowly, as if in a dream.

"Officer Jones?" the harsh accent mangled the pronunciation but the voice was flat and controlled, devoid of emotion, empty of life.

Jones froze, his bowels turned to water and the scream died in his throat. He instinctively knew the stick could be a weapon. On the edge of his consciousness he heard a car approaching, but he knew it would not faze the old man. He was locked on, like a stalking snake. He took a pace forward and the walking stick brushed at Jones's shoulder like a caressing fly. Jones stared at his death in those bleak eyes and had nothing to say. Then the car engine gunned and a horn blared and the old man blinked and spun away with a snarl. As the car mounted the kerb he threw himself sideways and over the hedge of the garden next to them. Garelli's eyes stared wildly behind the windscreen. She crashed the hedge and flung herself out of the car but he was gone, lost in the night.

"Damn!" cursed Garelli, "He's quick! Was he pulling on you? Did I see that?" She paced around angrily, like a predator cheated of its prey. "I daren't go after him, I'm unarmed."

Jones was breathing in short shallow gasps. "Slow enough for me," he croaked and laughed shrilly, like a hysterical child. Garelli moved in close and slapped him hard.

"Christ, Jones, you stink!" she muttered.

"I've shit myself," he admitted, and started giggling again. This time she let him go.

Garelli backed the car out as best she could. There was no serious damage, at least not to the vehicle. The hedge was wrecked.

"Get in!" she ordered Jones, "We'll go to my place."

"I need a change of clothes," Jones was sheepish.

"Just get in!" insisted Garelli, "You stay out here and you're a target. I'll pick up your gear tomorrow. Now move it!"

He did, and sat in embarrassed discomfort.

"Christ, Jones," complained Garelli, "wind down the window."

She reversed savagely out into the street. The tyres squealed as she accelerated down the road. "That's better," she breathed, "I was worried he might try to shoot it out. Silly old devil couldn't have realised I wasn't carrying. Aren't old bones supposed to be brittle? You'd think he'd break a leg?" she added as an afterthought.

".22 smoothbores are hardly appropriate for gun battles," commented Jones, "They're very weak and inaccurate. And it's old women that get brittle bones. It's a calcium deficiency due to pregnancy."

Garelli snorted, "So Jones, your wits are recovering, are they? It's about time. You were like a stunned rabbit back there. What was that he was holding you with?"

"A shooting-stick?" presumed Jones, "probably a single shot .22 with a silencer encased in cane. They used to be very popular in Europe with poachers. Lethal close-up," he shook his head weakly. "So how come you came back for me?" he asked.

"Typical woman!" grunted Garelli, "thinking of your stomach. While I was waiting for the lights I realised you'd probably need a takeaway. I came back to save you from your landlady."

"Thanks," said Jones simply. It was heartfelt but he did not know what else to say.

"Don't take it personally," said Garelli, "I just didn't want you folding on me in the morning. I had a heavy day planned."

"So when are you going to report it?" Jones sighed.

"Let's think about that," said Garelli. "We'll discuss it after you get cleaned up."

*

Jones sat at the breakfast counter in Garelli's flat drinking steadily. Garelli had provided the whisky. It was old and mellow and warmed like fire.

"You don't get violent when you're drunk?" asked Garelli.

"Not with women," muttered Jones.

"Good," said Garelli, "I know I can take you but I wouldn't want to trash the flat."

Jones groaned. She was hopeless but he owed her a big one now. He scowled sullenly, sat there in her bathrobe and pyjamas. The legs were too short and the arms too tight. He felt like a fool.

"I don't understand why you don't call it in?" he slurred.

"Information is power," said Garelli. "Lack of it, in your case, was nearly fatal. How and why is what you've got to ask yourself."?

"The how's easy," muttered Jones, "He'd only have to follow me from the station."

He remembered that uneasy feeling from the other day. So it could have been real after all.

"How would he know you're over here?" persisted Garelli, "Someone must have told him: who and why?"

Jones shrugged, he had no idea.

"Think about it!" demanded Garelli, "There has to be a connection with the force. Who else could know?"

Jones was shocked; he felt his mouth drop.

"Why?" he queried, feeling the sense of it slip away like a wriggling eel.

"I don't know!" admitted Garelli, "Perhaps we should start with the other question. Why should the old man want to kill you?" She made him go through that first meeting again and again. The only thing he could think of was that he could recognise and thus identify the old man. But neither he nor Garelli could believe that was enough to justify murder.

"What about the language he spoke?" mused Garelli. "You said he spoke in foreign, to the daughter. Can you repeat it?"

Jones shook his head. It had been momentary gibberish. He recalled a sense of softness contrasted with the harshness of the accent when the old man spoke in English, but that was all. It had been a lifetime ago in another world. "It was probably European," he guessed, because they were white, "but East or West I wouldn't know. Their pasts are full of forgotten conflicts and broken promises."

"A refugee from a foreign war?" said Garelli. "We could go down to the foreign languages department at the university and run it by them."

"I can't run anything I can't remember," said Jones. "It would be easier to ask the daughter. Have you tracked her down yet?"

Garelli nodded, "Good one Jones, I'd forgotten all about her. I'll run some checks in the ACT. Name of Smith, wasn't it? But hey, she might even be in the Telstra directory? Of course she might deny everything over the phone."

"We could go and visit," said Jones, refusing to be baited, "take that ride in the country you were on about."

"Christ Jones, this is the mainland," said Garelli, "if she does live in Canberra it's hundreds of kilometres away. Somehow I'll have to try and get a phone number first. I don't like long distance travel. I get homesick."

"I know the feeling," nodded Jones, suddenly feeling overwhelmingly sorry for himself. Garelli dropped the interrogation and poured him another drink. They sat there drinking steadily, listening to music while the night died. Garelli looked all mellow and cosy in the firelight.

"You're not a bad sort, Jonesy, for a bloke," she ventured, "How come some smart woman hasn't taken up your option?"

"Never been with a woman," Jones blurted. The words sprayed out before he could stop them. He never meant to talk about that, ever. He glanced at Garelli, expecting derision but only finding sympathy.

"I've never been with a man," she said, "only an animal."

Jones did not know what she meant. He was faintly disgusted.

"Do you live at home with Mum?" she probed gently.

"No, I'm an orphan," he replied curtly.

"I thought you said you lived on a farm?" she continued.

"Fostered out!" he muttered. He did not want to talk about that either.

"Don't you keep in touch?" asked Garelli.

Jones shook his head. "The past is a closed door," he said, "I don't want to open it." Or remember it, he thought. But of course it was impossible to escape entirely. One had appearances to keep up, and expectations. Like the wedding, best man, and the obligatory annual hunt, a kind of primeval male ritual that for some reason he could never refuse. "Put the notebook away, detective," he suggested, "I thought we were trying to unwind?"

She apologised and poured him another drink.

"You know something, Jonesy?" she hazarded after a while, "if you'd been born near a city you would probably have been a street-kid."

Jones shook his head and stared at her. Her eyes were wide and unguarded, the sadness spilling over in glistening tears.

Her words were still turning in his mind when he finally passed out.

*

"Damn!" cursed Garelli, throwing the phone down on her desk. An echo hissed around the office, whispered off the walls to fade and die in a cluttered corner. "That f...ing surname. It's impossible. Do you happen to know her Christian name?"

Jones shook his head despondently. He had never thought to ask. But it would be known by people in the community, and of course the truck had been registered to her. He could ring home and ask his replacement to find it out. Only that would make him look such a fool. He offered anyway, but Garelli had another thought.

"Maiden name of Smith!" she suddenly popped the comment, "What if she's married? Did you happen to notice a wedding ring?"

Jones shook his head again: he had not noticed. He tried to make an excuse about the awkwardness on the occasion distracting his attention, but in the end he just gave up and accepted that he had failed once more.

She simply said to put it on hold while they concentrated on the son.

Jones sighed. Little hammers were driving spikes into the back of his eyeballs. His stomach churned; the knot was not unravelling, it was disappearing. The daughter could be anywhere now. They had rebuilt the son's file. It was meaningless, nothing for years, and before then only incidents:

minor assaults and drunkenness. The last recorded was a charge of possession. A Detective Constable Mulligan was the arresting officer. They could only assume it was one and the same; the name was not that common. Garelli said she would check it out, as it was a connection of sorts, albeit a long time ago. But all in all, it just looked like a young bloke's wild oats, and it seemed as though he had outgrown them years back. The only obvious fly in the ointment was the lack of a tax file number, which Garelli could not extract. She said she would follow that up with the tax office.

"So what do we do about Honey?" Jones had asked Garelli. He was trying hard to hold himself together, but it felt as though the dykes were crumbling.

"I've thought about that," said Garelli, "When our friend comes in we'll get her the check through the current Youth File. If Honey's on it we can resurrect her as a missing person. If she's not on it we can put her on it. Either way we can put out a legitimate APB on her as a missing person. We can fabricate some urgent family reasons. We don't have to publicise the connection with the old man at all. That way we don't put the girl in jeopardy.

"That's good," said Jones. He was impressed; that should hold the tide for a while.

"I want to go down to the mortuary to check up on something," said Garelli, "You wait here for the girl and start her off with the identikit."

Jones started to shake his head but it hurt too much. "She trusts you, not me," he stated the obvious, "That's not a good idea. Find another errand boy."

"No way," said Garelli, "We keep this in the family. But you're right. I'll stay. We'll both go together later, after the girl's finished."

"If it's the dates of those deaths," said Jones; "Surely we can get them without going out?" He was feeling paranoid about leaving the sanctuary of the station.

"No, it's not them," said Garelli, "but that's good thinking. I'd forgotten. Check them out while we wait."

Jones did. Drug killings were not a rare occurrence in the city, so he went back to the first known use of the .22 as the method of execution. It coincided roughly with the time frame of the girl's story. Jones thought he should probably have felt good about that. It was another part that fit the puzzle. But in fact it just made his headache worse. He had the mother of all hangovers, on top of a squeamish stomach. And Garelli was insisting they go to the mortuary. He felt sick to death but she maintained it was important.

*

In the afternoon, after the girl had been and gone, Mulligan stopped them on the way out. "So what's with all the V.I.P treatment for that ugly mole? She's not even in the files; I couldn't forget that plate in a hurry!"

Garelli handed him a flyer. "She came in to help us with this missing girl," she said, "She's got recent information on her whereabouts. I've made it a priority. The father is facing open-heart surgery."

Mulligan glanced at the poster. "Well at least she's good-looking," he mumbled, "I wouldn't mind finding her myself." He handed the poster back. "Next time get authorisation from me before you proceed," he ordered. "We have an official priority list here, and it comes from upstairs. "I'll need a written justification for this: on my desk, a.s.a.p!" He sniffed and retreated into his office.

126

Garelli was taut as a coiled spring.

"Ignore him," said Jones, "He's an insect."

Garelli nodded, and ground her heel into the carpet.

"One day!" she promised on the way out.

*

At the mortuary Garelli wanted to know if anybody could remember the son's body. That was easy, everyone could. Headless corpses were not that common, even in the big smoke amidst the perennial gang wars. The technician who had seen them before came over.

"Have you come to see the latest arrival?" he queried.

He took them over to a table. Under the sheet was another Asian, but older looking than the previous. This one had a neat round hole drilled in the centre of his forehead.

"When?" asked Garelli?

"Came in yesterday," said the mortician.

Jones swore, thinking of himself the previous night.

Garelli inspected the arms. "Drugs?" she queried. There were no track marks.

"Possibly," said the expert, "the pupils are dilated," he peeled back an eyelid, "but fear can sometimes do that."

"I'll take your word for it," said Garelli.

"Autopsy's this arvo," said the mortician. "I'll confirm after." He covered the body up again. "Now what did you want to know about that other affair. We call him our Missing Link: until the head turns up of course."

"His files have gone missing," said Garelli. "We wondered if you could help?"

127

The mortician shrugged, "The autopsy reports go to the coroner. Then the police take over, pending the verdict. We don't keep copies. Space is a dying luxury around here."

"What about photographs?" asked Garelli?

"With the files," said the mortician; "The negatives will be around somewhere upstairs. Check with filing on the way out. Mind you, don't expect them to drop anything, they'll want an authorisation to release them."

Garelli winced. "Can we look at the body?" she asked

The mortician stared at her, for once seeming to be lost for words. "It has been released for cremation," he said, "last week I believe."

Garelli shook her head as if in disbelief.

"It would only have been processed with the proper authorisation," the mortician almost seemed defensive. "A woman arranged it. Over the phone I seem to remember, and the paperwork sent by courier mail. You'll have to check with the office."

Jones wondered if the daughter had intervened, and if so, why had no one seen fit to inform them?

"Can you describe the body to me?" Garelli asked, relentless in the face of apparent adversity, refusing to be stalled.

"Of course," he replied, "only the face wasn't so memorable. Excuse me," he cleared his throat, "I can't remember the stats, but I was assured that they matched the presumed I.D. In fact I did the measurements to confirm it. I had to guess the size of the head of course, but within normal parameters it was spot on."

"There was nothing else?" asked Jones, disappointed again.

"Only the usual track marks on the arms," said the mortician.

Garelli raised her eyebrows.

"He was a heroin addict," said the mortician, "quite a heavy habit too by analysis of his blood. Oh yes, one last thing; there was a random pattern of knife cuts on his right pectoral. A bit like noughts and crosses from a demented surgeon with a scalpel."

"Fresh? Or scarred?" asked Garelli.

"Well sort of fresh actually," he replied, "but after death. That's what we couldn't figure. At first we thought torture, the death of the thousand cuts, etcetera. But why would you torture a headless body. But it was probably a fruitcake. That would explain the head. Who knows with nuts?"

"Could you draw them for me?" asked Garelli.

He shook his head, "Sorry Officer; like I said, it was a scribble."

Garelli sighed and thanked him. They both turned down the offer of joining the mortician for a coffee break.

"Hey don't upset me," was his parting shot, "you'll both end up here one day."

"You should be so lucky!" retorted Garelli, "I'm younger than you."

"But I'm immune," said the mortician, "Death doesn't affect me any more."

"No?" Garelli had to have the last word, "What about your sense of humour?"

\*

"Are we going to try for the negatives?" asked Jones on the way out.

"You heard the man," said Garelli, "We'll need a piece of paper: probably in triplicate. That will mean going through Mulligan. I don't think I'm up to that today."

"Pity we can't bypass him," muttered Jones, "write our own requisition."

Garelli smacked his hand. "That would be forgery. Besides, they might check the signature."

Jones swore silently as they pushed out into the sunlight. Garelli suddenly announced she'd see the D.I.

"He's in hospital," said Jones.

"So I'll go in visiting hours," said Garelli, "I'll sort it tomorrow."

\*

They checked back in at the station for messages. Jones had one to call Theo from Drugs Squad. He rang and was put through to a mobile. Reception was poor, somewhere with traffic in the background, mind that could have been anywhere in the city; it was a car park.

"Meet me downstairs at 3 a.m." Jones thought he deciphered, but could not quite believe it, so he asked for a repeat to confirm.

"What's the matter fruit?" the voice broke in and out, "I thought you country boys got up with the sun?"

"No, I've been polluted," Jones tried weakly for a riposte, "I can't see it anymore."

"We're on dawn patrol," crackled Theo, "Action Man, you're going on a bust, the whole squad's on the rock n' roll!"

For a moment Jones considered crying off, then he decided he could not let his paranoia get the better of him. After all he would be in the company of other cops. If that was not as safe as anywhere in the city, then what was?

Jones tracked down Garelli in the canteen getting a coffee fix, and begged off for the rest of the day. Said he needed an early one to recover from last night. For some reason he did not feel like telling her about his plans for tomorrow. He had a gut instinct she would not approve. She gave him a latchkey, told him to feed the cats and not to wait up for her.

*

# Chapter 15.  Busted

Jones woke up in the small hours, a cat purring on his chest. He had not heard Garelli come in during the night, and did not dare stick his head in the bedroom door to check. He had not had an alarm to set either, and had dozed off worrying about waking up, relying on his tendency to insomnia and bad dreams to rescue him in time. He left a simple note for Garelli on the table, about catching her at the station later. He figured it would probably all be over before the day shift started, and with luck she would not even hear about it. He snuck out as stealthily as he could, with one eye open for strange men and dark shadows, but nothing apparent seemed to disturb the slumber of the sleeping neighbourhood, so he set off on foot with nervous glances over his shoulder, and managed to flag down a cab within a couple of blocks. The streets were quiet with hardly any traffic. It was a weekday.

Theo was waiting in the basement. The squad room seemed still, only a few desk jockeys slouching at their consoles.
"The crew's already on their way," said Theo, "I said we'd meet them over there."

Jones apologised for holding him up, although he did not actually think he was late. The cab had seemed to take no time at all to get there. The Greek looked wired and urgent, as though he had been up for hours. Jones wondered aloud if he ever needed sleep?
"I'm a fucking vampire!" Theo crackled crazily, and led Jones out to his car, chattering like a magpie, and laughing like a

kookaburra. Inside he belted up and put on some soul music; an unexpected choice but Jones did not comment. The Greek was finally silent and Jones did not want to disturb the peace. The night was empty and the streets deserted. It was like driving through a ghost town. The warmth of the heater encouraged Jones to relax, he forgot all about the old man and started to doze, cocooned once more and rocked back to sleep.

"We've arrived," Theo's voice cut through the layers and prised open his eyes, "Quiet with the door."

He went to the boot and passed Jones a flak jacket. It was body armour, with POLICE in bold white letters blazoned across the back.

"If it's not on, it's not on," grinned Theo, wagging his finger and slipping his arms into one himself.

Jones struggled into it reluctantly. It reminded him of something he had once refused to be. The weight of it dragged him down. He looked around to settle and centre himself. They were parked in a side street, and had to walk to the proposed scene. Streetlights were few, and as they approached other members of the team flitted through the dark to join them in the garden of a house with a high wall and bushes edging the street. There was a large tree on the nature strip in front. It was across the road from the target.

"What are you doing here?" the weary sergeant from the other day accosted Jones.

Jones shrugged, if the i/c did not know then how the hell should he? He would much rather be tucked up.

"I brought him, Sarge," Theo rescued him, "All in the spirit of inter force co-operation. He's Special Ops trained."

That caught Jones short; he had not mentioned that to anyone.

"A fucking cowboy!" snorted the sergeant in apparent disbelief, "This I do not need!"

"I'm just sucking arse, Sarge," said Theo, "Keeping upstairs sweet. I'll hold his hand and smack him if he's a naughty boy."

The sergeant shook his head and looked away. Jones did not want to get caught in the crossfire. He looked across the street at the target. It was a big old weatherboard on a large block, with a high chain link fence topped with razor wire all around it. Two high metal gates chained and padlocked blocked the access to a large side garage. There did not seem to be any other entrance. The lawn to the front door was only accessible through the driveway. A few chopped and polished Harleys leaned nonchalantly on their stands. Jones also noticed security cameras set up on strategic corners of the house. He realised then that he was looking at a compound and waved the neighbourhood goodbye.

Just then the front door of the house of the property they were trespassing in opened and the elderly owner came out, threatening to call the police. His English was not too good and he was angry and very agitated. The sergeant tried to get him to keep it down. Theo interrupted, rattling away rapidly in what Jones presumed was Greek. He turned his back to the owner to show him the lettering on his black armour. The whole squad had to turn their backs before the owner got it and finally went back inside.

The sergeant thanked Theo by handing him the bolt-cutters and telling him to get the gate. Theo slipped across the road to attack the chain, accompanied by one of the other team members as backup with his sidearm drawn. Two dogs started to bark. Theo left the gate closed and ran back to the sergeant. "I've cut the chain but there's two pit-bulls loose in the yard." The racket made that statement obvious.

"I'm not fucking deaf!" said the sergeant but he looked stumped for a moment.

"Shoot the dogs," muttered Jones from the back, half in jest, but more in retaliation at his indifferent treatment.

"Shoot the dogs!" relayed somebody and the backup still by the gate shot the dogs through the fence. One went down but the other began to limp away howling. The backup finished it off with a third shot.

"Fuck!" said Theo and he ran for the gates. He kicked them open and raced for the front door. A window slammed open and a shotgun thundered out. Theo's legs were cut from under him and he crashed to the ground. Jones assumed it was a low shot, aimed to deliberately miss the body armour. The backup ran back over the road to rejoin the others across the street. Theo was left on his own in a spreading pool of blood. Jones ran without thinking for the open gates. As he entered the yard another shot crashed out and caught him in the chest. He was picked up and thrown backwards, momentarily stunned, then he pulled himself to his feet and ran forward again. All hell broke loose behind him, guns opening up in a barrage. He could see the walls of the weatherboard being peppered with shot holes as he reached Theo. The young bloke was lying on his face towards the front door moaning softly. Jones went round to his head, turned his back to the house, and bent over to lift Theo under the armpits. He dragged the dead weight round and started hauling him backwards towards the open gates and safety. Rounds of fire whistled all around him. He watched the walls of the house splinter and disintegrate as he reached the gates and started across the pavement. Then they were on the nature strip and heading for home. He thought about calling it there but a stray round hit him in the back. He stumbled forward, nearly falling on Theo, but managed to

135

recover his balance at the last minute and carried on dragging the boy across the road. At the nature strip on the other side he put him down under the shade of the spreading branches of the tree, and crashed down himself to lean with his back against the trunk. He began to laugh crazily when he realised the sun was not even up yet. He looked at his watch. The whole thing had gone down in only a few minutes.

In the meantime the rest of the team had poured across the road. There was empty brass everywhere all over the pavement and in the gutter, but at least it was quiet now. His ears were deafened. Jones watched a pair rush the front door of the clubhouse with a ram and smash it in. The rest were ranged at the back in a loose semi-circle with weapons drawn. Sirens began to wail in the distance. Theo was drifting in and out of consciousness.

"Cross over Apples, and get me a tally," he whispered weakly.

Jones shook his head, not knowing what was required and not wanting to leave the boy on his own. He could not believe the rest of the squad had rushed on by without even a look in.

"I want to know the score!" insisted the Greek.

Jones assumed he was talking about the body count? He shook his head again, "Later, Ackers, later; I'll keep you company till the ambos arrive." Something else occurred to him, "How come you know about my background in Special Ops?" he asked.

"I pulled your jacket," Theo tried for a grin and a spasm crossed his face.

Jones must have looked confused.

"I made some phone calls to the Apple Isle," chortled Theo, "a little birdie shit in your file and whispered in my ear."

"So you knew I'd jacked it?" asked Jones. The logic was beyond him.

Theo nodded barely.

"So why today?" Jones had to ask, gesturing at the chaos and carnage over the road.

"I wanted to see if you had any balls!" said Theo.

The answer was so completely inane and so obviously in character that Jones did not know whether to laugh or just lean over and strangle him. The whole invite had just been a windup.

"Fucken A!" swore Theo, "I don't know about your equipment, Big Boy, but you've definitely got no brains. You are fucken mad!" he cackled insanely and started to giggle.

Jones did not like the swearing and told him so. That set him off again. An ambulance finally arrived and Jones stood up and waved them over. The medics ran up and asked him for a quick rundown. One knelt down to remove Theo's shoes, and started to run a pair of shears up his trouser legs.

"Lie still or you'll lose your bass notes," Jones warned the boy, trying for payback.

"Is everything alright down there?" Theo asked with his first hint of worry.

Jones leaned over with a serious face to inspect the crotch. "Can't even see it?" he pronounced finally, "I should have brought my magnifying glass."

"Bastard!" Theo hissed sharply.

Jones leaned back on his heels and smiled happily for the first time since he had dragged himself off the couch that morning.

The other medic opened a case and produced a syringe. She loaded it up from a phial and bent down to inject it in Theo's bare thigh once the trousers had been cut away. The young bloke smiled broadly and sighed deeply.

"That's good product," he breathed, "I can see me crossing to the dark side."

"Made in Tasmania," said Jones. He explained the opium fields.

Theo laughed weakly, "It's probably fucken organic," and cackled again.

Jones did not get the joke and told him again to stop swearing.

Theo laughed so much at that he was almost hysterical. "Love your priorities Big Boy," he called as the medics stretchered him away, "My legs have been shot to shit but you're worried about my mouth!"

Jones walked with them to the back of the ambulance. Theo started rambling. As they loaded him up he suddenly became lucid again. "Get me the score!" he insisted of Jones.

Jones promised and waved him off. Then he crossed the road to keep his word. Part of the team was busy hauling bodies out of the clubhouse, kicking them flat facedown on the ground in the yard and cuffing their hands behind their backs. Others were jemmying the garage, finally kicking the roller door in to get inside. Jones caught glimpses of chrome and metallic flames and a tangle of bikes and pipes. One of the cops came up to the sergeant and said loudly while staring at Jones; "Can't find the lab, Sarge!"

"Pull all the bikes out, put them in a heap and fire them," snarled the sergeant standing over the line of bodies.

"You fucking dog, I'll fucking sue!" one of the bikers screamed and cursed and spat.

"Can we get away with that, Sarge?" the cop queried, quieter now, and nodding over at the growing audience in the street. The neighbours were out sticky-beaking now the shooting had stopped.

"Fuck!" said the sergeant, "Someone set up a perimeter, keep the vultures away."

"We're shorthanded," insisted the off-sider, "we're still looking for the wedge."

"Rip up the fucking floorboards, and kick in the plasterboard!" ordered the sergeant, "And someone call traffic. They can check all this shit," he gestured at the chopped bikes, "and impound the lot. That'll settle the natives." He glared down at the complaining biker.

Jones did not know what was going down. He felt he had escaped hell to stand on the edge of purgatory.

"What's the score?" he asked the sergeant, fulfilling his promise to Theo.

The senior stared at him blankly, "What the fuck do you want?" he asked nastily right in Jones's face.

"What's the score?" Jones repeated, not backing down; a promise was a promise. "The Greek wanted to know the body count," he explained, "and I'd appreciate you cutting out the swearing. I find it offensive."

The sergeant looked at him strangely. "Nobody's dead," he said at last, "bloody miracle; nobody to pay off except the RSPCA."

One of the crew ran out and gave the sergeant the thumbs up. "We've got it," he said.

The sergeant nodded, and told the cop to move it. Then he dipped into his pocket and pulled out a roll and peeled off some notes. "Take off the armour," he ordered Jones.

Jones complied hesitantly, still at a loss.

"You got any damage?" asked the sergeant.

"Bruised," admitted Jones, "hurts like hell," being brave, acting cool.

"Take an aspirin," said the sergeant, "No hospitals, no records." He leaned forward into Jones's face again and stuffed the notes into Jones's shirt breast pocket.

"Here's a monkey," he said, "Hear no evil, see no evil, speak no evil. Now fuck off out of here."

Jones stared at him in disbelief.

"You saw nothing, you know nothing, you weren't here," emphasised the sergeant.

Jones still stood rooted to the spot.

"We'll cut you a bigger slice when we split the wedge," the sergeant must have misconstrued his reluctance to leave. "Now fuck off out of here before the toe-cutters arrive, or do you really want to spend all day in interrogation and the rest of the week buried in paperwork?"

Jones finally began to move. As he turned to walk away the sergeant called after him. "There's a cab rank two blocks to the east," he paused, "And Jones, about the Greek," Jones turned back and tried for humility; he had never been one for plaudits, public or private. "Next time let the little turd bleed out, he's a pain in the arse," the senior's final shot.

Jones walked off into the sunrise. No one commented, no one even noticed; he was just a little boy lost again, with nobody to care.

\*

He caught up with Garelli back at the station.

"Jones," she said, "you disappoint me. Underneath that sensitive exterior, you're just another macho man at heart."

Jones winced, so much for the code of silence; the wires must have been humming.

"Jones," she rescued him from his evident confusion, "you've got the heads up. Somebody's told Mulligan you're O.K."

Jones sat down and told her all about it. After it had all spilled out of him he realised it had at least been good to debrief to somebody. "What I don't understand?" he tried at last, "is how such a cock-up could happen? Don't you guys have a Tactical Unit trained for stuff like that?"

"It would have been an unsanctioned action," said Garelli, "to keep the circle tight, maximise the result."

Jones must have looked totally at a loss.

"You're acting on a tip-off, anonymous of course. Something's being moved, now. So you have to make an on the spot decision, put a team together, instant response or the opportunity's lost. Some of the crews are independent, but if you're coy a quick call and someone upstairs can sign off on it, your butt's covered and you're gone," Garelli on a roll, outside the loop but wanting the action, a street junkie, Jones could see it.

"Someone mentioned a lab," he said.

"They don't cook in clubhouses," said Garelli, "even bikers aren't that dumb."

"But it was all planned in advance," said Jones, "Theo rang me yesterday."

"Thanks for telling me, partner," stressed Garelli.

"So what were they after?" asked Jones, still in the dark.

"Cash," nodded Garelli, staring into space, "somebody must have got the word a deal was being put together."

Jones pulled the notes out of his front pocket and counted them, $1000 in hundred dollar bills.

"You're cheap," said Garelli. "But now at least you can pay your share for the informants." She took one note off him.

"And you can pay for the rest as they come," she said, "as penance for holding out. We'll call it the future fund."

He did not see it as a laughing matter, and said so.

"Who you going to tell?" Garelli pointed out.

Jones stared at her and finally nodded. "I'm a fucking monkey," he said at last.

"Jones," she said, "Go wash your mouth out."

*

"There's a rave going down this evening, a midweek special," Garelli informed him when he returned. "I've heard that Honey might be there. I'm going over there to check it out, see if I can pick her up."

Jones shrugged, it seemed like a long shot, and he said so. They were not even sure exactly what she looked like? He was not even sure what a rave was himself? So he asked.

"It's a giant party for techno-kids," explained Garelli, "lights, loud music, lots of ecstasy to dance the night away."

"Not more drugs!" groaned Jones, "I've bottomed out!"

"You don't have to come, you've had a busy day," Garelli gave him a way out.

"No, I'll come and hold your hand," said Jones,

"I'll break your fingers," Garelli retorted.

"Somebody needs to keep you out of mischief," Jones persisted. He did not want to hang out on his own, that was the long road to boredom. Plus he did not want to be restricted to the station. If he was with Garelli he could at least keep his paranoia at bay, or maybe not?

"I am tired," he admitted. It had been an early start and the day was already more than long.

"Take a siesta," said Garelli, "we'll sign back in for the evening shift."

"I'm just a lonely boy," hummed Jones. "Lonely and blue. I've got no where to go?"

"Jones, I'm not sure if you're mangling the words, the tune or both?" said Garelli, "Are you some kind of country'n western throwback?" she tossed him a key. "Don't let the cat out of the bag," she said. "I'll pick you up later."

He wandered off to catch a cab and crash for the afternoon.

*

"What if we're followed?" Jones anxiously watched the rear view mirror.

"Doesn't matter," said Garelli, where we're going age is more than a barrier, it's beyond the bounds of probability."

Jones glanced at her, wondering if she was playing games with his mind?

"How is that possible?" he asked cautiously, not wanting to provoke her.

"You will see," said Garelli, "Wait and see."

The site was a giant warehouse in an industrial zone in the eastern suburbs. It was a vast grey prefabricated building with an even bigger car park, surrounded by a clutter of smaller factories and storage facilities. Loud music was throbbing from a roller door like an open mouth howling in pain. There were kids everywhere, crowds and crowds of them mingling and mangling in apparent confusion. The logistics were overwhelming. Jones figured there had to be a Met station somewhere nearby, and train and bus stops. A continual succession of cars were pulling up and dropping kids off and then pulling away again in to the traffic jam, or at least queuing

143

in the attempt. Was that really what modern parents did, deliver their kids to the devil in SUVs, and then drive off into the sunset? Jones started humming, "Trains and boats and planes."

Garelli told him to shut up if he did not want his taste in music to start a riot. Then Jones started to notice a pattern in the chaos; somehow the swell was pressing inwards, like liquid swirling round the inside of a funnel's edge, as it spiralled slowly towards the restrictive centre. Craning over their heads he noticed two rows of stalls set up in the car park funnelling a passage down to the entrance to the building, the huge roller door. Cashiers sat just inside at trestle tables each side of the door were taking money and stamping hands and arms. Bouncers big and bruising lounged intently waiting to pounce.

The kids and their outfits were all the colours of the rainbow and extremes of fashion: butterflies beyond the exotic fluttering distractions in the last rays of the sun. Many of the girls wore wings on their back, fairy wings and angel wings bobbing and weaving in the pulsing throng. Jones trailed in Garelli's wake as she slipped and eeled somehow ever forward through the milling crush of bodies.

"We'll never find anyone in this!" he tried to shout to her above the babble.

She did not, could not, or would not hear him. The din from the music inside was growing the nearer they got to the door. Then they were in amongst the stalls. They were selling an assortment of glow sticks of all shapes and combinations; wands, headbands, wristbands, bracelets and neckbands. Then there were masks and face paint, torches and lights. There was even a stall selling bottled water. When Jones saw this he realised that most of the kids were carrying water bottles; many had them slung in pouches like quivers or bandoliers across their shoulders. Many also carried water pistols, holstered at the waist like the outlaws of old.

Then they were at the doors and a cashier was harassing Garelli. "What's up, Grandma, or are you the big bad wolf today?"

She bared her teeth in a crocodile again, "What do you think, little boy?"

The cashier demanded $50 off her. She waved her warrant card under his nose.

"I've got a free pass!" she said and marched in imperial, queen of the moment.

The cashier fronted Jones. "I'm with her," he tried, but she was already ahead of him. He fumbled in his wallet for his own warrant card, and ended up producing it without Garelli's flourish. The cashier actually scrutinised it, and then laughed.

"You're well out of your box, mate," and waved over a bouncer when Jones protested. He ended up forking out the fifty before he lost all sight of Garelli's head in the milling throng. He scrambled after her with a fluorescent stamp on his hand, forcing his way through mildly protesting bodies, before she was gone forever, swamped in a sea of juveniles. He caught up with her in a burst of concentrated violence, brushing kids aside like reeds in the marsh, and made the mistake of grabbing at her arm to get her attention. She nearly broke his in return.

"Please don't leave me, let me go!" he tried to croon through the pain. He was still bruised and sore from the morning. She released him but he sensed some reluctance.

"Don't walk on me! Stand by your man!" he pleaded genuinely terrified of getting separated in the crush. He hated crowds, tight places and the intense claustrophobia of massed humanity.

145

"If we get split up!" she shouted in his ear, "keep in touch by mobile!"

She flashed a pink and fluorescent compact under his nose.

"I don't have one!" Jones shouted back.

She stared at him in disbelief, her mouth dropped open.

"Close your gob," shouted Jones, "You'll eat flies!"

She shook her head in exasperation or despair. "How do you communicate over there, carrier pigeon?"

"There's no coverage on my patrol," he said, "black spots everywhere actually."

She looked at him in consideration.

"We could hold hands?" he tried again, "it would be good cover, I bet everybody here over the age of thirty is either a dealer or a paedophile?"

"Are you implying I'm over thirty?" Garelli pretended outrage.

She put her hand in his. "You're sweaty!" she decided, "Hang onto my bag," and she towed him in her wake before he could protest.

Strobe lights flashed and stuttered flash bulbs in his eyes and coloured displays projected and swirled on towering walls disappearing into a lost ceiling, the smoke haze playing rainbows in the clouded air. Rows of supplicants locked mesmerised onto a makeshift stage, where the D.J enthroned took homage from the faithful, weaving spells of rhythm out of the cacophony of noise. The kids wore white faces staring out of shadowed eyes, gaunt and hypnotised balancing on the very edge of oblivion. Jones watched a boy covered with tiny lights and a battery in a backpack watching the bulbs on his fingertips in wrapt concentration as he waved to an imaginary audience.

Jones's migraine was beginning and building, an intense point of pressure at the back of his eyeballs waiting to explode and spear shrapnel into his brain. He anchored his feet and pulled Garelli towards him.

"I can't do this!" he shouted in her ear. It was all pointless anyway. There was no way they would ever locate anybody in all this chaos and confusion, let alone someone they had never even met. "Wait for me by the squad car in the street outside!" she shouted back.

He let her go, to be swallowed up in the glittering throng, and forced his way back to the roller door and the promise of fresh air. It was a hard swim against the current, the crowds still pressing in. Outside it was dark now, and the glow sticks fluttered fireflies in the meadows of the night. Jones found the squad car by its flashing roof lights. He had not seen it on the way in. Perhaps they had only just decided to join the party? He wandered over and introduced himself. The uniforms were disinterested and after a cursory reply ignored him to concentrate on the parade.

Jones leaned back against the car and watched with them, mesmerised by the ebb and flow. The numbers were mind-blowing. The inadequacy of the lone patrol car was beyond bizarre; the potential for riot seemed as astronomical as the numbers they were shepherding. He pointed this out to the uniforms, attempting once more to breach the divide and make conversation.

"It's a non-starter, mate," one said, "They're all mellow. They're all popping Es. The only action will be the bodies dropping as the night wears on."

As if on cue an ambulance arrived, lights swirling and siren squealing, to attempt to breach the ramparts of the crowded traffic still trying to break the jam.

"Dehydration!" one uniform answered his unspoken question.

Jones looked at them, looked at the sky, and hardly knew what to say. He could scarcely cope with the magnitude and folly of all this big city insanity, how on earth did the old man? He reflected that Garelli was definitely right about his personal security in this place: here and now was certainly no country for old men. Then he considered that he himself was not so completely out of his depth. Back on the island the drought was affecting everything, the sheep especially were suffering from a lack of water. Perhaps he was not so far out of his element after all?

Eventually Garelli came back out to join him. "What was the point of that?" he asked.

"Lighten up, Jones," she said to him, "Don't you like to party?"

He stared at her in amazement. "Do you enjoy this?"

"It's a fashion parade," she said, "I thought you might want to unwind after all the excitement this morning?"

"Can we go home?" he pleaded for absolution.

*

# Chapter 16.  Tunnel Vision

The adrenaline was long gone and Jones had truly bottomed out. He was sat at the kitchen counter again in Garelli's, and back to what seemed to have become his usual obsession, the old man.

"It's got to be revenge," he pronounced.

Garelli had decided he should move in with her, but she had given him a spare key to symbolise his independence. He was not happy about it. His chest ached, and his back was sore. He had mentioned the hit in the back to Garelli, saying it was fortunate it was only a handgun round.  Her response started making him feel paranoid again. He felt vulnerable, and he wanted, even needed protection. But Garelli was adamant there was no one he could turn to, especially after the events of the morning.

"Look," he tried again, "Let's hand over what we've got, and I can get a flight home."

"You think you'll ever be safe?" asked Garelli.

Hell she was more paranoid than he was.

"It's just an old man," he persisted, "Who thinks that drugs have killed his son. So he's knocking off dealers: an eye for an eye. He's probably crazy. Perhaps he blames me for bringing him the bad news? Perhaps he associates me with his son's death? Why don't we see a police psychiatrist? Get a personality profile. For land's sake he's been a hermit for years. It wouldn't take much to knock him off his trolley."

"You're forgetting something," said Garelli.

"Oh yeah, what?" asked Jones. He was tired, depressed and homesick.

"The old man never showed at the mortuary. He never viewed the body. How does he know his son was an addict?" Garelli was relentless.

Jones stared at her. His mind was numb.

"Obviously someone's been feeding him information," said Garelli.

Jones shook his head. He had been down that track before and got nowhere. Nothing made sense.

"But why?" he found himself repeating the tired refrain.

"Where there's drugs there's money," said Garelli, "We just have to find the connection."

Jones sighed, his hand straying self-consciously to his wallet, which still carried the remnants. It was not what he wished to hear but he supposed it was an answer of sorts.

"What arrangements did you make for the old man to see the body?" asked Garelli.

"The phone number," he said, it came to him suddenly. "I left a police phone number with the old man before he left. To contact when he arrived."

"So who's was it?" asked Garelli.

Jones felt himself back away from that. "Do you know what you're saying?"

"This is the city. You can't trust anybody. Who's was it?" she insisted.

"I've no idea," admitted Jones, "I just presumed it was the station's?"

"Was it an extension?" prompted Garelli.

"Yes," hesitated Jones, "I believe it was."

"Have you still got it?" asked Garelli.

"I made a note of it, obviously," sighed Jones, "but it will be back in the watch-house on the island."

"So do you think you could track it down in the morning?" asked Garelli, "phone home?"

"Maybe?" muttered Jones, "if I can remember what I did with it. I might just have torn it out of my notebook to give to the old man. I'm not much on paperwork."

Garelli was calm and patient. "So who gave you the number, Jones?" she asked.

Jones shrugged, "I don't know, it was just called in from our headquarters: could have been anybody, even an auxiliary? We employ civilians for some clerical duties. I don't log official calls; only citizens'."

Garelli swore. "Shit! I need another drink." She poured one for each of them.

Jones wandered over to the side window drink in hand. The outlook was a wall, with more windows. Some of the bigger ones had balconies. In the middle of the courtyard grew a tree. Its branches sighed and rattled in the evening wind. Someone had tied a wind chime to its upper branches. If it was not for that and the background hum of the traffic Jones could close his eyes and almost imagine he was out of there. But of course it did not pay to breathe too deeply.

"Do you think I'm in danger of becoming an alcoholic?" he swirled the amber liquid in the bottom of his glass. The whisky glowed with the promise of oblivion.

"I shouldn't worry," said Garelli, "the job will probably get you before your liver does."

Jones must have looked hurt.

"I'm sorry," she apologised, a rarity for her. "I'm often told my mouth is my only open orifice." She got up and walked over to join him at the window. "Look at the night before last another way," she said, "From an overall perspective, don't you think the old man was acting out of character? It was rather desperate. We must be putting pressure on them somehow."

"Them?" queried Jones, "I'm not too sure about this conspiracy theory. It's just too bizarre."

"Jones, don't be obtuse, do I have to rub your nose in it? It's O.K to be cynical about human nature. Here it's essential. There's no value for anything out there. But in the shadows the price for everything is all the shades of grey."

"I'm not an idealist," Jones stated stubbornly. How could he be? He had been crippled long ago. "But I can't see a motive?"

"Sex and drugs and rock n' roll are all commodities out there," said Garelli, "They're the currency of the night. They pay for the electricity bill."

Jones could not even raise a snigger. He thought of all those butterflies, trapped by the neon sun, unable to rest until the lights turned out. What had that cab driver said? "Of an evening 90% of fares are under the influence; drink or drugs or just plain insanity."

Why else would they roam these streets? They were not safe in the moonlight: all those fragile butterflies, sipping at the nectar of the night, and in the morning, how many broken wings?

"It's hard for me to imagine a man who doesn't think about sex," said Garelli. She was looking at him through the bottom of her glass. Her eyes were huge, like bruised flowers. She was cutting deep tonight. Was she that pissed already?

"Would you like some help?" she asked next.

He stared hard at her, it could not be a come on, that would be completely out of character. Was she trying to annoy or destroy him?

152

"I've got some contacts in the hospitality trade," she continued, "You know, working girls. They could break you in gently."

He felt his face flush with anger and his jaw tighten.

"I'm sorry," she said. She reached out and touched him on the arm, softly, like the caress of a leaf. He was not sure if she had ever touched him before.

"I'm not trying to hurt you," she whispered.

He looked deep into her eyes and saw the truth of it, and relaxed into the whisky once more.

"I'm sorry," she repeated, "I guess I'm drunk, and I'm tired, and I'm lost and a little bit frightened."

"You?' he queried, "Frightened?"

That had to be a first.

"It's a lonely world out there," she said, "when the lights go out. I keep having this dream; I'm in a tunnel in the pitch dark. The tunnel's curved like a tube. I don't know whether I'm going backwards or forwards, but I have to try to find my way out. And there's no one to help me."

She stared at him again. "God I must be pissed, I'm going maudlin. I'm going to bed." She left abruptly.

He stretched out on the couch and stared at the ceiling. He too was tired, but his mind had long since gone beyond exhaustion and now roamed in the twilight zone where distorted perception blurred the edge of reality and could only focus on half-imaginings. He drifted on the swirls and eddies of the night till the old man reared out of the dark seas and poised over him. His eyes glowed with the half-life of the phosphorescent tide and his breath stank of seaweed and decay. Jones instinctively knew his touch was death and woke up screaming. The sound of Garelli's snoring brought him back to earth. He stumbled into her room and stood at her

153

bedside paralysed. She was on her back with her mouth open like a gaping wound. Her eyes fluttered open as if she could sense his presence.

"What the fuck do you want?" she snapped.

He was crumbling. "N…nightmares!" he stammered and sank to his knees. "I just want to be held."

"Well I don't!" she hissed. "You're like a little frightened boy. If you're having bad dreams sleep beside me on the floor. And keep your hands to yourself."

Jones curled up on the floor beside the bed, his knees tucked under his chin.

"Idiot!" muttered Garelli from above, "you'll catch cold."

The bed creaked as she stamped out and back from the living room. She threw the blanket from the couch over him and climbed back into bed. Moments later she was asleep. The floor was hard but firm and the sound of her breathing reassured him.

Eventually he must have slept.

*

When he woke up the room was full of light and Garelli was gone. There was a wry note for him on the breakfast bar. "You know what they say about sleeping dogs, and I thought you needed your beauty sleep. I'll cover for you. There are a few things I need to check at the station. Don't open the door to any tall dark strangers. I'll be back around midday to pick you up. If you're awake, G."

It was already late in the morning so Jones showered and got dressed. He had a leisurely breakfast while he waited. He still was not thinking too clearly but his mind was not as fogged as yesterday. He figured another good night's sleep and he would probably catch up with himself. It was something to look forward to. He made a deliberate decision to take a break from the old man, the investigation and everything, and switched on the T.V and himself off. In a commercial break in amongst the litany of trivia he reflected that was one of the advantages of his character. It was useful to be able to block things off and carry on as if they had never happened. He was good at that.

It was nearly three o'clock before Garelli showed to collect him. He was glad to see her in a way because the television was wearing thin, but on another level he was also embarrassed about the previous night. He supposed he was getting claustrophobic about the flat. And their relationship was becoming almost incestuous. Really if he analysed it he was already beginning to feel the need to move out, even though he had hardly been there very long. But he did not want to think about the where and how. She also seemed a little strained and distant. She said she had received a call a call off the street about the girl they had nicknamed 'Honey', and had arranged a meet at an address across town. She was running late so they had to leave straightaway. On the drive over she said little, just complained about missing lunch and being hungry. On impulse Jones offered to shout her a meal in a restaurant after the meet. He was a little hurt that she did not seem to acknowledge the effort that cost him. Then he reflected that she would think he was flush after the payoff from the bust, and he let it go. But he felt she was holding something back so he asked her if she had any leads but she said she wanted to contact Honey before she jumped to any conclusions. So he sat and brooded in silence for the rest of the way.

The address was in a plush neighbourhood on a corner block, big old Federation houses and bigger blocks with stately trees. The driveway they wanted was almost overgrown. Garelli motored on regardless and pulled up in an unkempt turning circle in front of the house. Weeds were growing through the gravel and a tangled climber straggled across the porch. The front door was shrouded in shadow.

"It's a squat," Garelli stated the obvious. "She said use the back door."

"Did she say who she was?" queried Jones.

"Get real," said Garelli, "what's in a name? A tag now, that could be relevant." She said the girl was really nervous and looked at Jones decisively, "It's probably better if you stay in the car," she declared, "you know what these girls are like in front of strange men. She'll relax more if it's just me."

Jones did not like it.

"You'll be right," she patted his knee, "Just drop the door catches while I'm gone. And look, we weren't followed. I checked the rear mirror all the way."

She got out abruptly and disappeared in the wrangle of shrub round the side of the house. Jones deliberately did not drop the catches. Instead he got out and stretched his legs. The air smelled almost clean, and the ramble of trees and arched branches almost reminded him of a forest. If only they were not all weeds. It took almost a second before he could react to the sound of the gun. With the next shot he realised he was not the target and he did not have to duck for cover. He raced for the porch and shoulder charged the front door. It smashed open and he ploughed into the hall screaming and roaring. Another door he kicked apart and then there was only the body and he could see nothing else. Out on the edge somewhere he could hear footsteps and then a door slamming and he knew he should follow.

156

But her voice held him. "Is that you Jonesy?" she whispered, "I told you to stay in the car!"

He knelt beside her. Somewhere outside a car revved away with squealing tyres. A side street, back street, he did not know? The red stains pumped between her shoulder blades like crimson flowers opening.

"The bastard wouldn't let me get close," she hissed. Her voice was like reeds rustling and rattling in the breeze off the marsh. "In the back the fucking coward!" her voice strained with contempt.

"I'll get to a phone," he croaked, "call an ambulance. I'd better run."

"There's a mobile in my bag, idiot!" she cursed, "don't leave me!"

Her hand snaked out and caught his in a vicelike grip. He pulled her bag over with his free one and rang the emergency services. All the while he watched the strength fade from her face and feed into her hand.

"I can't see Jonesy," she whispered after a time, "Don't leave me, I don't want to go into the dark all on my own."

He sat there watching the light go out in her eyes. When it was finally gone he pulled her to him and folded her in his arms. He had never held a woman before; not that he could remember. When they finally arrived he was still rocking her gently.

*

## PART THREE: Agitation.

*The fast and repetitive beating of the untried wings by the stationary imago to harden and dry them in preparation for flight.*

# Chapter 17. Anaesthetic Hours

He sat in the chair and stared at his feet. If he looked up the light bounced off the antiseptic walls and hurt his eyes. He was numb and empty, a drained glass after hours.

"She was dead on arrival," a disembodied voice said from somewhere above and to the side. Jones did not bother to look up. He knew that already, but then he had only been along for the ride, the siren wail of death through the clogged arteries of the city. She had got shot just before rush hour, how inconsiderate.

"Officer!" insisted the voice, "We need to know what happened. Come on man, pull yourself out of it. You are a professional. We have an officer down. We need to respond."

Jones looked up. It was the superintendent from CIB. His face was white and drawn, stretched taut like strung wire, and his eyes were angry, hard and barbed. Of course, thought Jones, it was murder; they would be handling her now. Now at last they wanted her back. Mulligan was behind him, his face a blank cipher, puffed and pasty, a doughboy. The location reinforced how overweight he was. What indeed was Missing Persons: a last refuge for the unfit and incompetent, an accounting or a financial rationalisation? Cheaper to paperwork than pay out and pension off?

"She was out there on her own without a weapon!" snarled Jones. "She was unarmed because of your frigging regulations, because of you!" he lurched to his feet.

The superintendent backed off.

"So where were you, Apples?" asked Mulligan. He was impassive and immobile as an elephant.

Jones slumped back in his seat. "In the car," he admitted.

"We have operational procedures for a reason," Mulligan was remorseless, "What happened today is why we work in pairs," emphasising the last word.

"Not now, sergeant," the superintendent admonished quietly, "that will all come out in the enquiry. So you saw nothing?" he asked Jones.

Jones shook his head in defeat.

"So what were you doing there?" asked Mulligan, "or rather, what was she doing?"

You cannot trust anyone, that was what she had said. "She was checking out a tip about a missing girl. Said the girl might be nervous about strange men. That's why I stayed in the car. She was good with the street kids: had a way about her. Said I put them off. Too stiff-necked," that was safe enough, thought Jones, only lie by omission, hard to get caught out then.

"So this had nothing to do with the other inquiry then, about our mysterious senior citizen?" the superintendent was casual, a man tidying his desk at the end of the day.

This was the moment of truth. If he said yes he could come in from the cold, get back up and support. If he said no he would be out on a limb without protection, a man on his own.

"No!" he shook his head emphatically. He had been on his own all his life. If in doubt, act in character. Then at least you would be consistent. Garelli could not criticise him for that.

"Sergent Mulligan says Officer Garelli exceeded her authority with this APB yesterday," the superintendent appeared mildly puzzled, "apparently she fabricated some fictitious parental crisis?"

162

Mulligan's eyes gleamed with a sudden flash of malice. So he had checked it out; very efficient.

"Like I said," Jones prevaricated, "she was really good with the kids. She was a bit of a maverick but she really put out for them. I guess she was just trying to help?"

He lumbered to his feet again and turned away because he did not want to look them in the eye. He must have seemed all choked up because the superintendent came over and draped an arm across his shoulder.

"I'll get you some post-trauma counselling," he said.

"Thank-you, sir," mumbled Jones. Been there, done that. Talk about what you've seen, talk about what you're feeling. But it doesn't bloody go away. It just hangs there, in your mind's eye, till your brain gets blasé and changes the scenery to suit. And all your mates and acquaintances get sick to death of hearing you talk about it.

"You've had a rough trot, son," the superintendent released him and gave him a gentle pat on the back; like a bloody dog, old faithful. "We'll get this mess sorted, and then we'll send you home. It hasn't achieved much, your being here, but I suppose we had to try." He shook his head sadly, said, "Hang in there!" and left Mulligan to administer the last rites.

"Take tomorrow off, special leave," the sergeant granted magnanimously. "I'll clear her desk out, inform next of kin. Make all the arrangements. You can come back to a clean slate."

Jones shook his head. "No," he said firmly; how could he ever be clean after this? "I'll be in. She'd expect that."

"Suit yourself," said Mulligan, "I can't make it an order. Do you want a lift to your digs?"

"No," repeated Jones, "I think I'll hang around for a while. Catch a cab later."

He was not ready to say goodbye yet.

Mulligan shrugged and walked away after the superintendent. Jones sat there and counted cracks in the vinyl tiles. Some time later a nurse came up to him and said sorry but they needed the room in casualty and they would have to move the body to the hospital morgue. Jones said he would ride shotgun one last time and escorted her down to the butcher's. He lifted the sheet off her face and apologised to her, "I wasn't much of a bodyguard, was I?" he said.

"You weren't much on the thinking side either!" she said without moving her lips. He thought that was a good trick and wondered how she did it. Maybe she was a ventriloquist as well as a black belt. They kept up this conversation all the way to the morgue in the basement. The hospital porters kept giving him these funny looks and he could not understand why.

"They're crazy!" explained Garelli, "it's their work environment and the anti-social hours. It's affected their health."

Jones thought that was hilarious and laughed insanely. How could working in a hospital be unhealthy? Hospitals cured people.

*

The thing about sanity, reflected Jones after he had finished off the bottle, is that you don't question it until you realise that you are losing it. And then it is too late. Or is it? Does insanity question anything?

He lay on the floor of the bedroom of their flat and watched the lights from the traffic broach the open blinds and chase shadows across the ceiling. One of her cats sat on his chest and washed its face. The shy one was still avoiding him. Garelli would have to feed it herself. He needed to see a pattern in the shadows and then perhaps he would find the answer to everything. But the more he thought the less he perceived. In the final analysis the only thing he felt sure of was that it was all his fault. The modus operandi was all wrong and so was the target. The old man wanted him; he had proved that the other night. Which begged the question; had Garelli walked into an ambush set up for himself, or had she done something that morning which had precipitated a crisis? Jones felt like a headless chook running around in circles. And the circles would keep repeating till all the blood pumped dry and then it would be too late to do anything. Eventually he realised that all he had to do was ask Garelli what she had been up to. He was a bit worried about her reaction after the last time, so he was a little hesitant about waking her. He stood by the bed puzzling over where she had got? He had not heard her leave and the bathroom light was not on. The bed looked comfortable but he thought he had best crash on the floor. The shy cat jumped up on him and he fell asleep hoping she would be pleased.

*

At the station in the morning people were treating him as though he had the plague. Normally he was hardly acknowledged, just by-passed, bumped into or simply stepped around, like unwanted furniture that they knew would eventually be given away or removed to the skip. But now for the first time everyone seemed aware of him, they were all talking in whispers about him, and whenever he stepped into a corridor, room or office, everybody present would fall silent and look away. The superintendent dropped by to check up on

165

him, but seemed more concerned with his memory than his well being, and left in a flurry of platitudes that shrivelled in the silence.

Jones insisted on going through Garelli's desk and current files but had the distinct impression that it was all a lot tidier and more ordered than when he had last seen it. Her scribble pad was gone and her trash basket was emptied. He could not find the 'Honey' file at all. He knew Garelli would be really annoyed about that. Then two detectives from CIB dropped by to go over his statement from the previous evening. He had not realised that he had been making one but he supposed that either the superintendent or Mulligan had been taking notes. The questions turned into an interrogation and Jones got angry and wanted to know who had been at Garelli's desk and why? They told him not to be stupid; the murder of a police officer took precedence over everything and half the department had dropped what they were doing to go through Garelli's caseload the previous night to try to get some leads. And it was all very inconvenient because they were up to their necks in a major investigation of a drugs war that had erupted out of nowhere. They wanted to know if Garelli's death was part of it or just incidental. Jones had the distinct impression that they thought it was in fact irrelevant and was beginning to feel really angry when they terminated the interview and left.

He had barely the time to ask Garelli what she thought when Ethical Standards arrived and he had to go over it all again. Plus they wanted to know if he had seen any evidence of Officer Garelli taking bribes and hinted that it was quite a common scenario in the force. Jones was very clear on what he thought about that. Then they suggested that she might have been blackmailing someone. Jones snapped at that point and became very abusive and had to be restrained. After he had calmed down they explained that a procedural check of Officer Garelli's bank balance had shown that a cash deposit of $5,000 had been paid in the previous morning. The deposit slip was signed 'Smith.' It had been paid in at the main city branch where most of the major retailers banked, so the size of the amount had not attracted undue attention. It was well under the $10,000 limit so did not have to be reported to the Cash Transactions Agency, and the particular teller could not remember enough to give a description, just a nondescript female of average height and age wearing sunglasses. The security surveillance cameras were little help either.

"It's all too pat," said Jones, "Can't you see it's a set-up?"

One of the investigating officers appeared to ponder this. "The money was paid into the same account that her wages are. It is a little too convenient," he considered, "We would expect a corrupt officer to cover their tracks better than that. But then if she hadn't been shot we would have no reason to look, now would we? And the description could apply to her, if she had dressed down for the occasion? We have a rundown of your current caseload from CIB. What particular line was your partner pursuing?"

It was the first time that someone had acknowledged Jones as her partner, and that made him feel less defensive.

"So you are sure there is nothing you can tell us?" the officer was repeating.

Jones realised that he had been wandering and had not listened to what was being said anymore.

"No!" his answer was abrupt and instinctive. But later, after they had gone, he wondered if he could trust them after all. He decided to talk to Garelli about it. At one point they had actually sat and told him to lie about the line of their enquiry. They told him to tell anyone that asked that Ethical Standards

167

was only involved because Jones had not followed operational procedure; the argument they rehearsed was the one that he should not have let Garelli go in on her own. That re-opened the wound, but they told Jones in confidence that he should not hold himself responsible for the on the spot decision of a senior officer on home ground. He was surprised they considered her senior but of course words were easy. He could not hide behind them.

They concluded by asking about his transfer and secondment from interstate. He told them about the fed that was concerned about the anomaly of a man with no I.D, and Superintendent Campbell from CIB who in retrospect was probably concerned with the brutal murder of the son. Finally they thanked him. Gave him their card and told him to contact them if the need should arise, and left him in turmoil, hardly at peace.

He sensed there was a lot left unsaid, and sat there trying to fill in the blanks, but he realised that he still did not speak the right language. So instead he sat there staring at his feet, and the plain carpet they rested on, and he created patterns on the floor, circles within circles all going round and round but leading nowhere.

Then Mulligan came over and said Forensics had finished the ballistics report on Garelli, and it was two 9mm bullets that had shot her. The two shell cases found on the scene had no fingerprints, but they were fired from an automatic at a range of about four meters. Garelli would appreciate that; it was an ambush, the killer must have been frightened of her, and had taken out insurance; a bigger gun, accurate over a greater distance. So Jones made another circle alongside the others on the floor, but the more he stared the less he knew whether it should go inside, or outside, or just interlock. Then Mulligan came back and said he had just got a call and had to go to the mortuary to look at a John Doe that had just been brought in. And no Jones did not have to go because it could not be the old man because this corpse was Asian and besides it was a real mess, and he, Mulligan did not think Jones was up to it at present. And any rate did not Jones remember he had an appointment with the headshrinker? Finally, and this was reinforced with a stabbing forefinger that would have done credit to a hot-dog, Jones on no account was to go anywhere outside the station without Mulligan's express permission.

Then the post-trauma counsellor turned up and asked Jones to tell her all about it. And Jones was so sick of telling and talking about it that he blew up and told her where to go. And she said it was really healthy to vent his anger and she did not mind at all. He tried again to get rid of her and she said it was really good to express all his feelings and get his emotions out in the open. It was the first step on the road to recovery. So he screamed at her that it was not him that needed to recover because he was not the one who was fucking dead and she could not really help with that now could she?

It was then that he realised that Garelli really was dead after all and he broke down and cried. The tears fell like rain but the pain would not go away. Eventually he looked up and saw that she seemed embarrassed. Were grown men not supposed to cry in this brave new world of embracing one's sensitivity? She said he would feel better now and got up to leave. He shouted at her that he did not feel better and he never would. So she sat down and asked him when he had felt these emotions before. So he told her about the husband in the kitchen and the brains decorating the wall, and the boy whip-lashed through the windscreen and the shattered skull with more brains slopping out. Then she asked him to describe his final scene with Garelli and so he did.

The counsellor pointed out gently that it was not the same because Garelli's head was intact and she still looked beautiful. And Jones nodded and agreed that she did not look dead at all, just sleeping. Then the counsellor asked him if that had ever happened in his life before? Had there been someone who was dead but looked to be sleeping? And Jones relived the holding of her and the blood weeping and he rocked her in his arms again and the memories rolled back and he was a small boy once more in a yellow room with a white ceiling. She was lying there in bed and she would not wake up. He brought her a glass of water but he could hardly lift her head and she would not open her mouth. So he poured it between her lips as best he could. It ran over her face and wet the bed. Then he lay there and held her head. The pillow was damp as though she had been crying. He lay there for hours and the sun shone through the curtains and played shadows on the wall.

Eventually the shadows won and they came and took him away and he never saw her again. He could picture her now, before the sunset, so still and so beautiful.

The counsellor held his hand and stayed with him for a while. Then she said she had to be somewhere and got up to go. She advised him to go home and rest. He smiled and said he would be O.K now. After she had gone he sat back and thought about it. He had not had a home for so long that he could not quite be sure of the meaning of the word. Was it somewhere safe? He went and moved to Garelli's desk. At some point the phone rang and he answered it. He told the caller he was Garelli's partner and he would take a message. It was an instinctive response, out and spoken before he could think about it.

She said her name was Marge and would Garelli contact her as soon as convenient, it was important. Jones asked for her number but she said Garelli already had it and put the phone down. He decided there was no point in kicking himself but the best thing to do would be to look for Garelli's address book and hope that it was not too cryptic. He had already been through her desk and drawers and knew it was not there. It had to be in her shoulder bag. And she had that with her yesterday. It could be at the mortuary with the rest of her effects. So he disobeyed Mulligan and elected to go out. He consoled himself with the argument that he would be able to ask for the sergeant's permission when he met him there.

At the vehicle pool they let him take the car assigned to Garelli without any hassle. As he drove out he realised that it was the first time he had driven independently in the city since his arrival. He had a momentary qualm as he wondered if he could cope, and then it was too late and he was in it. As he tried to fit himself into the rhythm and flow of the traffic he found himself wondering about the old man again. How had he felt driving on the mainland after all those years of seclusion in the wilderness? Why on earth did he hire a car instead of taking a bus? If he really was frightened of flying how come he had the courage to take on urban traffic? As Jones wrestled with the one-way system the answer suddenly presented itself. It was so obvious he wondered why he had not thought of it before. It was the old man's armaments. He had come carrying weapons, at least two with the shooting stick and the automatic handgun that had killed Garelli, and what else besides? He predated the firearms crackdown after Bryant by decades, not mere years. The damage at Port Arthur had been done with an AR 15, brought over the counter legally in the laxity of the old days. One could only imagine what else the old man had in reserve. Of course he could not go on the plane. And maybe he did not want to be separated from his arsenal on the coach? They would have had to go in the luggage compartment.

So he had come prepared, expecting to kill, with an unknown armoury. Who or what the hell was he? Which triggered another question: surely one needed a current licence to be able to hire a car? So the old man must have had one. How could a man with no I.D have a driving licence? Unless the daughter had hired the car for him? But then she had not been on that ferry, had she? How come the investigating team had not picked up on that? Surely Garelli would have, but at what stage would she have been brought in? And who was there that Jones could dare ask? Neither he nor Garelli were exactly experts at this line of work. Had they been set up as presumed incompetents? Wheels turned within wheels as the traffic shunted in the choked streets. Jones had a growing headache; from excess of thought or fumes he did not know.

*

# Chapter 18. Long Tan

At the mortuary Mulligan was long gone and Jones realised that time had run away with itself without him noticing. Garelli's effects were gone to. In fact they had never arrived. The mortician surmised that CIB had collected them from the hospital before the body had been moved. It was logical to check for possible leads as soon as possible in a murder investigation.

"A woman's bag contains her life," said the mortician, "What better place to look for clues?" It was the only reference he made to her at all, and she had only been there alive and well some few days ago. Perhaps he was too blasé to offer condolences? Jones felt he would like to dance on his grave.

"I can chat, but I can't stop," said the mortician busily cutting into another cadaver, "Mustn't keep the customers waiting."

It made Jones feel quite ill. Purple and pink organs floated in a pool of cloying froth. Perhaps on reflection it was not a good idea to mention Garelli, Jones realised. She had probably been up on the self-same slab in the morning. The mortician could be more sensitive than he appeared? Jones decided to give him the benefit of the doubt and took back his thoughts about the wake.

"This one's a horror story," said the mortician, "been tortured systematically before garrotting. Fingernails, eyeballs and genitals in that order, we think? Do you want the gory details?"

"No thanks," said Jones. He felt strongly that he needed to keep his imagination suppressed at this juncture.

"Funny thing," continued the mortician, conversing comfortably as if he had been sipping a beer at a barbeque, "after our conversation the other day about our Missing Link." "Do you mean he would have been tortured the same?" asked Jones.

"No means of knowing," said the mortician cheerfully, "all the bits were missing, weren't they? Still it's a thought though, one I hadn't had before I must admit. No, it's this," he picked up a sponge and swabbed away at the corpse's chest. On the left pectoral was a tattoo. It was slightly mottled and blurred around the edges, as though it had been imprinted in the man's youth, and had spread and faded with the passing years. The man looked middle-aged. The tattoo was like a capital Z with a vertical slash through it. "It's the same as those slash marks on the headless wonder," confirmed the mortician, "as soon as I saw it, it brought it all back, the pattern of those cuts. Exactly the same!"

"What does it mean?" asked Jones.

The mortician shrugged, "How should I know? I'm only a butcher, preparing the meat!" he reached into the cavity and pulled out the liver. "Now look at this," he said, "that's not bad. You've got to hand it to these Orientals. They don't abuse themselves the same. Now if that had been Caucasian of the same age and gender it would be pickled. We just don't look after ourselves," he shook his head sorrowfully. Jones felt sick again, and tried hard to swallow down his protesting stomach.

"So this guy was lean and clean?" he managed to ask.

"Not exactly," said the mortician, "he was doped up to the eyeballs, but he didn't drink."

Another link in the chain, pondered Jones. But who had killed him? There was no trademark .22 in the head with this

174

one, but it seemed to fit the pattern. He wished Garelli were there, to bounce ideas off. But she was there, was she not, in one of the vaults? This time he had to leave.

*

The car was as hot as an oven. He had forgotten to park it in the shade. When he opened the driver's door the air hit him like the blast from a furnace. He rushed around opening doors and winding down windows to let out the heat, and then stood there panting like an old kelpie at the end of a long drive. After a while he ventured in and the seat burnt him through his trousers and the wheel scorched his hands. He turned on the air-conditioning and then had to scurry round winding up the windows and closing doors so that it could take effect. It was like sitting in a sauna. Sweat ran down his face and stung his eyes. He got moving to take his mind off the feeling of oppression and swung out into the road. He had to steer with the tips of his fingers on the spokes of the wheel because the rim was too hot to handle. The traffic grumbled and worried like an old steer in the midday heat as cars and trucks stuttered between the lights in fits and starts. Tension hummed like power lines before a storm and tempers frayed in bursts of horns and spraying curses. The lines of the buildings and the power poles melted in the heat and wavered in the haze. Pavements sweated tears and the roads made shimmering pools to trap the traffic, and the traffic was a huge old snake, slow and powerful, fighting its way out of the tar pit, defying dissolution. Jones became as one with the serpent, one scale in the chain mail that linked the body armour, and finally found patience and lost himself in the flow.

At CIB headquarters they would not give him access to Garelli's address book, because it was now part of their murder enquiry, outside the jurisdiction of Missing Persons. A team of detectives was going through it item by item, checking out every address and phone number. They brushed Jones aside as if he were no more than a fly. But he found Mulligan wandering the corridors, and pre-empted his complaints by telling him that the book contained information vital to one of their current missing persons investigations. Mulligan was easily persuaded to intervene, and the detectives were O.K with him, almost deferential, and at his asking granted Jones's request for a quick look through the book. It only took a minute. Marge's name was there, and he copied down the phone number. Mulligan was watching him like a vulture. Jones tried to act casual but as soon as he had handed the book back Mulligan was all over him.

"So what's this all about?" he asked as he took the number off Jones.

Jones could only tell him that he did not know but he had been assured it was important. Mulligan stared at him with hooded eyes, his face expressionless.

"I know this number," he said at last, "it's a brothel in the suburbs. In fact I know it well. Marge is the madam. We'd best go and check it out. I'm overdue for a visit anyway. I can imagine what she wanted with Garelli. Most whores are bleeding dykes."

Mulligan drove, silent and brooding, as oppressive as the heat outside. He took all the short cuts through the backstreets and avoided most of the traffic. Even so Jones could sense his resentment building with every minor interruption and hold-up. What a penance, to be trapped in such a gross body in such a climate. It almost made Jones believe in natural justice.

He chuckled silently to himself, knowing that Garelli would appreciate the scenario. The sweat stains under the armpits of Mulligan's shirt spread steadily. Jones could almost smell the fat melting.

The brothel was a weatherboard set back off the road next to a motel. Its veranda was festooned with a string of coloured lights. At night, thought Jones, it would be lit up like a Christmas tree. Mulligan heaved himself out of the car and shambled to the shade. He was mopping at his brow with a handkerchief almost as big as a tablecloth, and wheezing like an old horse with broken wind.

"Give us a minute," he muttered, "must look me best for these bitches, else they might think they can't take me for a ride."

When he had recovered himself he led the way in, mincing his steps with a swagger that Jones would not have thought possible before. For an instant the eyes of the woman at the reception desk narrowed to slits. Then they opened wide in apparent pleasure and surprise.

"Well, well, sergeant, where've you been? We've missed you."

"G'day Marge," rumbled Mulligan, "you old whore. How's tricks?"

"Oh not bad, you know," her smile seemed brittle, "we have or ups and downs. But of course most of our customers prefer the former." She laughed shrilly, like a kookaburra courting.

Jones decided she looked slightly apprehensive.

"I, err, didn't realise you were still on the books," she hesitated, "I thought you'd moved, one of the boys told me."

"So I have, Marge, so I have," Mulligan smiled complacently, and settled his bulk against the counter, "but that doesn't mean I'm out of it, now does it?"

"Of course not," Marge's facile charm caressed him carefully, "I'll take you through to the girls; we've got a few new ones.

But you always liked variety. I take this visit is pleasure?" she enquired adroitly, "not business?"

"Business is always a pleasure with you, Marge," parried Mulligan.

"So who's the new boy?" asked Marge, "you haven't introduced him yet."

Mulligan turned ingratiating, his mouth a crocodile set of teeth.

"Oh this is Apples," he announced, "he'll bring a glow to any girl's cheeks."

She led them through to the lounge. Four scantily clad girls lolled on the settees and armchairs. Jones was too embarrassed to look or take much in.

"As a visitor and a guest," Mulligan was all abundant magnanimity, "you can have first choice. Take your pick."

Jones did not know where to put himself.

"Come on man," muttered Mulligan, obviously regretting his impulsive generosity, "time's a wasting."

Jones forced himself to look at the girls, trying desperately to think of a satisfactory excuse. He glanced up at an Asian girl, and then beside her focussed on a blonde with smooth creamy skin and a ponytail. She looked young but her eyes belied her innocence. He realised it could only be Honey.

"That one," he tried not to stammer, taking a step forward.

"Well at least you've got taste," grunted Mulligan, "she's the best of the bunch. I was beginning to think you're a faggot. Still, you can oil her up for me. I'll come back for seconds. I don't like slants," he dismissed the Asian with a flick of his head, "so I'll take these two," he said to Marge and dragged the two remaining girls off to a side door. "Watch the walls shake, mate," he said over his shoulder on the way out.

Honey stood up to follow but with Mulligan on his way Jones's wits seemed to return to him. He motioned Honey back to her seat and turned to Marge.

"I took your call," he said, "I'm Garelli's partner."

Marge looked at him carefully and made her decision. "I wanted to talk to Garry," she said, "I thought I made that quite clear."

"Garry's dead," Jones said simply, "yesterday, in my arms." He looked Marge straight in the eye.

She sat down and stared back. Then she asked a question. "Are you really with him?" she nodded at the side door.

"No!" he said sincerely, "We're not even on the same force."

Her eyes made another decision. "I'm sorry love," she said to Honey, and turned back to Jones. "She's underage," said Marge, "I didn't know till I saw Garry's flyer, I swear. But I know the girl doesn't want to go back out on the streets. She's frightened of something. I wanted to talk to Garry about it. I could lose my licence over this."

Honey sat up on the sofa, her eyes wide and frightened. The Chinese girl beside her leaned forward and took her hand.

Jones did not know what to say. He thought of Garelli and made a decision.

"I guess it's a moral call," he said, "it's out of my sphere. I can only make legal judgements. And I'm way out of my jurisdiction, so I pass. I just want to talk to you," he said to Honey, "about the old man. I know you stayed with him. Maybe I can help. Is it O.K to talk?" Here, he meant, in front of them.

"They're my friends," she said, "Lee's my lover." She squeezed the Asian girl's hand and looked up at him. Her eyes were faded blue, lifeless, without expression now the fear had gone.

179

"He didn't do anything with me," she said, "sex or nothing. He wasn't like that."

Jones nodded sympathetically. He assumed that already, as though it mattered in the scheme of judgement.

"He was looking for his son. I knew a good scam so I played him along. He had this photograph. I said I knew him, had seen him around. Funny thing was, in a way I had."

What the hell did she mean? That was impossible.

"I knew a dealer who sort of looked like him, but much older. I kind of put out to him when I first hit town. He was big time. I was thirteen years old and queen of the night. I haven't seen him for the past year or so. Some megabitch showed on the scene and pissed me off. Said I was jail-bait!" She laughed harshly, a woman scorned. "I heard since he died of AIDS."

"Did you tell the old man this?" asked Jones.

"Yeah," said Honey, "only I kind of made out he was a lot younger, more like the photograph. I mean he looked after himself, worked out and everything, but he had to be in his forties. But I guess the photo might have been kind of old. It looked sort of faded round the border. I didn't mention the AIDS, just that I hadn't seen him around for a while. It was only a rumour anyway."

"Did you ever get yourself tested for HIV?" asked Jones.

Honey shrugged; "Whatever for? I'd rather not know. When you gotta go, you know?" the fearlessness of youth or the death of innocence?

"So the old man asked you to move in with him?" Jones returned to firmer ground.

"Yeah I guess I was like a daughter to him," Honey laughed, a cynical sneer that marred her beauty, "There's no fool they say!" she left the conclusion unspoken and paused and stared into space. "Actually he kind of reminded me of my Pops, same kind of eyes. My Pops was in Vietnam. He was at Long Tan. You heard about that? My Pops was proud of that. Never talked much but you could tell, Anzac Day parades and all that. But he had those dead eyes, killing eyes. I guess he'd done a lot of that. The old man was the same. The eyes I mean. That's why when I saw the photographs I got scared, really scared."

"What photographs?" prompted Jones.

"I was going through his things," she said. "He was out one day and I needed to score. I mean he gave me money for food and stuff and I suppose he thought it was enough. But of course it didn't support my habit. So I was looking for something to sell. I found some guns and shit. And these big blown up photos. Really sick. This headless body. All cut up. I was shacked up with a psycho! A real sicko! So I lit out."

Jones took a deep breath and tried to take it all in. There was one more thing.

"The photos of the body, the chest," he asked, "were there any marks on it?"

"Yeah," she said, "sort of cut marks like a pattern."

In his notebook Jones drew the tattoo he'd seen on the dead Asian in the mortuary, and showed it to Honey. "Like that?" he asked.

She nodded, her eyes wide again. "What does it mean?" she asked.

"What it means," considered Jones, "is that you saw the photographs of the body of the old man's son." And that somehow the old man had got them from police files?

Honey frowned, her forehead wrinkling with the strain. Lee was looking at Jones's sketch.

"That is the Chinese ideogram for the Ox," she said.

Jones tried to digest this, but could not for the moment. There was something else he remembered. Honey was looking puzzled, unfocussed and staring into space.

"A friend of yours," he said to her, "said that you were giving the old man information about drug dealers?"

"That's right," confirmed Honey, "I thought he'd sussed my habit. I got a bit paranoid," she laughed nervously, "it would have been a bit like Daddy finding out his little girl wasn't so sweet after all."

"But he must have realised to have asked you in the first place," declared Jones.

"Suppose!" frowned Honey, "but he definitely didn't like it. I think I told him I was in a programme or something, going straight."

"But you did tell him?" asked Jones.

"Yeah," said Honey, "I saw no harm in that. I gave him a couple of faces, regular dealers on the strip. I thought the old fart wanted to abuse them, you know shout at them. Let off steam!"

"Are they still around?" asked Jones, "You know, still dealing?"

"Dunno," shrugged Honey, "but I don't go to the strip so much now. It's a bit out of my way. Dealers don't last long on the street anyway. It's a business with a high turnover." Her voice was pensive, seemingly unaware of the irony. She paused, considering something. "If it was his son," she said, "I guess he wasn't so sick after all."

"Perhaps not," agreed Jones, "at least not in the way you think. I don't think you need to be scared that he'd torture you or anything."

"He'd still be pretty pissed," said the girl, "I sold one of his guns."

Jones stared at her in amazement, "You're crazy!" he muttered.

She laughed at him. "I'm here for a good time," she said, "not a long time," she smiled at him, "You want to get laid, it's on the house."

He shook his head and didn't know what to say any more. Marge saved him from himself, and talked trivia while they waited for Mulligan. Jones suddenly realised that they had not been interrupted by other customers.

"We're closed," said Marge, "until he's gone. It's a quiet time of day anyway."

Jones tried chatting to Lee, asking about the significance of the ideogram, but she didn't seem to comprehend. Her English did not seem so good now. But that was O.K. His Chinese was a lot worse.

Eventually Mulligan showed. He was red-faced and sweating, his eyes glazed and hard. "Those bitches won't be any good this shift!" he crowed, "Now they've had a man." He leaned across to Jones, "I split them till they screamed," he boasted. Then he looked across at Honey. "I'll save you till next time, bitch," he said, "so you've got something to look forward to." The folds of fat round his eyes crinkled as he sniggered.

Jones gave an involuntary shudder. Honey gave Mulligan a vacant smile.

"Any time, big boy," she crooned.

Mulligan was staring at Jones as if he had just realised something.

"You haven't fucked her, have you?" he accused Jones. "Mr Neat and Tidy, you haven't even unbuttoned your shirt. You pick the best-looking bitch in the house and you do fuck all? You wanker, what have you been doing here, holding hands?"

Marge tried to placate him but he would not have a bar of it. He paid out on Jones till he ran out of breath. Then he stumbled out, threw the keys at Jones and told him to drive. He sat in silence all the way back to the station. They were more than halfway before Jones realised he had not asked Honey for the address of the flat the old man was staying in. still, he rationalised, he could always phone for it. It was no big problem. The problem would come when he got the address. What would he do with it? He certainly would not want to give it to the likes of Mulligan. What the afternoon had given him was hard evidence that someone in the department was releasing information to the old man. The question was who, and what to do about it?

As he tried to weave the car through the cluttered lanes of the city with the brooding bulk of Mulligan simmering beside hi, Jones felt lost again, lost and afraid, a small boy in a strange environment, alone and confused.

When they reached the station it was the end of the shift at the end of a long tired day. Mulligan heaved himself out without even a grunt of acknowledgement and Jones decided to sign himself off and head for home. As he struck out in search for a cab he reflected that he did actually regard Garelli's flat as home. Here and now, in this alien city, his only safe haven was the flat of a dead woman where he had a latchkey but no tenure. He did not even know what the rent was, let alone when it was due.

The cabs seemed thin on the ground so he had to keep walking. He started to get that feeling between his shoulder blades again, that feeling of tension that meant he was being followed. He hurried for the busiest section of street, so that he could lose himself in the scurrying crowds of the shopping plaza. The mall loomed like sanctuary and he ducked inside to cocoon himself in the security of its enclosed humanity. But then he realised it was closing time and he was contradicting an exodus. So he turned and headed for an exit himself, all the while darting furtive glances over his shoulder, or ducking into boutiques to check the throng that streamed past. Outside in the plaza again he felt exposed and vulnerable under the mousing sky. So he slipped into a souvlaki bar and ordered a takeaway. Actually he was not at all hungry but he knew he ought to be, and he rationalised that it would save him from fending for himself later back at the flat. So he sat down on a chrome stool at a bench bar at the window and forced himself to eat. Outside the crowds marched into the oblivious evening and inside the owner fussed and sweated over his spits and grills, his rounded features melting in the heat. Customers slipped in and out barely breaking stride. In, queue, order, pay, wait and takeaway; the rhythm of the city stomach gnawing at the remains of the day. Ritualised greetings made meaningless with repetition, fast food to sewage, the essential cycle of urban decay. Jones sat there sliding his eyes over the current, focussing on the eddies. But there was never an island in all that cascade and flow, and eventually he had to admit to himself that he had been imagining things. No one could remain stationary in that without drawing attention to himself. So he could not have been followed, could he? Unless, he thought as he slipped back out to rejoin the thinning stream, the pursuer had, like him, also taken temporary refuge in one of the countless shops.

But Jones managed to catch a lone cab off the ranks on the far side of the mall, and decided that would be a hard act to follow. Even so he kept watching the cars behind, all the way back to the flat. They chopped and changed at every set of lights and intersection, so he had to be safe, did he not?

# Chapter 19.  The Wrong Side of Midnight

Once inside the flat Jones decided to phone Marge to get the address of the old man's place off Honey. He had intended to ring in the morning but now he thought about it he reasoned that the brothel would more than likely be empty at that time of day. When he got hold of Marge he could not get a word in edgeways. In her words Mulligan had 'damaged' one of the girls that afternoon, and she spent a good while complaining to Jones about Mulligan and his behaviour. Jones switched his mind off to the details. He did not know what to say anyway. How did a brothel complain about a rogue cop? Perhaps he could mention it to Ethical Standards; he had almost made up his mind to go to them on the morrow anyway. He managed to suggest this to Marge, but she shied off, muttering about Honey being underage. Jones said Ethical Standards did not know about that and surely between them he and Marge could keep Honey out of it? But Marge said there were other considerations and would not elaborate, except that she felt better now having talked about it. Jones did not, he felt lousy. Mulligan had only gone there because of him. And what did the 'damaged' girl feel? But he saved that for later, for the private pain of his inner darkness, got the address he wanted, and put the phone down.

He stared at the four walls and the prowling cats and the flat became a cage without bars. He wondered what made men like Mulligan and he wondered at the obsession with sex that seemed to enthral so many. And he wondered at himself and why it meant so little. He had never really faced that before. But the walls gave him no answers, just reflected his shadow pacing. And outside was that other shadow, stalking the byways of the night, that terrible old man, that demented prophet from an Old Testament past, extracting his eye and tooth with clinical precision. For Jones knew now what he would say to Ethical Standards in the morning, it would be up to them to fill in the details and organise the arrest. He would give them the address and leave them to it. As he sorted all this in his mind he realised that at some point he must have accepted that he could trust Ethical Standards and hand over to them. Garelli could not object. Perhaps tomorrow he could go home, catch a cancellation on an afternoon flight? In twenty-four hours he could be breathing fresh air and watching the mountains. He would be safe.

Then he remembered Garelli's funeral and knew he could not miss that. But afterwards? He watched the patterns flutter on the walls and breathed in deeply, trying to take in the possibility of escape. As he tried to relax another question nudged to the surface of his mind. One that, as he thought about it, he could hardly answer back in his real home. The lure of the butterflies was goading him to tempt the night, and the walls shrank in around him, and pressed him to take flight. He ordered a cab to the door and scurried out defenceless into the dark. The lights of the strip pulled him and he lost himself in their neon glow. The cab set him down and he toured the pavements holding close to the lights, darting through shadows and avoiding the mouths of alleys and dark places. When at last he came to the gay bar he walked a way past it and then crossed the street. He found a shop doorway more or less opposite where the shadows were not deep enough to alarm him, and settled in to watch.

He watched for hours, lounging against an archway. They flitted in and out, in singles, pairs or groups. It was not all sequin and leather, a lot of them, perhaps a majority from a distance, were dressed like him. Thanks Garelli, he thought. But still he could not make up his mind whether or not to go in. Finally, in the small hours the wrong side of midnight, a slightly built youth approached him.

"Been watching you," he ventured, "fancy some action?"

Jones stared at him. He was sallow, with greasy slicked back hair, and acne.

"$50 for a blow job," volunteered the youth, "I give good head. Don't do the other." He shrugged, hands in denim pockets, cool and casual, out of the Fifties, he wished.

Jones felt sick. "How old are you?" he asked.

"What's it to you?" the youth backed away slightly, poised on the balls of his feet. "You a bull or something?"

"Yeah, I'm a cop," said Jones, "if that's what you mean?"

The youth fled into the night. Jones stared after him and off into the dark. The street was long and straight, knifing into the distance. Opposing lines of street lamps lit up the cutting edge and parallelled perspective till they met at a far away destination. The taillights of a lone cab ran the gauntlet and dwindled to disappear over the horizon. Eventually Jones decided to go home. He walked along abstractedly, staring at his toes, kicking at the odd can or crumpled paper. At last one piece of litter rolled out of the light and into the shadows and Jones looked up and around himself and realised he had left the strip streets ago. He looked behind him and saw his shadow stretching and leering in the circle cast by the streetlight. Then fear hit him and he started to run. Every time

188

he crossed a light his shadow overtook him and leapt away into the darkness. Then he turned into a street and all the lights went out at once.

Finally, somehow, he found his way to the flat. He flung himself inside, his chest heaving, his legs jelly. He felt as if he had been running for hours, and collapsed on the bed exhausted without even bothering to change. The friendly cat jumped up to join him again. Later some soft scratching noises the other side of the bedroom door woke him up. Jones rolled silently off the bed and crept across to the door and flung it open behind him. Framed in the doorway was the old man, his eyes glowing green and luminescent in the half-light off the street. Jones screamed and snapped awake and realised he had been sleepwalking. The other cat, the shy one was winding itself around his ankles, purring softly. He could not get back to sleep, and spent the short remainder of the night praying for the dawn. When at last the sky lightened outside his window he felt himself relax and let himself uncoil and sink back on the bed. He was convinced that he was safe in daylight, that if the old man should get caught out in the sun he would shrivel up and die. He had seen that in some film, and felt that it was more than appropriate. Garelli's suggestion that he should go to the Foreign Languages Department at the university crossed his mind. He had always felt that Eastern Europe was a strong possibility.

\*

Jones really did not want to face any kind of inquisition from Mulligan, so he forced himself to get to the station early to clock on before the usual time. At his desk he immediately contacted one of the officers from Ethical Standards, a

Detective Sergeant Fletcher, who had left him a card the previous day. Fletcher told him to come straight round. Mulligan was not in yet so Jones left a note to cover himself by saying that Ethical Standards wanted a further statement from him regarding Garelli's death.

Ethical Standards was actually in another building across the city. Jones really did not feel up to driving, and it was too far to walk so he caught a cab. For the first time it occurred to him that it was probably the way the old man travelled round the city. Cabs were so convenient and anonymous. The old man might even have sat in the very same seat. Jones sat there, trying to sense any imprint, soak up his essence. Then Garelli's voice told him not to be so silly, this was the big smoke, there were thousands of cabs out there, not just a few dozen, and the odds of him following in the old man's footsteps were beyond the bounds of probability. Still he wondered if it were possible to trace the old man's movements by checking through the cab fleet. Then he had another thought, and asked the cabbie it he would be willing to switch off the meter if Jones paid cash? The driver said that was fine with him if he could have the money up front. Jones, now the point was made, told him not to bother as this was only a short fare, but he would remember it for next time. The driver gave him his private number, to his personal mobile phone. So it could well be a blank trail, not that it really mattered now, it could only corroborate his scenario. Jones was sure of what had happened, most of it any rate. He stared out of the side window. The sky was clear, cobalt blue above the smog-line, and the city buildings stood sharp and proud with razored lines.

Ethical Standards was in back of a nondescript building of tired brick walls and sandstone lintels. It looked neglected and

190

unwanted, almost like a squat. The doors tended to jam and the floorboards creaked. It felt like a heritage building too ugly to be open to the public but too historical to be pulled down. Fletcher's office was small, cluttered and gloomy. It even boasted half-panelling round the walls. Jones sat in a real upholstered chair and tried to remember everything. His mind was fazed and strained but he thought he presented it well. They taped him to save taking notes. He concluded by implying that it was the photographs of the son's body that gave the old man a starting point. What he did not know was who gave them to the father. He thought that Garelli had been killed because she was getting close to the truth, either through the phone number or through her attempted resurrection of the son's files.

Fletcher's partner, an Officer Stravitis, said that fitted in with what they had made of Garelli's movements the morning prior to her death. She had gone to the hospital to visit the D.I to get written authorisation to view the negatives in the mortuary files. The other thing that she had been doing was to attempt to check how many office extensions in the station were continually manned. Stravitis's assumption there was that Garelli's line of reasoning required the police contact to be present when the old man's call came through. The landline would have been set up because reception to a mobile could not be relied upon. Garelli had also asked the telephone company to check calls rung in from the island to those numbers. There had not been any.

"Now that we know what she was looking for," said Fletcher, "we will put together a short-list of officers who fit. We'll also run a check on mobiles, though as we've said we think they're less likely because of the black spots. Until then it looks like a dead-end, being as you can't remember the number you were given?"

"It definitely wasn't a mobile," said Jones, "but it might not be necessary in any case," and he gave them the old man's address.

That got them going but after the first flurry of excitement they sent Jones back to the station to allay suspicion about his movements. They said they would organise things and contact him later, hopefully when the old man was safely under lock and key. They said they would only involve officers from Ethical Standards and the Tactical Response Squad so that the informer would not get tipped off. On the way back Jones hoped that they did not kill the old man. That really would be a dead-end.

Back at the station Mulligan was waiting for him, gross and threatening. He got into Jones instantly, wanting to know about the boy that he and Garelli had brought in the previous week, and stuck one of the youth files under Jones's nose. At first Jones could not place the kid, it all seemed so trivial and long ago now, an incidental point buried in the avalanche of much larger happenings. Mulligan refreshed his memory.

"You must remember a pretty boy like him," he insinuated, stabbing at the photo with that massive forefinger. "What I want to know is why you and that bitch recommended his release back into care? Now he's done a runner again and the parents have laid a complaint against us for not informing them of his apprehension. They want him back! Claim the State's incompetent!"

"It was a Community Services decision," said Jones, "You know that."

"Sir!" insisted Mulligan, "you call me Sir, you maggot."

His piggy eyes glared at Jones through the folds of fat as he waved another document in Jones's face.

"This is the Community Services report, Jones," he said, "It says that it acted on your and Garelli's recommendation that the boy be put in care because of allegations of parental abuse. Allegations, Jones, unsubstantiated! What gives you the right to usurp the prerogative of the courts?"

Jones did not know what to say, it had been Garelli's call, not his; he had not even been at the meeting, but he really did not want to pass the buck, not with her being unable to answer back. Garelli would not be able to forgive that.

"I'm not too familiar with procedures, sir," he prevaricated, "it seemed a good idea at the time. Best for all concerned, a safe compromise."

Mulligan snorted like an angry bull, his chins quivering with indignation.

"No you're certainly not too au fait with procedures, are you, Jones?" he spat, "which is why Garelli got killed the other day!"

Jones flinched under that blow and felt the blood drain from his face.

"But now, maggot," continued Mulligan, "I'm stuck with you cause I've got to sort this mess out," he waved the file in the air and then threw it on his desk, "cause as the superior officer I cop the blame!"

He sat back heavily on the edge of the desk and glared at Jones.

"So!" he said, "you had better revise your memory, Jones, and remember what brilliant operational procedures led you to this delinquent in the first place. And then you and me can go out and pick the little faggot up, and put him back under lock and key till Mumsy comes for him."

Jones stared back at Mulligan. "It was accidental, Sir!" he stressed, "routine street checks." On their own time and unpaid for too, he seemed to remember, but did not bother to make the point. After all it had really been Garelli's altruism, not his.

Mulligan swore and looked up at the ceiling.

"We did get some addresses of current squats out of him," Jones added. "I suppose he could have gone back to them. He'd need to go somewhere. It would at least be familiar territory."

Mulligan looked at him without expression.

"Pull the addresses then, Officer," he said, " and we'll get out there. And you had better pray he's holed up somewhere on that list. I do not want to roam the streets all day. And you do not want to be with me!"

He levered himself back onto his feet and glared at Jones.

No, thought Jones, he certainly did not: Mulligan forced to pound the pavements was not a pleasant thought, not if he had to be with him.

"I'll go through Garelli's files," he muttered, "if you can get them released to me. I'll see where she wrote down the squats. It might take a while, Sir!" he added as an afterthought.

"Didn't you take notes?" Mulligan was incredulous.

"No," said Jones shortly, "It's not my city. Sir!"

*

# Chapter 20. Maggot in the Apple

Outside the sky was growing overcast. Cloud cover was building rapidly and the air was getting sticky as liquid tar. It pressed down smothering and crushing, squeezing the lungs with remorseless pressure. Mulligan's breathing was laboured, and he shuffled and snuffled like a tormented bull.

"What a mother of a day to get lumbered with the shit end of the street!" he groaned, and shunted up against the front door of the second squat they had visited. The first had been bare, derelict and deserted, and Jones hoped desperately that this one would pay off. Mulligan's fuse was getting shorter by the minute, and Jones did not want to be around when it finally blew.

"This one's a window job," Jones pointed out diplomatically, "I'll check them out to find a way in."

"Right little ferret, aren't you, Jones?" sneered Mulligan, "pity you can't give yourself a run?"

Jones tried to ignore him and left him leaning against the door while he went round the side. He remembered the point of entry from before. As he scrambled in through the unlocked window a huge crash from the front shook the house. Jones rushed through the rooms to see what had happened. In the hallway Mulligan was sprawled on his back on top of the door and frame and side-panels. His weight must have pulled the whole shebang free of its fastenings. Glass from the sidelights was shattered across the floor. The pane above the door, with the house name printed in gilt upon it, was still incongruously intact. Jones did not know whether to laugh or cheer. He certainly was not inclined to cry.

"Get me the fuck up!" rumbled Mulligan.

He was stranded on his back, like an unshorn ewe in lamb fallen on a wet day. For a moment Jones considered leaving him, but reflected that if he did, and Mulligan somehow managed to get free, the retribution would be colossal. So he brushed aside the shards of glass with his shoe and knelt down beside Mulligan to try to turn him on his side. With Mulligan's writhing and cursing they eventually made it, and Mulligan flopped over onto his stomach like a beached whale. Jones suddenly felt overwhelmingly sorry for the girls at Marge's the previous day. Mulligan managed to lever himself onto his knees, and then again required Jones's assistance to get to his feet. When finally upright he refused to go and get himself checked over, but insisted on continuing. There was of course no one about as they checked out the squat. The dead would have long fled.

It was all downhill from there on, not that the day had been too auspicious to begin with. They slogged through squat after squat, from mothballed construction sites to abandoned warehouses, from peeling weatherboard in the streets to federation brick in the boulevards. Some had occupants, but never the one they sought, and Mulligan would take out his frustration by kicking the squatters into the street and throwing their gear out after. Jones was appalled but felt powerless to intervene. As the day dragged by Mulligan's anger smouldered like a dormant volcano. At one point Jones persuaded him to look at the city storm drains. He was hoping to cool him off, but Mulligan would not reconnoitre to any depth, saying the weather was far too volatile. Jones figured the stooped shuffle cramped his style too much. Besides the rain if it came would flush out all and sundry soon enough. It was certainly no place to lie up in, strictly just a one-night stand. But the afternoon was waning, and the nightshades were out there somewhere on the edge, waiting for the death of the sun.

"It's getting too late," said Jones, "they'll all be out on the streets now, for the evening trade."

"So we're an expert now on rent-boys, are we?" sneered Mulligan. "You think this scum clocks on like shift-work? Some of these night birds don't even wake up till the moon rises. We'll check them all, and then tomorrow we'll check them again. And in between we'll check the streets, you on foot, me in the car, kerb-crawling."

It was funny, reflected Jones, that Mulligan's burst of determination and dedication should remind him so much of Garelli: perhaps once he had been a good cop?

They had two addresses left to go when they came to a fibro shack on the side of a rundown and deserted looking industrial estate. It looked like the broken down victim of a forgotten recession. One of the front sashes was up, probably because of the heat.

"Careless," muttered Mulligan, "might let the cat in. I'll go round the back."

He moved off silently, surprisingly quiet for a man of his bulk, gliding on the balls of his feet. Rising to the occasion, thought Jones, and knowing full well that he would not be able to keep it up. He slipped in through the window and made for the partition door. It was almost too dark to see now. Jones cursed himself for not bringing a torch. Out into the hall and then a glimmer of candlelight under a door at the back to the right. Something crunched under Jones's foot as he crept forward and the light snuffed out and a dark figure slipped out of the door and in through another. Jones rushed forward and found himself in a small kitchen with the shadow scrabbling at the back door. As he lunged the door flew open and there was Mulligan framed in the twilight. The shadow bounced off him and Mulligan's hand whipped out and grasped the struggling figure by the hair.

"Well now, what have we here?" he grunted and pushed forward and kicked the door closed behind him. Then he fished out a lighter from one baggy pocket. The boy's face twisted and frowned in the flickering flame, his eyes dark pools of fear. He reached up and scrabbled ineffectually at Mulligan's massive hand locked in his hair. Mulligan spun him round and backhanded him across the face with the hand holding the lighter. The boy screamed and sank to his knees. Jones shouted for Mulligan to leave him alone. Mulligan laughed and wrenched the boy's face up to the light.

"It's Cutie Pie, isn't it, Jones?" said Mulligan.

The boy spat at him and Mulligan hauled him upright almost onto his toes and smashed him in the stomach. The boy whimpered and doubled up and sank down in slow motion, the collapsed weight of him pulling down on Mulligan's outstretched arm. Jones screamed and Mulligan laughed.

"For Chrissake Mulligan, he's only a boy!" Jones cried.

"That's right, Jones, I forgot, he's a boy, a nancy boy. Perhaps you fancy him do you?" Mulligan sneered and hauled the boy upright again. "You don't like women do you, Jones? Is this what you like?"

He reached down to the boy's waist and unbuttoned his jeans and yanked them down. The boy's white buttocks quivered in the warm air.

"Have a good look, Jones," taunted Mulligan, "This is what turns you on, isn't it? Have a good look!" he repeated, and held the lighter near them.

The boy twisted away sobbing.

"Stop it!" shouted Jones, "just stop!"

"You faggot!" sneered Mulligan, "maggot in the apple, that's what you are, Jones." He flung the boy aside and slapped Jones across the face. "Gutless faggot!" he sneered, "gutless fairy faggot!"

Jones staggered and came back with fists raised.

Mulligan laughed. "You want a piece of me, little boy?" he boomed, "Fat chance, your arse is mine!"

Jones snapped and charged. He feinted at the last moment, dropped his guard and sidestepped to kick in Mulligan's kneecaps, and as he toppled smashed his shoe into the fat man's stomach. Then as the head hit the floor Jones kicked it again and again. Then he moved down the body, booting hard into the rolls of flesh. It was like kicking into a sponge, and soon he tired and staggered back wondering at what he had done. The boy tiptoed forward, re-buttoning his jeans.

"Wow!" he muttered, "You put the bastard down, but good eh!"

He poked tentatively at the hulk with his foot. When there was no response he kicked Mulligan hard, and then again, and again.

"You fat bastard!" he screamed, "You're not so fucking flash now, eh!"

Jones sagged exhausted against the kitchen door, too washed out to intervene. Eventually too the boy tired and stopped. It was too dark to see well, but Mulligan's body was blocking the back door and Jones the other. The boy seemed to come to his senses and he shrank away against the far wall.

"Have you got a light?" Jones asked at last. He had no idea where Mulligan's lighter had gone in the tussle.

The boy fumbled in his pocket and brought out a box of matches. They rattled as his hands shook.

"I can get a candle," he offered.

"Just make sure you come back," said Jones, and he stepped aside to let the boy through. Instinctively he knew the boy would not run. They were joined now, a tenuous link as fragile as life itself. He knelt beside Mulligan and lit a match. Mulligan's face was bruised and bloody and swollen and motionless. Jones probed for a pulse in the carotid artery but could not feel anything in amongst all those layers of fleshy neck. The match scorched Jones's fingers and he flung it away cursing.

"Is he dead?" whispered the boy from behind him.

Jones took the candle and lit it without replying. Mulligan did not appear to be breathing.

"Is he dead?" repeated the boy but an octave higher.

"Probably!" muttered Jones.

He was not really sure. It was in a doctor's jurisdiction, not his. He remembered something about mirrors over the mouth and the condensation of breath, but the day was so warm and Mulligan so fat. That could not be conclusive either. He stood up slowly, his mind going blank, not knowing what to do.

"You started it!" accused the boy, "You hit him first!"

Actually he had not, Jones clearly remembered Mulligan initiating his own demise. But that was hardly the point.

"And you kicked him last," Jones retorted quietly. "Does it matter?"

They were both accessories before and after the fact. Jones did not bother to mention that in law, as the adult, he was the one culpable, not the juvenile.

"You killed him!" insisted the boy, "Not me!"

He began to shake and sat down on the floor and started to weep, "Oh hell, oh sweet fucking hell!"

Jones went through Mulligan's pockets and removed his wallet. He was hardly thinking clearly but on reflection he considered that it was probably better if Mulligan was actually dead. It was less complicated. He took out all the cash. It was a lot, mainly hundred dollar bills. He wondered for a moment what Mulligan had come prepared for? But he did not bother to count and held it out to the boy. The candlelight shadowed the planes of the boy's face and transformed it into a skull. Jones was unconscionably reminded of Garelli's comments about slow suicide on the streets, and wondered if he were merely offering a quick solution, but in the end he judged that he could not be responsible.

"Take it and split," he decided, "Another city, another state: a fresh start. If you stay here they'll keep looking. Your mother is insisting."

"What about him?" asked the boy, nodding towards Mulligan's bulk?

Jones shrugged, if Mulligan was not dead now he probably soon would be if he did not get medical attention. He bent down to remove Mulligan's gun. The boy shrank away.

"No, no," Jones reassured him and pocketed the weapon. It might come in handy, another time, another place, but not here and now. Jones could never kill in cold blood, could he?

"We leave him," he decided, "perhaps no one will notice the smell for a few days. This isn't exactly the popular end of town. That will give you plenty of time to get free and clear. After all, this is a squat, who's going to report it?"

He did not know if he was trying to persuade the boy or himself?

"What about you?" asked the boy?

Jones shrugged again. "I'll say nothing," he declared, "I clocked off at the normal time and he went off on his own. I thought he'd gone home."

"That'll be enough?" queried the boy.

"Yeah!" decided Jones, he was improvising, but it was best to stay positive, "As long as you keep your mouth shut. Come on, grab your gear; I'll walk you to the coach terminal. I have to leave the car, make it look as though he drove himself."

He lifted the candle to the boy's face, "And wash off that make-up," he ordered, "this is a clean slate."

As the boy tried to clean himself up, Jones went through Mulligan's pockets again and removed his I.D card. He thought it might slow the identification up, if only the flies were given time to start their business. Then he used a handkerchief to take the car keys out. He hoped that if he left them in the car someone might do him the favour of stealing it. It was an unmarked after all, just another unremarkable from the pool. Then he wondered if that would simply encourage the discovery of the body? Then he wondered about all the fingerprints he had left in the squat. But he realised if necessary he could tell the truth and honestly state that he had been there with Garelli previously. It would have been logged. Then he worried about the boy's fingerprints everywhere; but the boy was a minor, and would they have his prints on record, and if so what for? Then he decided the hell with it all, he would let nature, and the flies take their course. After all, who would suspect Jones of anything, most of the time he was an inconvenience, simply to be ignored?

He walked the boy part of the way into the city, keeping to the shadows and trying to be as unobtrusive as possible, hardly a father and son out for a stroll, but a couple of siblings going for a game somewhere? Actually it was feasible: now that the boy was cleaned up, he was just another teenager with a backpack on a journey. No casual observer would realise that he carried all his worldly possessions on his back. Eventually Jones decided it was better to leave him than risk the continuation into the busier parts of town. So they parted on a street corner, a couple of relatives saying a casual goodbye. Jones caught a cab.

*

When Jones finally got back to the flat he collapsed against the counter and started to shake. It seemed to go on for ever so he poured himself a drink, knocked it back, poured another, and another. The cats were irritating so he slung them out and stumbled to the bed and mercifully passed out. In the depths of the night he dreamed the dream again, that the old man was in the kitchen. When he opened the bedroom door the figure's face changed and became Mulligan, gross and threatening. Jones stared to plead and the figure became his foster-father. He snapped awake running with sweat. The humidity was too oppressive for him to get back to sleep. He could not get this image out of his mind of Mulligan buried alive in a vast double-sized coffin and clawing remorselessly at the lid with huge stubby fingers.

Jones suddenly realised his clothes and especially his shoes could be contaminated by Mulligan's DNA. He undressed himself in a panic, and threw all of the discarded clothing in a black garbage bag. Then he panicked again and tipped it all out. This time he picked up a new bin liner with a dishcloth covering his hand, and he loaded his old clothes into it carefully, making sure his fingerprints were not on it. But he knew his shoes probably held the most compelling evidence. He thought of scrubbing them in the sink, but recognised the futility of trying to hide blood trace from modern forensic technology. In the end he elected to wipe them down thoroughly to remove any of his own fingerprints, and then he dropped them in a separate plastic bag. Then he dressed himself in a dark tracksuit, slipped on a pair of trainers and snuck out into the night with the bags. He walked for ages, hoping for a street somewhere with a morning garbage collection. He had no idea of the city's routines, just kept wandering through the dark, a night moth flitting through the shadows, avoiding the lights, on the look out for patrolling cars. Finally he turned into a street where the bins were lining the pavement for the dawn kerbside collection. He dumped the clothes first, and then walked over to another street for good measure to bin the shoes.

The air felt like a storm was brewing. He walked back quickly, somehow feeling liberated, a weight taken off him. But Garelli's funeral was in the morning. When he finally got back to the flat he was too wired to sleep. The rest of the night was another long lonely wait for the dawn.

*

# Chapter 21. The Deluge

The rain was remorseless, as relentless as death. The drought had finally broken. It seemed to wash down in waves, with an intensity that seemed impossible compared to the showers of home. No gentle nourishing here, no soft moisture nurturing the soil, this was one of the horsemen, this was a flood. He peered over the edge and stared in. The grave was actually filling up with water. He wondered if the coffin was watertight, whether it would float? Perhaps this would be the nearest that Garelli got to that river cruise she had promised herself, promised him. Waves of sadness washed through him, threatening to drown him. He gulped down his pain and tilted his face to the sky. No need to feel ashamed, the rain would hide his tears. Real men do not cry, do they? Real men carry on and extract a biblical vengeance. Real men were heroes. He glanced surreptitiously at the mourners, to see if they had noticed him. But they were all shrouded by their umbrellas, black personal canopies shielding them from the rain, from seeing his tears. There were only a few of them, too few really to acknowledge her death and justify her life.

He wondered if that was how you measured a life, its significance and its meaning? By the number of people who turned out to witness the passing? He wondered how many would turn up at his own funeral, if any? He thought that this today should have been a police funeral, with all the trappings. Officer killed in the line of duty, and the parade through the city behind the hearse in slow time, and the honour guard in dress uniform, and a volley from standard issue revolvers over the graveside. But perhaps that was not how they did it: another state, another country? He had never been to a police funeral before. Besides what was the occasion but a commemoration for the living, so that their own finite lives could go on? The dead could care nothing. Apparently the sister had insisted on a quiet ceremony, no show, and no trappings. Only the Superintendent was there as a representative from the force. Jones wondered if Mulligan would have shown if he had had the choice? Perhaps the sister was right, perhaps she knew Garelli too well to profess to hypocrisy. Who else in the wide world would really mourn her passing: only himself, the outsider from another state? Only himself, and the few odd humans that Garelli had touched in her brief span: the man from the local deli, the vet who treated Garelli's cats, an elderly neighbour who sometimes came to feed them, and the delivery boy from the local pizza shop. There was no one from her past, only her sister and no other family. She was a small mousy thing, with rounded shoulders hunched against the rigors of the world, and dull haunted eyes that darted nervous glances from beneath a plain-cut fringe. Jones felt obliged to try and make conversation, but she was too shy or too sad to do more than mumble at her feet. Trivia drowned and lost itself in the pouring rain.

A flight of seagulls soared overhead, screaming with raucous delight, twisting and turning in the gusts and flurries. There must be a refuse tip nearby, thought Jones, or maybe some market garden or farmland. The cemetery was out in the fringe suburbs, he was not too sure where, he had just taken a cab, handed over a note with a written address, and let the driver take over. Another objective achieved without awareness of the journey. Cabs were so convenient; steel cocoons to protect oneself from the metropolitan weal. Or just another leap of faith, like death, a last voyage to the final destination? The inner cemeteries were presumably full, or fully booked. The dead of the big cities must take up a lot of space. So many people lived in them, and they were all waiting to die. He wondered why she had not elected for cremation, and a crowded rose garden. But roses die, and do not give that measure of permanence in a transient world. Two meters by one meter, yours for eternity, the real estate agent's final dream. If it was not for cremation, all the world would be owned by the dead, and there would be no one to muse elegies over old histories in country churchyards, because only land feeds the living. He himself, he would ask for his ashes to be scattered over the oceans, to blow in the sea breeze, and finally fall to feed the plankton. Would that cause pollution? How much death could the seas absorb? And what of the air: with all those smoking furnaces and the whole world a vast crematorium?

Crazy thoughts on an insane day when the living do not come to respect the dead, because the dead when alive offended the living. Of course, that was it, he realised. Garelli's final finger to posterity: if they burnt her she would disappear, but if they buried her they would never be rid of her. He wondered what instructions were left in her will, what the inscription would read? He ought to come back to review the headstone. But he would never dare. Mulligan's pile of corruption would already be beginning to fester out there and Jones did not want to be around for the reckoning. If he got out of this, if he managed to get on that plane, to what gods would he pray? He probably should have caught a ride in with the superintendent. He could have asked then about that ticket. The superintendent had previously seemed a sympathetic ear in the urban wilderness, had said he should go home. He could at least have saved the cab fare. It was no good being alone in a dying world. One had to liaise with the living.

The mourners shuffled in the rain. The hearse had finally arrived. It must have been held up in the traffic: the dead held up by the living. The pallbearers hoisted up the coffin and hustled forward in the rain. Someone bustled alongside indecisively with an umbrella, tyring to shelter all and saving none: four strong men and true, the rain running into their shoulders and down their necks. They must have been hired, Jones reflected. What a job for your resume. And what about gender equity? Was that Garelli's final joke, making four jocks slog for her through the pouring rain? There looked to be half a metre of water in the hole by the time they arrived at the graveside. No one seemed to know what to do, but definitely no one wanted to hang about, so they lowered the coffin into the hole in any case. When they pulled the ropes free it bobbed and floated in its own wake. Then a hasty obituary was launched, all dignity curtailed, and the professionals beat a dignified but rapid retreat. The acquaintances mumbled embarrassed condolences and slipped their separate ways into the veil of rain. Only the Superintendent and the sister were left, and Jones, too mesmerised by the extraordinary to leave. He had this vision of Garelli's last rite of passage, her coffin rising out of the ground on a flood of water, and rushing through the storm gutters and drains down through the city and out into the bay and then on to the open sea: a Viking funeral, a requiem fit for a Valkyrie.

A workman wandered surreptitiously into view, cowled and shawled with a waterproof poncho and somehow managing to look furtive as he broached the pouring rain to approach the open grave.

"She'll be right," he attempted with surprising gentility to soothe the little sister, "you go, we'll take care of her."

Jones wondered who the 'we' referred to, since there was only the one visible. The workman sidled alongside and whispered in his ear, "Take her off, son," he muttered, "Give her a nice cappuccino. We'll sort this."

"How?" Jones felt constrained to ask.

"Pull the bung of course!" the workman gave a sardonic grin and nodded away into the rain. "I'm off to get some tools. You'd best be away. Sometimes the smell's a bit ripe."

The superintendent took advantage of the departure to approach Jones. He nodded seriously, his face sincere with the sympathy an obligation of homage to a noble occasion. He carefully steered Jones a small distance from the sister until he had been manoeuvred out of earshot, and then he muttered platitudes, not true condolences since Jones was hardly family, little more than a passing ship really. Then he surprised Jones with an apology of sorts and an invitation of a kind.

"I believe you'll be leaving us next week? But I don't want you to go with a totally negative impression," he pontificated, "I understand you hunt. Some of the lads are putting together an outing on the weekend, a sambar shoot in the High Country. The ultimate hunting experience in Australia apparently, or perhaps as a native I'm prejudiced?" a muffled laugh from a man evidently trying to sustain at least the appearance of gravity in the present situation. "You're invited. I won't take no for an answer."

Jones stared at him through the downpour, momentarily speechless.

"I've got no gear, no gun, nothing!" he prevaricated, not wanting to go anywhere but home.

"I'm sure somebody will loan you some fire-power," the superintendent would not be gainsaid, "after all we've got access to the police armoury!" Another throaty laugh: was that an attempt at a joke? "Sambar are surprisingly large. You'd need a heavy hitter. I gather police issue .308 will do the job."

Jones wondered at the serendipity: how much had the superintendent been checking up on him?

"Tomorrow night then?" the superintendent would not be turned aside. "What's your current address? I'll get somebody to pick you up."

Jones was too embarrassed to admit to living at Garelli's, and too paranoid to advertise it anyway.

"At night?" he stalled for more time.

"Yes," affirmed the superintendent, "well evening actually. It's a fair drive, and the hunt needs to start at dawn. So you'll be camping out overnight, under the stars. Do you the world of good."

"Overnight?" Jones was stretched beyond astonishment and further comment, but could not help gesturing at the lowering sky.

"We'll fix you up with a swag," the superintendent seemed to have an answer for every possible objection. "If it's raining they'll bivouac under tarps. The moisture's good for the hunt, makes tracking easier."

Jones felt bulldozed, that resistance was useless. "You can pick me up from the station," he said, finally folding and yet finding a partial solution at the same time, "I'll be finishing off some paperwork so that I can clear the desk and get away," fictitious of course, but it coincided with the advertised intention of going home. It seemed as though a date had been

210

set for next week, probably time enough to resolve Ethical Standards' fiction about Garelli and hopefully cauterise the old man, but hardly soon enough for him.

"I hope you're not billing us for the overtime?" the superintendent bought into the line and made a joke of it.

Jones just grinned sheepishly.

The superintendent held out a hand to shake Jones's. "Good man," he said, all bonhomie and effervescent cheer in the middle of a cemetery at a funeral in the pouring rain. "I'll be seeing you."

Jones watched the superintendent's back in disbelief as he disappeared into the deluge. "Not if I see you coming first," he mumbled, but quietly, under his breath, so as not to disturb the retreat of interfering hierarchy.

Jones made his way back over to the sister, rescuing her from her solitude, and walked her away through the rain, hurrying her down the serried ranks of stone angels and plastic flowers and marbled monuments braced against the elements. She said nothing, just scurried in his wake, watching the puddles and runnels as she minced and tiptoed on the waterlogged land. He found himself babbling inconsequences to keep the sound of the rain at bay, the clouds' tears washing away the ground from under their feet. Then they were out into the traffic and the cars stalling and tailgating and shunting and lights flashing and the rain still relentless in the gathering gloom. The pavements though were washed clean, all the litter swept away to clutter the stained currents of a swollen sea. The asphalt gleamed slate and pristine in the subdued light.

They sat in a small café, the furniture all faded plastic and tarnished chrome, and sipped lukewarm drinks off chipped Formica tables and murmured nothings into the vacant air. He wanted to probe the past but she volunteered nothing, and at last he released her. He pondered the absence of parents or any other relatives as she scurried out into the deluge, and darted off down the sidewalk, flitting from canopy to canopy, hugging the shopfronts and doorways. He was left alone, empty and unanswered, a lost soul in the void. But how long would it be till he was found? The countdown was already happening; Mulligan was waiting, and then what? He would be discovered eventually. Would the body just be designated another casualty of the current drugs war? The police should pull out all the stops for the killing of one of their own. But would they? Had they done so with Garelli? Would it pay to look too closely under every stone upturned? Or would it be politic for the reputation of all to look the other way and simply declare another fine officer lost in the line of duty?

But whatever the future had in store somehow Jones had to get through another bloody hunt before he could contemplate the possibility of escape.

*

# Chapter 22.  Unfinished Business

He had to front up at the station in the afternoon for appearances sake. Mulligan of course did not show but everyone simply assumed he was sick. Jones told anyone who asked that Mulligan had dropped him off at knocking off time. Actually very few even bothered. Conjecture about a multiple killing in the western suburbs the previous night seemed to have everyone's attention even though it was well outside departmental parameters.

Jones pretended to be conscientious and made a show of working on the youth file. He had this overriding compulsion to go out and check whether Mulligan's car was still parked outside the squat. He was trying to make an executive decision of whether to profess to work the streets or not, which would at least him an excuse to cruise by, when a call from Ethical Standards solved his dilemma. Fletcher told him to stay put, on no account to leave the building, and he would be straight over. Jones put the phone down and sat back sweating, wondering what to do. Surely they had not found Mulligan already, he was counting on at least a day's grace. He decided he had no choice but to wait and brazen it out. As the minutes dragged by he reflected that only yesterday he had dreamt of flying home in the afternoon.

"You look frigging awful!" was Fletcher's first muttered comment as he leant over to Jones. "We're trying to keep the lid on this, who let you know?"

Jones stuttered for time, not knowing what to say.

"Is there somewhere secure and private?" Fletcher ploughed on softly, glancing round the open plan office, "I don't want to be overheard."

Jones pulled himself together, trying to gather his wits. "Err, the ...err D.I's office is still vacant, I think. Over there, in the corner."

It was a box cubicle with a window and a door, a defined space to delineate the boundaries of power. Fletcher ushered Jones ahead of him as they crossed the floor to enter. Of course everyone else in the office saw them, and undoubtedly wondered what was going on: so much for subterfuge? Jones felt numb, he had gone beyond tension and dread into a blank automatic response. Fletcher dropped the blind and secured the door.

"I've been trying to get hold of you all morning. Where've you been?"

"Garelli's funeral!" snapped Jones. He felt humiliated for Garelli's sake. How could Fletcher not have known?

Fletcher stared at him. "Of course, I'm sorry," he said, "It slipped my mind. If I'd known, I'd have arranged security. You're the prime target now."

Jones must have looked as bewildered as he felt.

"We think you're the old man's only unfinished business," continued Fletcher, "You'll have to go into protective custody."

"You didn't get him?" Jones tempted the maze.

"No," said Fletcher, "I thought you'd been told. You look white as a ghost. I thought that was why?"

"No," confirmed Jones, "I just had a rough night. Things are beginning to get to me."

"That's not surprising," considered Fletcher, "and I'm afraid they're not going to get better. The flat you gave us was empty, cleaned out, completely bare."

"You think the girl was lying?" asked Jones. She had been so convincing?

"No!" said Fletcher, "We checked with the neighbours. An elderly gentleman had been there, very quiet, kept to himself, but very polite. But he hasn't been seen for days, and no one saw him move out."

"Who owns the flat?" asked Jones. His mind was beginning to clear, now he realised he had not been discovered.

"A paper trail," shrugged Fletcher, "a series of companies. We're on to it but it looks as though it might be leading offshore. Whoever it is, it will take time."

"So why the sudden panic about me?" asked Jones, "You didn't want to lock me away yesterday. What's changed?" If only they had, he thought bitterly. If only he could turn back time.

"My boss put a team on what you told us," said Fletcher, "and they pulled all the relevant files from C.I.B and the Drugs Squad. It looks like you were right; the old man has been working his way up a chain of dealers. We ran that tattooed ideogram by one of our second-generation Chinese officers. She says that in China the Ox symbolises patience and strength. They always plough forward and turn aside for nothing. And when they lose it they are uncontrollable."

"What's that got to do with the price of heroin?" interrupted Jones irritated. It might be of interest to a linguist or a zoologist, but how was it relevant here and now?

"I'm coming to that!" it was Fletcher's turn to be snappy. "The boss has contacts with Interpol and ASIO," he explained, "and they briefed us on the Chinese connection. Several triads

215

out of China have been trying to establish themselves abroad. It seems to coincide with the expansion of foreign trade encouraged by the modern regime.

The Ox triad is one of the most secretive and the most feared. They adopt a very low profile but are said to never surrender captured ground. Once in, they can't be shifted. They never recruit locals into their hierarchy and they are very hard to crack."

Jones stared into space, trying to get a grip with where this was coming from, where it was leading?

"It's very difficult for our police to get a way into the Asian community. They tend to close ranks, speak no English and look inscrutable. But they've been very rattled by what's going on: even the major suppliers of illegal substances. We're getting a flood of information now," emphasised Fletcher, "especially after last night."

"What happened last night?" croaked Jones, appalled by his own temerity.

"Last night someone broke into the house of the presumed head of the Ox triad in this city, and executed him, his son, and three bodyguards: twenty-twos in the brain, all point-blank. The wife is under sedation but she told the interpreter she heard nothing. She woke up in the morning with her husband dead beside her. This man is a real pro, Jones. It's hard to believe he missed you. Next time I doubt you'll be so lucky."

Jones was horrified. "Who and what in hell is he?" he breathed.

"That's what we'd all like to know," said Fletcher. "ASIO says his methods remind of a counter-intelligence technique, used by both hard-line security forces and terrorists alike to trace command structures. The victim always leads the killer to the next link before he is executed. That way there's no warning and no comeback. ASIO thinks we're dealing with a specialist trained to eliminate informers or underground cells.

The thing is, you must have the key to his identity. That's why we've got to protect you, and presumably why he wants you. So we're going to have to take you out of circulation while we work out what you don't realise you must know. We thought we'd start with Garelli's suggestion of a visit to the Foreign Languages Department at the university."

"That's all very well," muttered Jones, feeling totally paranoid by now, "But how can I ever be safe until we discover the police connection? If he's got someone on the inside, how can you protect me? You know what the force is supposed to be like, it has to be accountable, and so wherever I go will be recorded and therefore traceable. With the old boys' network it will only be a question of time before the security of any destination is jeopardised."

"I was getting to that," said Fletcher. He walked round the back of the desk and prised apart the blind to peer down the length and breadth of the open area. "We might have caught a break there. There wasn't a call from the island, but we tracked one down from the mainland ferry terminal to this station on the day the old man got off the boat. It was to Mulligan's desk. I gather he's off sick."

Jones nodded wordlessly. It fit, the contact would have to be fairly sedentary so as not to miss the call, and Mulligan certainly had been that. "I've sent round Stravitis to pick him up from home," said Fletcher. "Funny thing is, I know Mulligan well; he was with CIB for years before they pastured him off down here. Health reasons you know: not fit for active duty. What I can't understand is his motive. Just can't see him as a vigilante! Still, perhaps he'll enlighten us?"

A flood of emotions washed through Jones; fear, anger and then a profound sense of relief. Perhaps last night had been an act of natural justice after all? The fat sloppy pig, he thought, fancy using his own number?

"He took a risk, didn't he?" Jones said to Fletcher, "that's so easily traced!"

Fletcher considered this. "Yes and no," he decided, "if it ever came to light. But even so, there's no record of the conversation. Mulligan can invent one, even deny one took place. He could claim memory loss; just how many calls does he take in a day? He might just say, 'I remember now, someone rang and asked for the address of the station.' End of story."

He leaned over and gave Jones a gentle punch on the shoulder. "Look, I've got to go," he said, "I need to be at the centre of things. Half my job's collating information, the other half's liaising. We'd like you to stay here until we've interviewed Mulligan. Keep a highly visible profile in case he has accomplices. We don't want to tip anyone off. The old bloke only seems to operate at night so you could be safe in daylight, but don't on any account go out. It's not worth the risk.

I'd like to take you over to the university later to see if they can come up with anything. So I'll arrange that and pick you up later. In the meantime we're trying to arrange federal custody, to get you out of the clutches of the State Police. Hopefully tonight we can drop you out of sight."

"Did you ever find out how the feds knew the old man had arrived?" asked Jones. The mention of them had reminded him of the query that had vexed him before.

Fletcher shook his head, "Sorry, I don't know what you're talking about?"

Jones remembered that it had only come up between him and Garelli. He tried to pass his old concerns on to Fletcher, but that officer merely shrugged them away, "Remember that ASIO has a lot of programmes in place to counter the threat of terrorism. They'll only deliver on a strictly need to know basis. I'm not sure I've got the security clearance."

He shook Jones's hand and left before Jones could gather his wits and ask when exactly he could go home now, back to the island. As the opportunity slipped away with Fletcher's departing back he also questioned to himself the other officer's comments about ASIO security programmes. Did he refer to computers? And if so how could they pick up a man who on paper did not exist?

*

## PART FOUR: Flight.

*The butterfly takes to the air to maintain itself in independent motion but it can be carried by the wind, sometimes over vast bodies of water.*

# Chapter 23.  A Walk in the Park

Jones sat on the bench and stared at the horizon. The storm had blown through and the rain with it. Gulls circled on the thermals, spiralling higher and higher on the updrafts. White flecks on azure, snowflakes in the summer or litter on the wind? Skyscrapers trembled in the haze and the trees shimmered as the smog twisted the edges of the sky. Jones sighed and breathed deeply, and then wondered at what he had done. The leaves of the eucalyptus shading the seat rustled overhead in a sudden breath of wind off the sea, and he could almost sense the scent of gum and the tang of salt in amongst the layers of exhaust and decay, but the fumes won out in seconds. And the seconds turned into minutes and the minutes dragging with the sun climbing and he kept checking his watch but only the second hand moved and time seemed to stand on its head and mock the hour. So he sat there in an agony of frustration and suspense, feeling absurdly exposed: the third man or the spy who came in from the cold? Only he was sweating in the heat and his self-control was shivering on the verge of dissolution. He kept running through the instructions for the meet in his mind, re-checking the position of the benches, the trees and the power poles. He alternated between certainty and indecision; surely he was on the right bench under the right tree in the right reserve? Every now and then he would ask a passer-by the name of the park, just to reassure himself. They clipped by in a blur of motion; all sexes, ages and occupations, most hustling in time with the pace of the city, rarely strolling, never at ease. And the time was long past and still the kid had not showed and Jones cursed him and himself for fools, and wondered whether he should have killed the boy as well, to cover himself, but knew in his heart that his conscience would never have permitted it. Then an ancient pensioner shuffled into view hunched over a walking frame, to hobble along the path with a slowness and fragility that almost made Jones want to scream. The faded Panama on the bowed head nodded in slow time with each deliberate tread. Like an advertisement for euthanasia, thought Jones, the walking dead, one step from the grave and headed his way. Jones watched him creep alongside the bench and then turn with agonising effort to approach. With total disbelief Jones realised the bench would be a stopover, a resting place for the old fart to recuperate on his relay round the park. Eventually, with infinite patience he reached his goal and settled back slowly with a deep shuddering sigh, which rattled like dead reeds in the wind on the edge of a dried up dam. Jones was almost numb with tension, there was still no sign of the kid and now it looked as though the meet would be cluttered for eternity. The old fellow swivelled his head slowly to face Jones. Oh God he is going to make conversation, thought Jones, and expect me to reply. The old fellow removed his shades and the eyes were alert and unmistakeable.

"Good afternoon, Officer Jones," the harsh accent grated, "forgive the deception, it's remarkable what a bit of makeup can do. I heard you were looking for a young lad, so I paid a youngster to arrange the rendezvous. I thought if you knew it was I, you might not be inclined to visit!"

His laugh drifted without humour, without life into the urban vacuum of background noise. Jones shrank within himself, paralysed with fear. He found himself incapable of speech, incapable of movement. He thought the message had come from the boy from the squat, his accessory. The message for the meet had been relayed to him from the desk. They had all thought it was about the Youth File. Jones had privately assumed the kid had changed his mind about leaving, and perhaps he wanted more money?

"I see I have your attention," chuckled the old man. The eyes stared without laughter, without hope. "I trust you are still not carrying a gun?"

Jones nodded in reflex, responding automatically without volition, although the dead weight of Mulligan's gun pressed upon his thigh: a stupid risk to take if anyone had noticed, but one he had felt obliged to chance at the time. Even so the old man had him hypnotised: a stunned rabbit.

"Good!" said the old man, "Now I can relax."

Where did he get that information from, Jones asked himself?

"Why do you want to kill me?" he managed to get out, his voice barely croaking from a dry tight throat.

The old man looked genuinely puzzled, for an instant an expression of hurt seemed to flicker in the depths of those bleak eyes. "Whatever gave you that idea?" the old man's stare unnerved Jones completely.

"Th…that night, in the st…street outside my digs," he managed to stammer at last.

"I merely wanted to talk to you," commented the old man, "and then that fool of a girl tried to run me down. Do you really think I would expose myself like that otherwise?" His tone was incredulous, the professional insulted. "I only just got out of the way. I'm slowing down," the sigh seemed genuine.

"Is that why you killed her?" Jones sneered, outrage beginning to fuel bravery, "because a girl nearly beat your reflexes?" he slipped his hand into his pocket, surreptitiously feeling for the cold butt of Mulligan's weapon.

The old man's eyes blazed with a flash of anger. "I don't make war on women and children," he declared flatly. He looked away and stared at the sky. Jones followed his gaze. High cirrus was drifting in the stratosphere, forerunners of another storm?

"So you did not kill her!" it was a statement, not a question, for he had realised the truth of it. He pulled his hand away from the gun. It had never been the old man's M.O. The old man did not even bother to reply. So it was a police set-up, decided Jones, after all. Mulligan? That would be justice. He tried to take a pause, to marshal his thoughts, but the wheels kept turning. "Who are you?" he managed at last.

The old man shrugged. "Just a refugee from a forgotten war: it does not matter which one. The world is full of victims."

He continued staring at the sky. The streams of cirrus seemed to be drawing together, thickening into plumed trails across the azure blue.

"It is a wonderfully comfortable world that you live in, Officer, to be sure," he added.

Jones shook his head. Not any more, he thought, not by any means, if indeed for him it had ever been?

"Why did you want to see me?" he asked.

The old man did not reply for a while.

"I need to know who it was that asked you to transfer over here," he stated finally.

"My commander," replied Jones, stating the obvious. "Why?"

"No, no," said the old man, "I mean who was it from this state who asked for you?"

226

Jones shook his head again.

"Why?" he insisted. Suddenly that information seemed dangerous; he needed to make a judgement before he divulged anything.

The old man's eyes flashed with anger. Lightning before the storm? Then they clouded again, expressionless, bleak, a snow sky with the wind dropped, ready to fall. The old man seemed to consider Jones carefully.

"The reason that I would not want to kill you," he said slowly and patiently as if explaining something to a child, "is that I asked for you. You are my insurance policy."

Jones was lost, totally confused.

"What do you mean?" he asked eventually.

"Who gave you that number I was to ring?" asked the old man.

Jones shook his head hopelessly; he had already been asked that one. He did not know, and the only trail led to Mulligan, and Mulligan was dead, kicked to death in a dark room in an old squat.

"I was told to ring that number if I wanted help, or needed information," continued the old man.

"It was just a contact number for the station," said Jones, "so you could arrange a time to identify the body."

"No!" insisted the old man, "That it was not. I received a letter on the island, on official police notepaper. 'If you want justice,' it read, 'come prepared, our hands are tied.' They enclosed my son's driving licence, still blood-stained. A subtle push I thought. But I suppose the surname is hardly unique. I suppose too they assumed I could dye my hair and obscure the lines to defy the years. They also told me to contact them on that number, the same as the one you gave me. But only when I reached the mainland."

Jones did not know what to say, he felt the walls collapsing around him.

"When I got to the city there was a flat waiting for me, and some photographs of the body of my son. They also left a mobile phone, pre-paid of course. Whenever they want to contact me with information they ring me up. They wanted me to text actually, but I cannot be bothered with the technology, it seems so impersonal somehow. I say 'they', but actually it's always the same voice, a man's; very precise, very clear, and very bare." The old man was remorseless, grinding the fragments, leaving Jones nothing but dust. "I do not like being led by the nose, but there was no one over here I could trust. So I asked for you. You are from another State; you would have to be independent. I insisted on your transfer if he wanted my co-operation. I told him you could identify me, and I felt at risk. I said I wanted you over here so I could eliminate you to cover my tracks. He humoured me, I'm glad to say."

He patted Jones on the shoulder, and smiled reassuringly. At least the mouth curved upwards at the corners, but the eyes did not even blink.

Jones felt sick.

"And what exactly would you have done to me, if I didn't co-operate?" he felt constrained to ask.

The old man did not even bother to reply to that, just continued with his monologue. "I wanted you over here, because I want to find out what is going on. This person knows me, knows my past as well as I know myself. He predicted my reactions with total accuracy. It is as if he were certain I would pursue the road of vengeance. There must have been a leak. My identity is at risk now. I am an old man, with not much to look forward to but the grave. It does not matter much to me. But now the boy is gone, there is still my

228

daughter. I have to protect her from my past. She has always been so good at forgetting, pretending not to remember. I keep hoping that one day she will escape the shadows, marry, settle down and have children. I would like to be a grandfather. At the least I would like my seed to continue. What else is there?"

He was rambling now, an old man in his dotage, wandering thickets of thoughts that Jones could hardly reconnoitre. But there was one thing that was certain; the silly old fool had pronounced him a target. How vulnerable was Jones himself now? If he continued to live, would the puppet-master feel his operation threatened, and excise him himself?

"So what happens when I keep showing up at the station, alive and kicking?" Jones snapped irritably, "Will your master think you've lost your touch?"

The old man shrugged apologetically, "It was only a short-term response," he admitted, "It was the best excuse I could think of at the time. But I figured that you would be safe enough until the operation was over."

"So when's that likely to be?" snapped Jones, "When do I need to start getting seriously paranoid?"

"Last night," the old man yawned theatrically, "was a busy one."

"It's over?" Jones suddenly felt horrified. His stomach turned and cooled by degrees.

"That part is," agreed the old man, "which is why it would be advisable for you to leave. So just tell me the names of the mainland officers who asked for you, and book a flight home."

Jones stared at him speechless.

"I can't do that!" he recovered himself, "it would be tantamount to a death sentence, wouldn't it?"

The old man was impassive. "Do not be naïve, Officer. Your partner is dead did you not say? This is not about justice. Not as you practise it."

There was no answer to that, not after yesterday.

"There were two of them," said Jones, remembering back to that interview room at his regional headquarters.

"So give me their names," said the old man.

"One might be innocent!" Jones felt stubborn. "They were representatives of different forces, one Federal, one State: this State. I have to be sure."

"Only the Federal Police could have access to my identity," declared the old man emphatically.

Jones thought about that. The report of the old man's arrival on the mainland had according to Garelli come through the feds. But then Mulligan was State. Jones shook his head in disagreement.

"This person," stressed the old man, "might have arranged my son's death in order to involve me. I have to know. I have to know how he knew about me!"

"I'll check it out!" insisted Jones.

The old man stared back at him.

Jones held his gaze.

"I'll leave my number," said the old man. "Be in touch, the fuse is burning."

It was a command couched in the terms of a threat. He got up and shuffled away. Decrepit once more, a frail aging human, hunched against the gusting wind. Jones observed him closely, half-expecting him to drop the pretence at any moment, abandon the walking frame and march away into the bustling crowd. But he did not, and Jones was constrained to watch him till he disappeared from sight. It seemed to take hours.

In the meantime the clouds thickened, and the humidity returned. Then the wind dropped and the air clogged Jones's lungs and his shirt began to stick to his back. Sweat beaded his forehead and dribbled inevitably into the corners of his eyes. They stung and tears formed. He wiped them away angrily. Grown men do not cry do they, and certainly not in public?

Rubbing them made them worse and he stumbled into motion to take his mind off the irritation. He walked back to the station through the cluttered highways and byways, his vision blurred and his mind almost blank. He could not concentrate and he knew he needed to. The wheels kept turning and every time he thought they were about to mesh together they crashed and the answer wriggled away into oblivion. So someone knew the old man's past? He had never considered that.

Then at some point in his ramblings he realised that he had crossed the line. He had tacitly agreed to help a killer, a multiple murderer on a quest for personal justice. But what about the law: his duty was to the legal system he had sworn to uphold? But Garelli was dead. And so was Mulligan. But at least that had not been premeditated. In the end he kept coming back to Mulligan and those phone calls. But he could hardly picture Mulligan running, and he could distinctly remember fast footsteps exiting the scene of Garelli's killing.

Then the clouds broke and the rains came again. By the time he had reached the station he was soaked through for the second time that day, a drowned rat.

\*

231

# Chapter 24.  Dead Men Tell No Tales

Fletcher seemed a man in crisis, torn between rage and relief. He was in the company of Superintendent Campbell, so appeared constrained to hold his tongue. Jones shrugged off his black looks. He at least knew now he was safe from external threats; inside the station he was not so sure. He could not even look Campbell in the eye, especially when the CIB man made small talk about the funeral. For some reason he did not mention the proposed hunt, and Jones hoped that events had overtaken the possibility of the outing proceeding. Fletcher must have sensed his discomfort, and made an excuse to get Jones away.

"We're late for that appointment at the university," he told Jones, and ushered him out ahead of him.

Jones steeled himself for a tongue-lashing, but Fletcher maintained a stony silence as they strode through the corridors down to the car park. Outside the rain was relentless again and the traffic struggling. The windscreen wipers could hardly cope, visibility was appalling and Fletcher had to turn on main beam. They stuttered out into the main drag, and vehicles shunted and tailgated down to the intersection. Kerbside gutters ran like rivers and the wheel-spray from the car in front showered a fountain of rainbowed droplets in the headlights. They slid to a halt at the corner and waited for the lights to change.

"Stravitis couldn't find Mulligan this morning," Fletcher fractured the silence and Jones did not dare reply, "That call to his desk, the one from the ferry terminal." Jones nodded cautiously in acknowledgement. "Mulligan was in the middle of a three week vacation when it came through. Fishing, up north for the barramundi."

"So who took the call?" Jones felt his stomach lurch and his world spin again.

"It was patched through to a mobile," said Fletcher. "The mobile is billed to one of the companies that owned the flat used by the old man."

Jones swore, "How can a police station be damn well linked to a private mobile?"

Fletcher shrugged. The lights changed. "It was an extension," he commented, "obviously someone with front."

"And you don't know who?" Jones felt weary. He wanted to sleep, and wake to a world where all the shades of grey had been abolished.

"Most modern officers carry mobiles off-duty," said Fletcher, "on the mainland," he added as an afterthought. "The phone company would not think it a particularly unusual request."

Jones looked into the coffin of his hopes and fears. "Where was Mulligan when Garelli was killed?" the lid weighed heavy now, he could hardly keep it open.

"At his desk, he rarely leaves it," said Fletcher, "you know that."

"And Superintendent Campbell?" Jones picked up the last nail.

Fletcher glanced across at Jones before he pulled out and moved into the overtaking lane. "Where is this leading?" he asked shortly.

Jones stalled, needing to extract himself. "They were both at the hospital so quickly," he muttered. If that were a red herring, it would barely swim the creek.

Fletcher shook his head, "Jones, I know you're under stress and all, but…" he let the sentence drift in a sea of disapproval.

"Where was he?" insisted Jones. He had to know.

Fletcher sighed. "He's being groomed for Assistant Commissioner. He was at a policy meeting with our civic leaders, discussing ways to combat the drugs problem in our ethnic communities. He's an advocate for community policing, and wants community leaders to encourage their youth to consider recruitment into the service. Of course he was at Casualty quickly, he left the meeting as soon as he heard there was an officer down!"

Jones hammered on the lid, and buried his disappointment. Where did he go from here? The rain was still dumping down. Clarity was impossible.

"Do you happen to know the name of the Federal cop who arranged my transfer?" he asked Fletcher.

Fletcher shook his head. "No idea. Why do you ask?"

"I want out," said Jones, "I figure he owes me a flight home."

"We've unfinished business," said Fletcher. His voice registered all the tones of disapproval at Jones's lack of stamina.

Jones could not find it in himself to reply. Maybe not for long, he thought; he had a call to make himself now. He lost himself in the beat and stroke of the wipers, and the rain pouring down the windscreen. The streets were washed clean, but he never could be. He suddenly sneezed, and realised his clothes felt damp. Glancing down at himself, he realised he had been soaked through twice already that day. He rubbed at his temples; his head was beginning to throb. As the car slowed down for the next set of lights he glimpsed a woman on the pavement out of the corner of his eye. The rain wrinkled side window blurred her outline, but she swaggered along under the awnings with familiar contempt for weather and pedestrians alike. Her clothes, her hair, her style shouted for recognition. Jones stuttered into action and wound down the window to call out to her. Rain swirled and lashed into the open car. At the crossing she turned and stared across the street. He blinked at the pouring rain but her face was a blank cipher behind inscrutable shades. Fletcher swore at him, the rain was pissing in, splattering the upholstery, the dash, Jones and himself.

"Sorry," apologised Jones, "I thought I just saw Garelli."

Fletcher stared across at him, silent for a moment.

"Jones!" he emphasised at length, "they buried her this morning. You were there!"

Jones stared back at him, through him and into the rain. "So I was," he muttered, as if to convince himself.

The lights changed and Fletcher shook his head and pulled away.

*

The university was an oasis in the concrete desert. Trees mellowed the contours and softened the skyline. Jones stood outside the car, closed his eyes, felt the rain on his face, and tried to listen to the hiss and rustle of the leaves overhead. He was almost home.

Fletcher's complaint brought him back to earth, and Jones followed him into the warren of corridors that meandered through the buildings. A bored secretary stroke receptionist told them they were too late in the day and that most of the

235

lecturers had gone home. Fletcher was disgusted. It was not even 5 o'clock. He insisted that she check to see if anyone was available. She wanted him to make an appointment for some time later the following week. Jones was not interested. He did not care any more who the old man was, now he knew what he was. Jones wanted justice for Garelli. Then he could go home. Fletcher admitted to the woman that he had made an appointment, but was running late. Hours late, he glared at Jones. The secretary smiled bleakly, and shrugged with studied indifference. Fletcher flashed his warrant card and threatened her with obstruction. Jones stared out of a window and saw nothing but rain. The secretary chased down an assistant professor, just leaving after a late seminar. She delivered them up to her with a mechanical correctness. Jones could see her seething beneath the façade. He looked through the professor and saw contempt. It was all pointless; he did not need this now, or any of them. He had the old man; he could point him like a gun.

Fletcher had to prompt him to pay attention, and the academic repeated herself with brittle patience. But no, there were no key words that Jones could remember, just the context, and no mistakes in the spoken English grammar or diction. No jumbled pronouns, or verbs in the wrong place, and Jones was lost in a maze of subjunctives, participles, infinitives, reflexives and pluperfects, and began to wonder how the hell anyone ever managed to learn to speak in the first place, this silly cow was making it sound so difficult. So there were no clues, only the accent, and Jones could not get his tongue around that. He had never been a mimic. Too uptight, he mused. The professor proposed they brought her a tape recording of the subject, completely missing the point of the attempted exercise, and Fletcher gave up in disgust.

"I suppose it was a long shot," he admitted back in the car.

Jones did not reply; it was irrelevant now.

At a set of lights near a cab rank Jones got out of the car. Fletcher screamed after him about safe houses and protective custody but Jones just kept walking and Fletcher was trapped in the traffic. Jones knew he had forgotten something; he had to remember to feed Garelli's cats.

*

The friendly one wrapped itself round his leg like a furry second skin, while the shy one growled at him from the counter. Jones emptied the fridge, was reduced to a carton of milk well past its used by date, and prayed that it had not turned. While they were demolishing that, he ransacked the kitchen looking for tins. Garelli must have died just before the weekly shop, for the cupboard was bare, apart from a half empty packet of dried food. It looked as appetising as yesterday's soggy chips, and he thought cats were supposed to be fussy, but they ripped into that as well. He tried to think about time frames but could not wrap his mind around the moment, let alone the day. Then he noticed the smell, and checked the litter tray. He opened the door to throw that outside, and the cats, bloated now, bolted for freedom. Look out the local bird-life, thought Jones, and he left the window ajar so they could get back in.

He slumped down on the couch by the phone, and tried again to think back. Then at length he rang the old man. "When did you last hear from your master?" Jones asked the disembodied voice.

The terse reply rattled and grated in his ear. "Today," the old man's voice was dry and desiccated, a rasping wind of dust and heat. "He told me to get out if it was over: a ploy of course. Once it truly is over, he will want to eliminate me from his enquiries permanently."

"That would be a risky enterprise, would it not?" asked Jones.

"Oh it would be done at arms length to be sure," said the old man, "an all points bulletin, armed and dangerous, do not attempt to apprehend, shoot on sight, shoot to kill: exterminate with extreme prejudice and all that."

Jones was appalled at the old man's cynicism, but had to accept the logic. Surely the old man was a loose end that could not be allowed to wander off into the sunset. And in any case where could he go now, not back to Tasmania surely. But the phone call let out Mulligan for sure. Dead men tell no tales. He felt a pang of sadness, perhaps a twinge of conscience? It would have been so fitting, true karma. Mulligan had hated Garelli. How now for the voice of retribution?

The old man's impatient rasp snapped him back to the present, and a commitment to honour. The decision was made.

"Andrews is the name you want," he spoke the sentence, "Inspector Andrews, Federal Police."

Using the station phone number might have been a clever blind to mislead any possible enquiry, but it was impossible to hide his presence at that interview. In the end it had not been too hard for Jones to dredge the name out of his memory; he had relived that interrogation too many times for a relapse.

"So what's his address?" asked the old man, "That's a common name, I can hardly go through the metropolitan phone book."

Jones had not thought about that. He had meant to keep his distance, maintain the façade of innocence.

238

"You'll have to get your hands dirty," commented the old man.

Jones said he would ring back. He sat there sucked in by the whirlpool, watching his options wash down the tube. His life was flushing away, but Garelli's absence spoke to him from every wall and pore, and he knew he had no choice but to see it through. In the end a man has to live with himself, and his own nightmares. He called Federal Police Headquarters in the city, and claimed to be Sergeant Mulligan asking for Inspector Andrews.

No the inspector was not there, he had left for home, and no it was not policy to release officers' addresses or home phone numbers, surely he knew that. Ah, but if it were that important, it was possible he could be reached by his pager.

Jones struggled momentarily to concoct a suitably demanding yet cryptic message. "Missing Persons has found Granny Smith," was all he could come up with on the spur of the moment, and he left Mulligan's name and Garelli's number. Hell, what choice was there? Besides, dead men tell no tales, do they?

The call when it came was as fussy and precise as the image of the man he remembered. Andrews reprimanded him for being unnecessarily obtuse, said he had stopped at a phone booth on the way home, and demanded an explanation for the urgency. Jones spoke into a handkerchief to muffle his voice, and improvised a question around the one that had been bothering him for some time: how did the Federal Police know that the old man had arrived on the mainland? He said it was a matter of national security that had to be resolved that night, and asked if he could drop by his home to discuss it? Andrews hesitated, said that he had been ordered off that case, and then agreed if it did not intrude too much on his evening.

Jones disconnected, called the old man, and gave him the address. The old man told him to get a solid alibi, and hung up. Jones sat back and wondered at what he had done.

He felt sick, sick to the core, to the very centre of his being. He slumped forward and started rocking gently, his arms wrapped around his stomach. Slipping forward off the edge of the couch onto his knees, the pendulum of his head began tapping the floor. Then he remembered through the pain about Garelli's little helper. Somewhere in one of the cupboards over the worktop she kept a half of bourbon, a reserve for emergencies, in case the bar ran dry during closing hours. Jones stumbled to his feet trying to remember whether they had drunk it that last night together. But no, that had been a full one, had it not, and he had finished it off himself since. Was that yesterday?

He blundered into the kitchenette, sorting through the overheads, tossing and scattering packets and powders, dried foods and dried fruits: all Garelli's health food. He found the bottle hiding behind a clutter of jars of tahina, bulgur, pulses and beans. Garelli's fart food: slow entry but a fast exit. He spun the top and bit into oblivion but the room stood still and the fear remained. All of a sudden he realised what he had done in giving out Garelli's number. Sanctuary was breached and he panicked into action. His clothes, his gear, his fingerprints were everywhere. He found himself praying that Andrews was a bachelor, and then he cursed at his own hypocrisy. The Old Testament Jehovah and the prophets of vengeance must have been free of the niceties of modern conscience. He lurched to his feet unsteadily. What had Garelli done with his suitcase? He rummaged through her wardrobe, the tiers of designer clothes and the layers of shoes, and then remembered that she had dumped it behind the settee. He was only there for a short time, not a good time, was he not? He did not have much, and what little there was did not take too long to find, let alone pack. Garelli had given over the top drawer in the bedroom. He pulled it out and tipped the contents into his case. Some missed, and he scooped them up, and the zip got jammed, and then he could not get the drawer back on its runners. So he threw it on the bed. Then he realised he was leaving fingerprints everywhere, so he grabbed a tea towel and started wiping down door knobs and surfaces and such like. After an interval of scrubbing and rubbing the panic began to subside and he realised he did not seem to be getting anywhere. Then he reasoned that a clean flat would appear more suspicious than one with fingerprints scattered about naturally, and besides there was no reason why he should not have visited Garelli was there? The discovery could even enhance his reputation, since no one now could ever know the truth? All he had to do was take his suitcase and leave; the question was where to go? Then he remembered the old man's comments about creating an alibi, and the answer came to him. He would go to the station and log in, and leave his suitcase under Garelli's desk. If anyone asked he would say he was changing hotels. His excuse for being there was unfinished paperwork, because he was trying to clear his desk and leave. Then he remembered something else: it was Friday night.

*

# Chapter 25. The Elusive Sambar

Jones, half-cut and sore-headed, was in the station at Garelli's desk pretending paperwork. Actually it was more than pretence, he was writing up that report that Mulligan had wanted about the runaway rent boy, but obscuring all the details about possible squats and means of contact. A stranger walked into the office, surveyed the scene and approached Jones. He was a stocky man, who somehow reminded him of Theo, but older and more solid looking.

"Constable Jones?" the intruder queried. Jones wondered if the man had been waiting for him. "I'm Lucky Xanakaredapopoulis, I'm your chauffeur for the evening," a hint of wry amusement escaping an apparently serious demeanour. Hard eyes though: reminded Jones somehow of Garelli, eyes that had seen too much, and not too much of it particularly edifying. Jones had half forgotten the invitation to the hunt, but felt too indecisive to make it go away.

He suddenly remembered that he had not enquired after the young bloke's progress. "Lucky?" he asked to cover his embarrassment.

"Yeah, it's real," said the Greek, "First-born son in Australia. So I'm Lucky. School was shit."

Jones shook his head in sympathy. His own surname was so common it was a non-event as a target, but in school he had seen the aftermath of other parental follies. Children were never so innocent as to escape the propensity to tease and harass.

"I'm Theo's cousin," said Lucky, "pleased to meet you," he held out his hand.

Jones shook it warily. The grip was firm without being demonstrative. So many men seemed to like to crush a handshake to assert their authority, or perhaps defy their fears.

"You're invited to the wedding," Lucky continued, calmly packing away Jones's desk, before standing over him to escort him out. Not giving any avenue of escape.

"Wedding?" repeated Jones, completely overwhelmed and at a loss once again.

"Theo's," explained Lucky.

"Oh!" said Jones, nicely surprised for once. "I didn't know anyone wanted him?" he quipped deadpan to hide his pleasure.

"It was a shock for the family too," said Lucky.

"She a Greek girl?" asked Jones: it seemed the right thing to say. Clichés usually made for safe conversation.

Lucky looked at him in mock surprise, "Who else would put up with him?"

He walked Jones without a further word through the corridors and out into the car park. At the car he opened up without comment, ushered Jones into the passenger seat and slipped in to buckle up himself.

"You stink like a brewery," he commented, sniffing at the interior air.

"It's the end of the week," Jones offered in explanation but not apology.

Lucky said nothing. Jones was somehow surprised at the car. It was just an average family sedan, without obvious accessories, without pretension. He had for some reason been expecting at least a four-wheel drive.

"I'm hardly dressed for the occasion," Jones now apologised, trying to strike up a conversation again.

"I've got gear in the boot," said Lucky, immediately relapsing back into silence, closing Jones down. He concentrated on driving, leaving Jones to take in the scenery in solitude. It had finally stopped raining: the latest front must have blown through.

The veins of the city were still clogged, the end of peak hour tailing out into the suburbs. The cut and thrust of the traffic seemed all consuming. Jones watched the world go by, and was glad he was only passing through, and hoped he could soon escape from it. The smaller houses nestled in the inner-city blocks with established gardens, shrubbery and trees sometimes rioting over fences and into the streets. Eventually they made way for broad-acre estates where huge double-storey executive homes cramped tiny blocks to the boundaries, and bare pockets of yard stared devoid of trees in a derelict streetscape of dreams of grandeur. Some mansions fronted an entrance of a pair of columns from ground to roof that supported a portico under the gabled eaves of the top floor, and overhanging balconies overlooking nothing more than their neighbours' reciprocal challenge to extravagance and taste. Then eventually the developments ran out, and Jones was finally in open country, of a sort. Rolling paddocks, flatter, browner and far wider than those of home, or was that simply his innate prejudice and loss of perspective? He felt something change inside of him, as though a switch had been thrown.

Lines of sheoak and wattle began to hedge the roadside between the power poles, and in the fields the eucalypts thrust towering windbreaks above the horizon. Flocks of Galah and

White Cockatoo flapped raucously across a westering sky; going home to roost, thought Jones, wishing he could do the same. But at least he was in a landscape at last, which he could relate to. In the near distance the blue foothills quivered in the haze. He wanted to wind down the windows and breathe in the gum leaves, but the Greek was still wrapt in concentration, locked onto the asphalt highway, and Jones did not dare disturb his peace. Then they were into the foothills, and the road began climbing, a winding snake insinuating the contours of the land. The trees started to get closer and the mature growth heavier, with massive trunks lining the road like an avenue of remembrance. Then they were into burnt country, where skeletal tops thrust blackened fingers at the fading sky, monuments to a firestorm in a not so recent past that must have defied and destroyed the promise of spring. Bursts of green growth were thrusting out of the trunks, a clash of contrasts in the ruined woods: life out of the ashes, the essential paradox of the sclerophyll bush.

The road wound past a reservoir, with glimpses of water pulsing silver treasure through the trees. Then they were alongside it, and Jones could see how low the levels were, and that the promise was already turning to dust. Then they were back into denser forest with a heavy understorey of shrub and bushes crowding the road, the eucalypts towering now in the backdrop of the twilight sky. The bitumen turned to dirt, and the Greek flicked on main beam to light their way in the falling night. Jones felt trapped in a tunnel of light and constrained to follow its fading end into the outer darkness. The trunks of the eucalypts were like enormous grey pillars flanking the road, an honour guard saluting the passing of the sun. Jones was inevitably reminded of other journeys in a lost past he wondered if he could ever recover: night patrol on the edge of the wilderness, watching for poachers in deer season, or rustlers any time diverting the dark to their own devious desires. He drifted in a doze, lurching occasionally awake as the car swept into tight corners as the road looped up and beyond all expectation. If it were not for the size of the trees he could be home. His country was mainly small eucalypts, lots of snow gum, gnarled and twisted beneath the ravages of the constant wind. These giants though built cathedrals in the passing light. Eventually he must have slept, for he lurched awake as the car jolted and finally braked, and skidded into a clearing off a sidetrack from the road. Various vehicles were parked in, around and under the trees. A fire was burning in a stone circle off to one side. In the flickering flames he could see the studied faces of serious men drinking the night away. Their banter died as he awkwardly scrambled out of the car and stretched upright. They simply stared at him in sullen silence, not even bothering to greet him. He recognised several faces from the team at the bust, and wondered all of a sudden what the hell he was doing out here, in the wilds with a bunch of men that were definitely more stranger than acquaintance. For a moment he thought back to his final fling in the aftermath of the bust, and recalled the senior sergeant promising a bigger cut of the action than the pittance he presumed he could buy Jones off with. For a horrible instant Jones thought that they brought him out here to pay him off far away from prying eyes. Then Lucky was at his side and guiding him into the firelight. He introduced each of the faces, but Jones was too confused to take in all the names; he just nodded vaguely and mumbled pleasantries at the passing crowd.

"Pull up a seat," Lucky handed him a foldaway, "and have a beer."

He tossed Jones a can from an open esky. Jones peeled the tab and tipped back his head, hiding his shyness behind the upturned can. Then he was offered another, and another, and finally his nerves drained away and he could lose himself in the dance of the flames and no longer suffer in silence, but rock gently in anaesthetised peace. The talking resumed a quiet subdued rumble of background voices that he chose not to hear.

Somebody asked if anyone knew he was out there, and had to repeat the question to get his attention.

"Only the superintendent," Jones replied, slightly embarrassed to be mentioning friends in high places.

"Something to write home about then," smiled the face with unblinking eyes, turning back to his interrupted conversation to ignore Jones once more.

The only other sounds of the night were the crackle of the flames, and the occasional bark and snap of some dogs somewhere off in the darkness. Jones did not know what or whose they were, and could not be bothered to intrude to ask. Finally Lucky pointed him to a swag laid out off to the side on a patch of cleared ground under the trees. Jones crawled in with all his clothes on. It was cold in the high country and would only deteriorate as the night progressed. He lay on his back watching the constellations flicker and wink in a clarity he would never have dreamed possible back in the smoke. A shooting star flashed across the arc of the heavens, its flare and death inevitably reminding him of Garelli. Sadness washed over him, and somehow he fell asleep bathed in starlight, but hardly consoled by the overreaching sky.

The dogs woke him in the morning. Somebody was trying to quiet them with a series of curses. It was of course much too late. The camp began to stir. It was almost dawn. Some bell miner birds were chiming bell tones in the canopy overhead. Jones unzipped his swag and fresh air washed over him like a breaking wave at Ship's Stern Bluff in the depths of winter, the cold cutting sharp as a knife. A hangover drove pinpoints into his brain, and he prayed for strong coffee to succour him. But the fire was out. He scrambled upright shivering in his shirtsleeves, hoping for matches or at least salvation. For some unknown and obviously stupid reason he must have shrugged off his pullover in the night. Everybody was busy. Everyone ignored him, again the rank outsider. He stumbled into the bush to try and pick up dry leaf litter and small twigs dropped by the gums. In some of the denser undergrowth the ground was reasonably dry. Finally he staggered back with an armful of potential lightings, but someone had beaten him to it with an artificial firelighter and now the tang of kerosene tainted the air. He dropped the litter off to one side and wondered what to do with himself. Somebody threw him a can.

"Hair of the dog, sport," breakfast on the run.

The pack was frantic now, yipping and yapping madly. Jones wandered over to look at them, flapping his arms to try and stimulate some warmth: an uncouth fledgling trying to fly the dawn. The animals were in a trailer, which stank of faeces, urine and the overwhelming crush of dog. The hounds were surprisingly small. Jones thought he recognised them as beagles, hare hunters, surely much too small for sambar if the superintendent had been correct about the size of their quarry. Jones assumed it was the usual bullshit and exaggeration, a variation of the perennial one that got away. He wondered if the superintendent was coming on the hunt, and then looked around for the obnoxious sergeant from the Drugs Squad, but neither of the seniors seemed to be in sight.

Someone was hauling out the dogs one at a time, putting a lead on each and passing them over to another handler to be held. Eventually the pack was out and straining at the leash. Somebody else brought water over to try to quench their thirst if not their bark. Nobody seemed to be bothering to bring them food. Jones had never hunted over hounds before and did not know the protocol. Presumably they would be more eager on an empty stomach? He could not understand the size though. Then someone else came over with a couple of bigger dogs with much longer legs.

"Harriers," said Lucky coming over to join him, "highly illegal."

"Somebody needs to call the cops then," said Jones, trying to lighten the day. Personally he thought deerhounds would be a better choice, and mentioned it in passing. Lucky just stared at him.

"The wets have banned any dog big enough to pull down a deer," he said. "There was a case a few years back. A pack chased a buck out of the forest into a hobby farm, and caught it on the front lawn. They ripped it apart in front of the lounge window. Quite ruined the rose garden."

"Wets?" queried Jones.

"Cry a lot," explained Lucky.

"I thought the bush was going green," said Jones, thinking inevitably of home.

"Yep," replied Lucky, "Rednecks are out. It's the colour of blood."

Somebody called them over to join the assembled crew. A plan of action was being laid down. The co-ordinator drew lines in the dust with a twisted stick.

"We'll run the pack through this gully here. We want shooters each side of the ridge at intervals," he pointed out positions to various members as he ran through the plan, "then we want a couple at the top end to block the escape route, and two back here in case they back-track and try and break out down here." He allocated each of the team, and told Jones to go up on the ridge to cover the valley below. Lucky interrupted and said, "No, he's with me. We'll stay down here."

The co-ordinator stared at him. "This is all arranged," he said, "It's agreed to."

Lucky shrugged, "Not by me," he objected. "He stays with me," he insisted, and would not be moved.

It seemed to be an impasse. Jones did not know what was going on.

"You can't send a new boy up in the scrub by himself," Lucky said at last, offering an exception and a way out, "He'd get lost."

It made absolute sense to Jones, but he could see the rest of the crew were angry at Lucky, and could not agree to the logic of his objection. In the end they backed down, weapons were produced, and hunters began stalking off into the woods. Most wore work gear, jeans and flannel shirts. Jones had expected camo, but few seemed to have it. All though wore some apparel coloured bright orange; either vests, waistcoats or simple beanies. Jones realised the sense of it; an obvious safety measure in dense country. Deer were colour-blind. It was something he had never bothered with back home. In fact he did not know any local hunters who did. It would be like advertising your private business. The old bastard would be horrified.

The dogs were beyond excitement now, running round in circles tangling up their leashes in a hopeless knot. The two handlers were cursing loudly. All in all the din was deafening. Jones thought that they had brought the dogs out at least an hour too early. Everything would be alerted for miles around. He said as much to Lucky.

"Sambar don't spook," said Lucky, "they lie up in thick undergrowth till you're right on top of them. Even then they won't move till you trip over them. If they're out there now, they're lying still. But if the dogs pick up their scent, they'll be forced up. And then they'll run. And then it's up to us."

It was the longest monologue Jones had yet heard from him. "Do you get much success?" he asked. He could not see much hope, personally. The density of the scrub and the under-storey seemed against it, as well as the steep terrain, all favouring the deer.

"Sambar evolved in tiger country," said Lucky, "They're super cautious cause they had to be. But that's why this is the ultimate. One or two per season is a good score. But the harriers give us an edge. They can pull it down for the ankle-biters to get in range."

Jones nodded sagely, trying to appear to savour the privilege of the experience on offer. He did not like to kill, but could hardly admit to it in present company. Perhaps the difficulty of the enterprise might redeem the moment without conflicting him? He tried to settle himself into contemplation of the environment and switch off to the chaos and cacophony of the pack and find some peace. But inevitably the problems he could not leave behind would not leave him alone if he did not divert them, and he hovered in a state of tension caught between the reality of the present, and the opacity of the past. Eventually though, it was time, and the pack was led off to find the gully's mouth.

"Ten minutes and they'll be into it," intruded Lucky, "come with me."

He led Jones back to the car and round to the boot and opened it up. He passed out an armoured vest to Jones and told him to put it on.

"What for?" asked Jones in considerable surprise.

"It's cold, you're shivering," said Lucky.

"I'll look like a dork," said Jones, trying to deny the offer. "Besides, these don't keep out rifle shots, do they?"

"Not at short range, but these are police issue," Lucky stated the obvious.

"So?" asked Jones, failing to see the relevance.

"Citizens aren't allowed body armour," said Lucky, "Courtesy of Ned Kelly. So this has to be accounted for. A bullet hole would have to be explained. It would cause as much paper work as a body, almost."

Jones stared at him, trying to read between the lines.

"Look upon it as insurance against accidents," Lucky insisted with immovable determination, and Jones surrendered to keep the peace.

"I'll get hot," he grumbled a final complaint.

"No you won't," said Lucky. "We're not walking any distance. We're the short-stop. And you can stand in the shade."

He fetched a couple of rifles out of the boot, both bolt-actions, nothing exotic. He handed one to Jones and started to move off. He had no camo, and no jacket.

"I'm Lucky," he said when Jones pointed this out, "No one will shoot me."

The danger of the hunt he was involved in suddenly occurred to Jones, especially the position on the ridge he had originally been allocated to. The potential there to be caught in the crossfire would be extraordinary.

"Do you get many accidents out hunting?" he asked Lucky casually.

"Not today," Lucky was laconic, "You're safe with me."

Jones looked at him wondering, increasingly aware of the extremity of his situation, right out in the wilderness on the very edge of the world. He wondered if anyone anywhere who mattered even knew where he was? A body could easily go missing out here and never be found.

They walked up the trail in the direction the others had taken. After a few minutes the track curved away and they were at the mouth of a high-sided narrow gully, somewhat over one hundred metres wide. The sides were fractured rock and tumbled scree, with scrub and trees clinging anywhere their roots could get a foothold. The bottom of the gully was fairly accessible, with a reasonably marked trail running up the middle, but the sides would be a bad climb, especially as the sun rose. Lucky led them over to a large gum at the side of the track, and got Jones to settle down in the shade.

"It will be a long wait," he said.

Jones suggested it would be better if they split up, one to cover each side of the gully's mouth.

"No!" was all Lucky said.

Jones simply gave up in the face of this intransigence, and slumped down against the trunk of the tree to rest his back against the solidity of its support. He did not even know why he had made the suggestion; it was not as if he had any real intention of shooting anything. He sat in the shade watching the day pass by and the land heat up. He was tired but too tense to doze without the aid of alcohol. Too many questions were crawling round in his head, irritating like bush flies on a sticky day tickling into ears, eyes and nostrils. The hours passed in slow-time on a long parade on a boring day where the presentation stretched into infinity under a beating sun. Then the distant dogs were barking with a new intensity, somehow sounding even more excited than before. Two shots rang out in quick succession, their echoes reverberating through the fractured gully to fade finally into silence. The forest strained with tension and the air seemed charged and heavy like just before a storm. Only the yap and stammer of the pack breached the stillness of the day, all the birds seemed to be holding their breath. Jones waited strung out with anticipation, but nothing happened. The dogs kept barking and the day droned on. He settled back down trying to regain the equilibrium he never had. Without sound or warning a doe as big as a pony stepped out of the brush at the side of the gully mouth, leading her fawn in front of them. Lucky nudged Jones with his foot, offering him the chance to take the shot. Jones sat mesmerised, not moving one iota. Lucky shook his head almost imperceptibly and began to slowly raise his rifle.

"No!" said Jones firmly and the doe vanished in the blink of an eye with hardly a sound at her passing. He did not even see the fawn move. One moment it was there, next it was gone.

Lucky stared at him in disbelief.

"We don't shoot does in Tasmania," explained Jones. A complete fabrication of course, the old bastard would shoot anything that moved, and run over anything that did not, but it made for some kind of an excuse on the spur of the moment.

Lucky simply looked to the horizon. Later a feral cat stalked out of the undergrowth at the side of the track and began to stroll across the trail as bold as though it owned the whole forest. Lucky shot it without warning. The bullet blew out its guts but it managed to sprint for cover dragging its intestines behind it. Jones was sickened.

"Shall we track it and finish it off?" he asked.

Lucky stared at the thickets surrounding them. "Whatever for?" he said, unmoved.

Later still the others straggled back, the dogs quiet now. No one spoke. Most seemed to ignore Lucky, some seemed almost openly hostile. Back at the campsite a ranger was waiting for them at the vehicles taking down registration numbers.

"Those dogs are prohibited," he pointed to the harriers. "You realise that your firearms and transport can be confiscated."

One of the team walked over to him, took the notebook out of the ranger's hand, and tore it up under his nose.

"I'll call the police!" spluttered the Ranger.

Everyone bar Jones produced a warrant card.

"Now fuck off like a good little boy," said one.

"You won't hear the last of this!" blustered the Ranger.

A deliberate rattle of rifle bolts being cocked underscored the unspoken response. The ranger backed away facing them all the while. Finally he disappeared into the trees. Jones thought he was either the bravest or the most stupid man he had ever met.

"That went well," said Lucky.

"Will he report us?" asked Jones.

"Who to?" asked Lucky?

They broke camp and the team split up to go their separate ways. Lucky drove Jones back to the city in silence.

"Thanks for looking out for me," Jones said when they finally got back.

"I'm Greek," said Lucky, "Family is everything."

Jones looked at him momentarily puzzled; he could not quite see the context. Then he let it go, not bothering to ask for a translation. He decided that sometimes, it was simply better not to know.

# Chapter 26. Purgatory

Jones got Lucky to drop him off at the station. Now that he was back, the interlude was over, and he was completely paranoid. The tension had been building inside him as they broached the suburbs. He did not want to know what, if anything, had happened overnight, but knew at the least that he wanted to retrieve his suitcase. He scurried in to get it, avoiding contact with anybody as much as possible. In the end he managed to get in and out without too much hassle. The place did not seem particularly busy; it was after all now part way through the weekend, but there definitely was none of the air of tension and anger like the aftermath of Garelli's killing, which he would always associate with the reality of an officer down. He sat for a moment at her desk realising that he did not know the old man's timetable or the degree of planning required for the execution of a senior officer. He pondered that he did not really know what was going down on many levels, and in retrospect never really had. He just wanted to get out. So he made at that moment the decision to simply walk away. He was going to use the desk phone to ring the airport to see if he could possibly book a cancellation, when the image of Lucky's casual despatch of the feral cat for some reason popped into his mind, and he realised something else. Despite the risk of going back to the flat he knew he could not leave her cats; that she would never forgive.

He caught a cab back to her place, not thinking clearly, but trying to plan ahead with the notion of something to put them in. He almost stopped off at a pet shop to buy a transport module, but his miserliness got the better of him. Surely there were boxes lying around at Garelli's free for the taking? But at the flat there was no sign of the cats. He remembered well after the proverbial bolt that he had left the window open. So he sat there in an agony of indecision and in the end turned to the bottle he had left on the counter only partly supped. He started drinking and carried on till the bottle died and the room turned and the floor flung up its arms in welcome embrace. Somehow he came to in his old bed at the farm, the old iron frame and the horsehair mattress and he was on his stomach and a pillow was over his head and smothering his cries. Then he woke up and the friendly cat was licking at his hair and the shy one was stood on his back kneading with its paws at his buttocks. He was numb and immobilised and the cat walked in smaller and smaller circles and eventually curled in a ball and settled down to sleep. Jones lay there for an age not daring to move, not wanting to destroy the trust, but finally the paranoia returned and he was compelled to move. He phoned the airport but there were no flights till the morning, and in any case they were fully booked. They said they could put him on a standby list in case of cancellation and asked for a contact number. It was then that he realised the call could be traced back to Garelli's flat and it was another link in the chain dragging him into the abyss and he dropped the phone before it burnt him.

It was much too late to try to get on the evening ferry, and in any case that would probably also be booked out at that time of the year. So he decided to rent a car and drive down to Port Welshpool overnight to embark on the fast catamaran in the morning. That meant getting to the airport anyway, because only there would the hire firms be open at that time of day on the weekend. He found a cardboard box and somehow got the protesting cats into it and taped it shut. Then he realised he could not risk phoning a cab, for that could be traced as well. So he grabbed his bag and the box and began to struggle for the nearest rank.

The land breeze bowled scraps of litter along the streets. Jones wove through the shadows towards the neon glare, clutching his case to his chest like an upturned shield, with the box resting precariously on top of it. It was precarious because the cats kept rocking it with their continual movement and miaou of disapproval. He told them they would like the island: no dingoes. After the second block the weight of it all began to drag him down, but he strove gamely on for the plaza. At the last he did not dare the inner circle, but stayed hidden in the outer darkness, frightened of the light. In any case the ranks were bare, so Jones found a booth with a phone that worked, and called a cab to the nearest intersection. The cabbie took one look at Jones, said he did not pick up drunks at that time of the shift, and pulled away vacant. Jones sat on his case accompanied by the cats and watched the taillights fade into the false dawn of the neon glare. The street funnelled an oil slick into the darkness and the streetlights winked out one by one. Jones was left with himself, the cats and the night. So he called another company, and this time the cab agreed to take him to the airport. Jones had one more curiosity to attempt to satisfy or at least subdue. He asked the cabbie if he would turn off the meter and not log the fare if he payed cash up front, and when a price was negotiated he asked for the driver to take a detour that would run through the derelict industrial estate where he had left Mulligan and the car. At first the cabbie refused with the mention of the area, and Jones realised that it probably had a bad reputation and that his own appearance only helped to enhance it. So he offered up another $50 and promised there would be no need to stop and the driver accepted the bait. Jones's nerves were more than fragile but he had no choice but wait and suffer in silence, apart from the screeching of the cats, once the decision had been made. Eventually they swung past the squat and there was no sign of the car. Jones took a while to digest the implications of this. As they drove off back onto the more direct route to the airport he considered the permutations. In the end he decided they could only be good for him, for there had been no mention of the discovery of Mulligan's body by anyone at the station, and as the car was now gone it could turn up anywhere, thus completely confusing the trail. Jones sat back and tried to relax for the remainder of the trip, but the cats were getting more and more restless and scratching at the box. Jones spent the rest of the way trying to pacify them. But at least, he reflected later, they made the time pass relatively quickly.

On arrival at the airport as a precaution he freshened himself up before he presented himself at the car rental desk. But the night clerk was tired and bored and cursory, and gave Jones the keys to a budget saloon with barely a glance. All that was left was to negotiate a way out of the city; homeward bound.

*

In the middle of nowhere the big boomer hopped into the highway and lost itself in the headlights. Jones was too tired, too pissed and too damned slow to react. The roo's eyes glowed red and accusing in the beam, and Jones locked onto them mesmerised. The body buckled round the bumper, slammed into the bonnet in a last leap, the head whip-lashing

259

through the windscreen. The car left the asphalt, onto the graded shoulder and then into the ditch. It rolled in slow motion, once, twice and then stayed, upside down on its roof. The cats burst out of the cardboard box spitting and screaming, and shot through the shattered windscreen into the night. Jones was too stunned to try and stop them. He knew he should call them or something, Garelli would be really pissed, but he just hung there by his seat belt, too shocked and confused to move. After a while his head started to hurt with the weight of all that blood, and he managed to pop the clip off his belt. He crashed down into the crushed roof and managed to crawl out through the screen. A flashlight was wavering through the bush towards him. Back on the highway he could see the running lights of a parked rig. One of the nightriders of the trucking fleets must have seen him flip and had taken pity. Then the ground was rushing up at him and all the lights went out. He felt himself shrink into a hard core of darkness, and then nothing.

\*

The light was harsh and sterile, the ceiling a whitewashed glare. Jones blinked and tried to look around. The walls seemed a lighter shade of grey through the chromed bars at the end of the bed. Was this purgatory or just another waiting room? A white uniform wandered through and flashed a sympathetic smile. Fletcher's voice cursed him roundly from somewhere behind his line of vision. Another voice, bored and pedantic, declared the possibility of a mild concussion.
"But he's fit to travel?" insisted Fletcher, demanding and aggressive.

"No broken bones, just minor abrasions and bruising," the voice droned on. Jones flexed his toes and fingers just to make sure. "But we'd like to keep him in for observation, to be safe."

Fletcher's face loomed overhead haggard and threatening. "Get your butt off the bed, Jones, and sign yourself out of here. You're wanted back in town."

Jones stared up at him, fearful and confused. He blinked away the up-welling of tears. So he had been found out already, but on what count?

"Am I under arrest?" so soon, it was not fair, he should have been able to get home first. He had something to do, some loose ends to tie up, he could not remember exactly what, but it would come back to him, when his head cleared.

"You drunken piece of chickenshit!" swore Fletcher, "You still smell like a brewery. If it was up to me you'd lose your licence, but the powers that be have ordered the charges buried. Lucky for you it was only a roo you cleaned up. Come on, let's go, we've got an afternoon appointment in the city to make."

Jones followed him out meekly, feeling too light-headed to be mutinous. He tried to make small talk, to draw Fletcher into conversation on the long drive back, but Fletcher was sullen and unresponsive. We have been here before, thought Jones, but he could not think where or when. The paddocks rolled by in drab monotony; rusted wire and bleached posts palisading the plains; imprisoned cattle sulked in skeletal shade and dead gums stood silent silhouettes against the ranging sky. Outside the closed windows you could almost smell the heat. Kamikaze bugs splattered little puddles of life across the windscreen and dust devils swirled at their passing. The road shimmered quicksilver and dancing in the distance but Jones had missed his way and could only feel saddened by the lost horizon. Only the city lay ahead and that had to be a dead-end. He fell asleep as the kilometres ate the day.

*

Fletcher escorted Jones firmly through the corridors of Federal Police headquarters, and then was refused entry into the actual meeting. He blustered and threatened, and waved his Ethical Standards card to no avail. He was told to contact his superiors and remove himself without further obstruction. Jones did not know what was going on; he was almost paralysed with fear. He obeyed his instructions woodenly, without sense, without volition. All he knew was that it must be very senior officers indeed, to shut Ethical Standards out. And on a Sunday too; they should all be in church?

The door closed behind him, and he was trapped in this room with these faceless, nameless men; three of them, a triumvirate, two seated and one standing at the back: men who could and would destroy his career and crush him utterly. He could not look directly at them, so he tried to focus on the room. A low suspended tiled ceiling, pressing and claustrophobic over walls of pastel grey. All these modern interiors seemed the same, functional and featureless, aesthetics lost to form. The rest of his life could be measured in anonymous rooms, with the exits shuttered by bars.

"Sit down, Officer," the voice snapped him back to the present, and Jones dragged his eyes down to find a chair. He forced himself to face them, but could not look any one of them in the eye. His gaze kept shifting to detail; colour of ties, shirt collars, and cuff links: formal, the anachronisms of age.

"It has just been brought to our attention the direction of your enquiries, Jones," the face opposite was turning a pencil end

262

over end with the fingers and thumb of one hand. Every now and then it tapped the table as if to emphasise a point.

"We've heard from Ethical Standards that you have been asking about Andrews."

Jones felt the blood drain from his face and forced himself to sit still.

"So we are telling you, asking you really, because in your case we cannot make it an order, to let this one lie."

Jones shook his head, completely confused; did they know about Andrews?

The other seated face stood up and leaned across at Jones, his hands resting heavily on the table. "Jones, this is off the record. Andrews is one of our statistics specialists. He has the mentality of a filing clerk, obsessed with anomalies. He exceeded his authority in chasing after Smith. We would never have permitted it, had we known. When we found out, we ordered him off. We are asking you the same, to give it up."

Jones found himself staring at them. Give it up: it had never been his idea in the first place? Did these departments not communicate at all? He had been on the way home when Fletcher dragged him back. A killing, and now an accessory to murder, and they would never have permitted it? He started to laugh, a brittle laugh that crackled on the edge of hysteria.

"Christ's sake, Jones," appealed the first face, "you cannot follow this through, it would be too embarrassing, to us and the government. Think about your career, the fallout would follow you forever!"

Jones ran his fingers through his hair. They were embarrassed? What possible lever did he have? Did they not know yet what he had done?

"So who is he?" he fired an arrow in the dark.

"For God's sake, tell the fellow," snapped the clipped voice from the suit at the back, the man leaning into the shadows by the window, "And then you can slap a D-notice on him," a posh accent, very proper, very British.

"We don't have them over here," said the first face, "We are no longer a colony, remember?"

"Really?" muttered the second, "then why did we agree to this in the first place?" He stalked around the table and planted himself in front of Jones, resting his weight against the edge. "Smith is part of our Witness Relocation Programme. Only in his case it is, or was, a favour to another government. His is a secure file, access only to our hierarchy. In fact it is closed. We only know about it because we inherited it. It is not known outside of this room, apart from your masters?" he queried of the shadow at the back.

An indifferent shrug was the reply. "Pensioned off years ago, or upstairs," he pointed out the window up at the sky

"So Andrews didn't know about it?" Jones was constrained to ask.

"Couldn't have," muttered the senior, "otherwise he wouldn't have got on his high horse, now would he?"

Jones felt ill again: what had he done?

"So why wasn't he given an I.D with all the paperwork?" Jones tried to turn the guilt aside. He could not carry all the blame?

"The offer was made; he simply refused to take it up, just wanted to drop out of sight. We knew where he ended up of course. We send him a monthly stipend; payment for services rendered, and all that," the faithful retainer.

Jones nodded; that would explain the money order, posted in Canberra, probably by the Embassy no less.

"Only thing is," the suit coughed up an attempt at clearing the throat, was it possible the man was actually embarrassed?

264

"When I checked the file I saw the silly buggers had not made it index linked; blasted bean counters, hoarding their masters' money when it ain't even their own. Accountants, eh: can't live with them, can't avoid taxes without them? Must have been a bit of a struggle with inflation though, especially lately, what?"

Jones shook his head more in disbelief than disgust.

"But of course we haven't kept track of him for years," was that an attempt at an excuse? "That way there are no junior officers involved, and no current records." The suit seemed to have retrieved his equilibrium, was sure of himself once more.

Jones tried to imagine what he would be prepared to give up to regain that sense of righteousness, that certainty. He thought back to the old man, to the choices he had made. Even so, something still did not quite ring true.

"What ever had Smith done, to provoke such an extreme retreat?" asked Jones.

He turned as one with the seniors to scrutinise the suit at the back. They were all intrigued.

"There were certain indiscretions that we would rather did not come to light," prevaricated the clipped voice.

"What else have you bastards done?" demanded a senior.

The suit in the shadows seemed still in contemplation. "Not outside this room?" he queried.

The seniors nodded in agreement.

"It was a long time ago, you must remember we were at war," the suit offered at last. "The boyos blew up the Shadow Secretary for Northern Ireland in the underground car park at the House of Commons. They nearly got the whole Tory government with a bomb at the Brighton Party Conference. Thatcher initiated her own war on terror. We had SAS teams undercover in Northern Ireland, as well as British Military Intelligence. Their mandate was to neutralise known and

265

potential IRA threats. Smith was a top Provisional assassin, specialised in rooting out informers and liquidating them and their handlers. We think he got to several of our boys?"

Jones was faintly disgusted by all the euphemism.

"The boyos got onto the trail of one of our top undercover operatives, but could never locate him. They knew he had a mistress. But her security was very tight. They also knew she was unlikely to give up lover boy. But they also knew where her mother was. They wanted Smith to get to the mother to get to the mistress to get to our man. Smith, man of principle that he is, refused.

So the boyos decided on a lesson or a provocation, and dressed themselves up as police, and ambushed Smith's wife at a fake roadblock, and shot her to death. Her and the twins, two baby boys. But the boyos were careless; uniforms were one thing, but it was harder to get police issue firearms. The boyos used AK 47s, left Russian brass everywhere on the floor at the scene. We let all the details slip out on the grapevine, and of course Smith heard and put two and two together to make five. To cut a long story short, he turned himself in to us, and offered to off the opposition if we guaranteed him and his surviving children a fresh start."

"It's hard to believe they were so stupid as to use soviet weapons?" said one of the seniors.

"That's the thing," agreed the suit, "that and the fact it was such a good result for us: it got Smith off the streets and the eradication of a whole hardline Provisional splinter group. Certain questions were raised, and certain accusations inferred in certain quarters. We would not appreciate anything contemporary reflecting back to the past."

"You mean to say you arranged it yourselves?" Jones was beyond horror.

"Not at all," denied the suit, "But you can see our concerns. We would never want any of this to get out. It's over thirty years; all those archives are now accessible under the Freedom of Information Act. If some news hack gets wind of Smith and starts to dig, well drug dealers are one thing, but what if he should turn to bite the hand that feeds him, eh? He must be neutralised."

"And just how do you propose to do that?" asked a senior, "we've got half the force out looking for him and we haven't found a trace."

The suit at the back nodded at Jones.

Jones suddenly realised the ulterior reason behind his invitation, and why they did not seem unduly concerned at what he, a junior officer had been allowed to hear. He was bait, and therefore expendable. The only question was his probability of survival.

"We think there might be someone on the force feeding him information," said Jones, reinforcing his own insecurity.

"All the better then," acknowledged the suit, "It should be that much easier for Smith to find you."

"Give us your assurance of silence," said one senior, "and when this is over we'll book you on a first class flight home. I'll write a letter of commendation to your local commander. It will help your career. And of course we will mention your discretion in the right circles; it will not go unnoticed."

"Perhaps you'll find yourself on the New Year's Honours List?" sneered the Pom from the embrasure.

The sarcasm washed over Jones like molten lead.

They said they would arrange a car to take him to a hotel, and suggested the one he first booked on arrival from the island. They thought it would be easier there for Smith to pick up his trail. They also told him to phone in his whereabouts to the station in case the old man needed pointing in the right direction. They promised they would keep Jones under twenty-four-hour surveillance. Then they let him run.

\*

The receptionist recognised him and flashed him a bright smile, but he was too emotionally exhausted, too drained and paranoid to even attempt polite conversation. He mumbled something entirely inappropriate as he booked himself in, then collected his key and shambled off to his room. Once inside he could hardly bear to close himself in, or lock the door. It was all too reminiscent of a cell. So he just dropped his bags and lunged for the bedside telephone. He called in to the station and made the excuse of leaving his present address in case of emergencies, and then went to make the call he could put off no longer. In the end he remembered himself, and realised he ought to go out and use a public telephone: untraceable. He was tired to the point of surrender, but forced himself out onto the streets. He was not sure whether the surveillance was in place yet, and did not know what they would make of his movements, but decided that at that point he really did not care, as long as they could not overhear him, he would be safe from fresh accusations at least. The light was so bright it hurt his eyes, and he stumbled along the pavements squinting against the glare, almost blindly searching for a booth. When he finally found one, it was almost impossible to hear against the roar of the traffic.
"The mobile phone you have just called is switched off. Please try again later."

He kept trying, but the refrain kept repeating. In the end his patience broke and he pounded the phone against the metal unit.

"Answer, you stupid old bastard, answer me!" he sobbed into the receiver.

A punter queuing to use the phone complained angrily. Jones turned on him viciously, and shoved him hard into the passing throng. The man floundered momentarily in a tangle of arms and bodies before he went down. Jones hurried away, embarrassed by his sudden violence. He wanted to run and hide, to escape the past. But he had to wait till it was finished, and he did not know when or what that would entail. His only sanctuary was compromised beyond redemption. There was only the hotel to go to for now. If only he could take it all back. He scurried away like a hunted mouse, desperate for refuge in a dark place out of the light.

When he returned, this time he did manage to lock the door, and he threw himself on the bed and collapsed in a heap. Sleep must have claimed him and the daylight eventually, because when a soft scratching woke him, the room was in darkness. A man in black with a shadowed face had entered, and he came and sat on the edge of the bed. It groaned with the weight of his body. Jones was lying on his side terrified, petrified with fear. The man pulled back the covers and gently but firmly turned Jones onto his stomach. Then he eased down his pants with one hand, the other pressing down on Jones's shoulders. Jones felt his bowels turn to water and started to cry. The man pulled back Jones's hair and twisted his face round to slap it. His eyes were large and leering. It was his foster-father. Then Ma was there slapping him too.

"You filthy little boy, you've dirtied the sheets!"

Then a final crack across the mouth and Jones snapped wide-awake. The old man stared down at him dispassionately.

"Lord, man," he muttered in that harsh accent, "I hope these rooms are soundproofed. You're screaming fit to wake the dead."

He sat back on the bed and leaned forward on his walking stick, clasping it with both hands.

Jones gasped and started to laugh hysterically. That was a good one. Perhaps he should try harder. If he did it would solve a few problems would it not?

The old man raised his hand again. Jones subsided instantly.

"I'm alright now," he mumbled quietly. "So how did you get in here?" he asked next, when he had gathered his wits.

"Through the door," said the old man, "I don't fly. I'm not Dracula." He held up a bunch of skeleton keys. "I can pick most locks."

"That's not what I meant," Jones shook his head. "I meant into the hotel. I'm supposed to be under surveillance."

"I figured it was his time to eliminate me when he rang with your current whereabouts," said the old man. "So I took precautions. I came in with a young lady of the night. We booked a room together. She's enjoying her beauty sleep."

Jones inspected him closely, noted the dyed hair, the fine suit, and smelled the cologne. He even seemed to have put on weight. They would not have been looking too closely at prostitutes with their clients.

"I know who you are," Jones risked finally.

"Good," said the old man, "Then you'll know I'm an expert."

"I've been trying to contact you," Jones said, "About Andrews, he's not…."

"I know," interrupted the old man.

270

"You didn't?" Jones could not find it within himself to finish the question.

The old man shook his head. "I'm a soldier," he said, "but I try not to harm the innocent. Too many civilians become casualties as it is." He sighed, "It is why I am here. I want the other name. You said there were two?"

"How did you find out?" asked Jones, "That it wasn't him?"

The first flush of relief was fading now, to be replaced by fear. How much had the old man compromised him with Andrews? Had he threatened him, tortured him even? He remembered that body back at the morgue.

"I received a telephone call when I had Andrews under surveillance: most inconvenient. I keep forgetting to switch the damned thing off. Advancing age I suppose: memory's going. It was my master's voice, not Andrews, because I had him in view at the time. He wants his flat vacated. He wanted to know why I was still hanging around, why I had not buggered off yet?"

"He set you up in another flat?" Jones was astounded at that.

"Of course!" replied the old man, "a safe house is only ever safe if one does not overstay one's welcome. It is best to have a selection."

"So what excuse did you give?" asked Jones, still trying to come to grips with the resources of the network.

"Unfinished business," declared the old man, "Yourself. Funnily enough he said it might already be a work in progress; that arrangements were in place. I am glad to see they have not eventuated. I would be upset at your premature demise."

Jones stared back at him, replaying the sambar hunt in his mind's eye.

"How did you know I was here?" he asked.

"I already told you," said the old man simply, "He rang."

271

Jones considered this. He wondered how much the surveillance team were involved? His stomach turned again. Someone was expecting another corpse in the morning: his.

"The name!" insisted the old man.

"It's not that simple," said Jones, and he explained what he had been told that morning. "They were adamant," he concluded, "that no one current could know of you. Your file is closed, too sensitive ever to be released."

He thought back to Garelli; she had said that the information about the old man's arrival had been passed on by the feds, but Garelli was State. If she had been told by a superior, it could simply have been disinformation. But there was no way that a member of the State Police could know about Smith?

The old man sat immobile, processing it all, motionless in inner contemplation as the minutes ticked by.

"There is another who would have known," he declared at last. He spoke softly, shrunken in on himself. His shoulders sagged and he suddenly revealed himself as a tired old man on the verge of yet another disappointment.

"But the fact remains!" he straightened himself and his eyes flashed once more, "That the officer who organised your transfer must be the one who is contacting me. Give me his name and I will go and ask him to confirm what I now must suspect."

Jones rubbed his forehead wearily. The old man was right of course; his logic was impeccable. But he himself would like to be sure, especially after the episode with Andrews. He wondered if he could get the old man to tape a phone conversation; even if the voice was disguised he could get the sound technicians in forensics to diagnose a match. But that would mean waiting for another call, and why should there be one, and in any case he did not have the authority and he could hardly explain his collusion with the old man anyway? Besides he could not see how he could arrange anything without alerting the target?

"I'll take you to his house," he said simply.

The old man shook his head. "You will compromise you own position, your career."

Jones had already considered this. "The bastard expects me to be dead by the morning," he declared, "I want to see his face when he answers the door."

"It is good to look an enemy in the eye before you kill him," agreed the old man, "But how will you explain your part in all this?"

Of course, Jones would be going on execution detail. "I'll claim I was a hostage," he decided.

The old man nodded in agreement. "Get his home number before we go, just in case we need it," he pursed his lips carefully. "One last thing," he continued, opening up his jacket. Round his waist he wore what looked like a weight-belt. A couple of wires ran from it up into his shoulder. "This is packed with explosives," he explained, "when I set the circuit a pressure switch in my left hand holds the contacts apart. If I release my grip, the circuit is completed. It is an old operational guarantee. If someone should shoot or incapacitate me, when my muscles relax I will blow up everything in the immediate vicinity. At the end of this, just make sure you keep your distance."

"How did you explain that to the young lady you were entertaining?" asked Jones.

"I never took my clothes off!" said the old man.

Of course not, thought Jones, the old man's compulsion was revenge, not pleasure. He nodded in resigned acquiescence; he could take a hint. He was no hero, and certainly no martyr.

"Is there any problem with the address?" asked the old man.

Jones shook his head. He knew where it was; Garelli had pointed it out to him on one of their excursions round the city, as a kind of antithesis to the squats they were targeting. Or had it merely been envy?

"I've got his number," said Jones. He had been given his card.

That was the easy part.

"How do we get out without alerting surveillance?" Jones asked.

"I'll wake the young lady," said the old man, "you can go out with her. They won't be watching exits closely, just entrances. She'll be pleased, I'm sure; you're much better looking. When you're away, send her back in for me. We'll just be another happy couple celebrating a successful transaction."

"They'll notice her if she goes in again," argued Jones.

"Why on earth should a busy working girl interest them?" asked the old man, "Is that not expected at this time of night?"

Jones acquiesced and they arranged a rendezvous. Then the old man went to fetch the girl.

"Why should she co-operate?" it occurred to Jones as the old man reached the door.

"Money without exercise?" retorted the old man, "Sometimes I wonder, officer, who of us is the real recluse?"

\*

# Chapter 27. The Sins of the Fathers

Superintendent Campbell's house was almost a waterfront block. Only the highway separated it from the reserve fronting the bay. The half-moon showered a path of silver across the oily estuary and wavelets soughed and blew on a hidden beach.

The old man nodded in appreciation. "A man with expensive tastes," he commented.

"His wife's independently wealthy," said Jones. He remembered Garelli saying something about it, how Campbell had scored an heiress. Even now he found it difficult to assimilate; Campbell had always seemed so considerate, so genuine. The only one who had seemed to have the time of day for him?

"So they do not need to keep up with the Joneses?" queried the old man.

Jones almost smiled. He did not know the old man had an ounce of humour in him. "Your English idiom is very good," he said.

"Why not?" said the old man, "I am a native speaker. English is my first or second language, if not my mother tongue. Gaelic is hardly international."

"How do we get in?" asked Jones, "he might have security."

The old man was impassive in the darkness. "You Australians are very blasé," he said, "Few of you bother with anything sophisticated. It is usually not too difficult, even for a dinosaur like me. Mind you, my training was very thorough, with regular updates."

275

"So where did you train?" Jones slipped in. The old man seemed to be relaxing, almost opening up, and he could not resist the opportunity. It had to be the moonlight, his natural element, nocturnal.

"The usual; the Middle East, and North Africa: we all went there in those days, money no object: we were funded on a tide of oil." He stared across the water, seemingly lost in a sea of memories.

Jones cleared his throat to break the mood. "So?" he queried impatiently, he was all hyped up now, the adrenaline pumping.

"So," repeated the old man, "I have you. Maybe I do not need to improvise anything technical. With luck you can just march right in and announce yourself. He will open up for you to be sure. I will be right behind you, in the shadows."

"What about his family?" queried Jones, "They might be there?"

"I hope so," agreed the old man, "that will make him all the more amenable to persuasion. Let me go ahead to check things out. If there are any difficulties, you can simply phone him on the mobile, plead an emergency, and get him to answer the door."

*

Campbell's face was a whiter shade of pasty grey in the light of the porch. He held the barking dog beside him firmly by the collar.

"What do you want, Jones?" he snapped, "Is this really necessary, it's really late."

"What's the matter, dear?" a female voice floated down from somewhere upstairs and inside.

"Nothing to worry about, go back to bed," Campbell called back over his shoulder, "Just official business." He glared at Jones again. "This had better be good," he growled. The dog was snarling now.

"Shut the animal up or I will kill it," the old man stepped out of the shadows and into the circle of light.

Campbell blanched and stepped back. "Who are you?" he blustered. "Who's this, Jones?"

The old man strode right up to his face. The dog whimpered and backed away.

"Good try," he whispered in that grating accent, "But it will not wash, not tonight. Best we step inside, eh? Do not want to alarm the family, do we?" The threat hung implicit and heavy. Campbell swallowed, and sent the dog upstairs. It slunk away with its tail between its legs. Then he led them into the study.

"Can I get you a drink, gentlemen?" he asked politely.

Jones was impressed by his recovery; the look of naked fear was veiled now, under control.

"Where is my son?" asked the old man without preamble.

"He's dead!" spluttered Campbell, "You know that!"

Jones sighed; the acknowledgement had condemned him. The old man did not even seem to notice, he was that sure.

"No head, no hands?" said the old man, "How convenient. Where is he?"

Campbell shook his head. The old man held his eyes, his stare hypnotic.

"Where are your children, Superintendent?"

"Upstairs," whispered Campbell, "My son and my daughter. They are nothing to do with this."

"I will give you one minute. Then I will go upstairs and kill the boy. Then I will come back and ask again. Then I will kill the

277

girl. I will leave your wife. You can explain it all to her in the morning."

"He said you would never kill women or children," whispered Campbell, ashen now.

"He lied," said the old man. "Now where is he?"

"He's dead!" whined Campbell, "A year or more; died of AIDS."

"So why the lure of that body in the mortuary?" the old man asked coldly. He turned and headed for the door.

"Wait!" pleaded Campbell, "I'll arrange a meet. I don't have an address, only a number."

The old man nodded, hand on the doorknob. Campbell's hands were shaking now; he had trouble picking up the phone. "Just yourself, mind," insisted the old man, "No mention of myself or my sidekick. Think of a good excuse."

Campbell nodded woodenly and punched in the buttons. The number was memorised, Jones noted; must be well used. They heard a woman's voice reply, high-pitched and tinny in the strained air.

"He always was a devil with the women," the old man muttered sadly.

Campbell's message was terse and to the point. "I need a meet tonight, at the Reserve, north of the beach, the usual place. One hour. You know who." He put the phone down.

"Very impressive," said the old man, "So he is at your beck and call. Write down the telephone number, and the street address of that reserve. What did you two manage between you: control of all the heroin trade in the city? Until the triads moved in, and you could not handle a piece of free market competition, so you set me up to do your dirty work?"

"He was always bragging about you," Campbell said bleakly, "Said you were the best, but dedicated, a man with principles, a man who could not be bought," he glanced momentarily at Jones, a flicker of annoyance creasing his brow. "Why didn't you kill this little prick like you said you would?" he asked bitterly, "it's all unravelled because of his interference!"

"Because, unlike you, he is innocent," said the old man quietly. He raised his walking stick and pressed the end against Campbell's forehead.

"Tell her I loved her," whispered the superintendent, his voice resigned and controlled at last.

The old man dropped the point a fraction and shot him between the eyes. The silencer hardly made a sound.

"A wife would always know the truth of that, without the need for telling," he said simply, and led the way out.

The smell of cordite mingled with warm blood and faeces drifted out of the room. Upstairs the dog whined softly. A woman's sleepy voice hushed it gently. Jones closed the front door silently behind him. As they walked out into the starlight Jones hardly knew what to say. He felt in shock, he had at least wanted to ask Campbell how he had involved Andrews; now the opportunity was gone forever.

"Here," the old man handed him the mobile, "make yourself useful, phone the taxi company, we have got to get to that Reserve. Get them to pick us up from the end of the road."

"You took a risk there," Jones managed at last.

"Not really," said the old man, missing the point entirely, "It is the prime rule in counter-intelligence; always sterilise your lead before you move on to the next rung of the ladder. Campbell did not lie: the stakes were too high. But at least he made a decent choice in the end. The boy will be there."

"What will you do to him?" asked Jones, "Your son?"

"He has forfeited his birthright,' said the old man bleakly. "He is a man grown now, more than adult enough to face the

279

consequences. I brought him into the world; who has the better right to take him out of it?"

Jones said nothing as they waited on the corner for the cab. He half expected sirens and a posse of squad cars, but evidently the wife had gone back to sleep after all.

*

They waited by the bushes at the perimeter of the reserve. Behind them a line of power poles silhouetted gaunt crosstrees against the horizon. The power lines were humming busily against the darkness, but it was late, in the lost hours the wrong side of midnight, for the street-lamps were out, and only the half-moon in the clear sky shone any light on the scene. Jones looked up and studied the heavens. A meteor soared and flashed and faded and fell to earth. He shuddered. He had heard it said somewhere that a shooting star was a departing soul flaring its last before flickering into oblivion. The old man was quiet and motionless, as impassive as the grave. Time hung heavily in the shadows, as the pendulum of the universe wheeled the nebulae of night so slowly in the death-watch of eternity.

At the last, when Jones felt beyond hope, beyond redemption, he sensed the old man tense up beside him. A soft tread of footsteps grew in the distance, and then faded as the nightwalker stepped onto the grass. A shadow moved slowly on the edge of the reserve under the opposite line of trees. The figure began to move out into the oval and the old man hissed sharply and motioned back with one hand for Jones to stay in the shadows. Then he leaned forward himself, as if his feet were unwilling to step out. He seemed to drag himself forth with reluctant limbs, a broken man held up by a

280

walking stick forcing crippled legs by a sheer act of will. Jones stared at the centre mesmerised as the figure moved out into the full focus of the moon. Her bouncing hair still fell in gentle waves that rippled as she walked, but now it glowed with silver fire in the moonlight.

"O Da," her words breathed clearly into the silence of the night, "I had a feeling it might be you. I am sorry that it had to turn out this way."

He stumbled towards her a collapsing puppet desperately trying to reach her before he fell. "Where is the boy?" he managed to gasp at last.

"Dead," she stated casually, "over a year back. He caught AIDS; always sleeping around, you know how he was. He wouldn't consider the retro-virals because they'd destroy his looks. I don't think he ever really believed he had it, but he went quite quickly in the end; pneumonic complications they said. I'd been advising him for years, doing his accounts, investing his money, checking quality control, networking, that sort of thing. Did you know I majored in Economics with a minor in Business Management?"

"I thought you were a teacher?" Jones could hear the strain in the old man's voice vibrating the darkness.

"A necessary fiction to maintain the charade," she said, "If anybody should ever bother to check my background from the gossip at home, it should mislead them. I do occasionally lecture at TAFE actually, to adults. You know, the real world." She laughed proudly, tossing her hair like a thoroughbred. "When he died I had to take over. But the triads moved in on us."

"Why?" his cry of anguish seemed to rip the heart out of the night.

She replied on a torrent of that soft foreign tongue that Jones had heard them use before, back on the island, when he had been innocent.

"Do not you dare use Gaelic with me!" the old man hissed, "Not now. You have betrayed our heritage. All I fought for."

"You old fool," she spat, "you silly, proud old fool. How do you think we managed to live all those years? You were too proud to query that pittance from the government. It was barely enough to feed us in the end. What choice did we have? He always sent me money when he could."

"We lived well," argued the old man, "A simple life, pure and healthy: no distractions."

"No money for anything extra!" she hissed, "Never a treat, never new clothes, never make-up, never ever anything special. Not even for birthdays, not even for Christmas. We never celebrated anything!" she wrung her hands in frustration. "The local kids used to call us the refo beggars!"

The old man's head sank into his chest. "I did not realise," Jones thought he heard him mumble, "You should have said."

"You never listened!" she replied, "You were switched off, a man closed in on himself. How did you think I got through college? You never paid for it. I could not apply for Austudy!"

"I thought you got an automatic grant?" he said.

"Not without paperwork," she replied.

"I am sorry," he said at last.

The silence stretched barbed and taut on the wires of the night.

"O Da," she whispered, "we were all hurting, for Ma and the others, but you, you forgot to live."

The old man raised his head and sighed at the stars. "It was not just that, it was the very fact they came after her to get at me. My own comrades, brothers-in-arms turning against me and mine over a question of policy. We were freedom fighters and they wanted to kill the innocent!"

Jones could almost taste the tang of bitterness in the black air.

"I have never tried to understand politics," she answered, "Only poverty and wealth. Oh Da, you should taste the freedom money brings. I can buy absolutely anything in the whole wide world!"

"I do not think so," the old man shook his head slowly, as if his neck could barely support the weight, "Not for long, not any more. You have lost your protection. I eliminated Campbell tonight."

Jones thought he could hear the wires strum with the tension.

"He was my lover, my shield," she breathed softly, "He had the whole force at his command: at my beck and call. How inconvenient!" She seemed to reach down into her bag.

"You were sleeping with a married man?" the old man spluttered outrage into the void.

"Oh God!" she spat, "You dinosaur, you obsolete old fool! I played him like an instrument. He'd dance to any tune I whistled!" Something bright and metallic glinted in the moonlight from the shadows at her loins.

"Your mother would be ashamed!" muttered the old man.

"Ma's long dead," she commented, "It was your intransigence that killed her. If only you had learned to bend, to move with the times."

Her arm stuttered up in fits and starts, an old projector running down the final frames in a black and white film. The something in her hand glowed silver to match the burnishing of her hair.

The old man let go of his stick and dropped to his knees.

"The sins of the fathers," Jones heard him mutter. He looked to be in prayer.

"Sorry, Da, you've become a liability," she commented, and pointed the gun at his head.

"NO!" screamed Jones as he flung himself forward, but the old man spread his arms wide and opened his hands as if in supplication. The sky erupted in a ball of fire and a giant fist plucked Jones into the air and threw him away. The shock of the sound wave was the last thing he felt before he fell into darkness.

\*

# Chapter 28.  The Homecoming

Only two uniforms were waiting behind the glass walls of the terminal. At least they had not made it a state occasion. The passengers hurried and hustled to disembark, a cramped huddle wedged in by the door. Such enthusiasm, they could only be tourists. The locals usually saved all their excitement for the other end, the bright lights of the big smoke beckoning a temporary escape from boredom and island fever. Through the window baggage handlers were unloading the luggage on to a convoy of trailers in a tractor train. So unsophisticated he was almost embarrassed. When the throng had finally cleared and he could be sure of freedom from the jostling crush, he wearily forced himself up from the window seat.  He was so tired and tender he felt almost mortally wounded. The steps down the mobile stairway were almost too much for him, but one uniform sorted his baggage and the commander himself walked him out through the terminal to the waiting car.

"Nice to see you are still in one piece, Jones," he cleared his throat as he settled himself into the back seat. "I understand there will be no official commendation," he began, "but it won't go unnoticed, we are all proud of you."

He tapped Jones a comradely punch on the shoulder. Jones tried hard not to wince.

"So did you ever find out in the end who he was?" asked the commander.

"I don't know all the answers, sir," said Jones.

"My opposite number would not tell me!" the commander sounded peevish, "Must think we're a bunch of bumpkins over here."

Jones would not be drawn.

"I have been asked to give your career all the support it deserves," the commander continued, "Have you thought what you would like to do next?"

"I would like to work in Missing Persons in the city," Jones said promptly.

"We don't have one, as such," said the commander, "You know that."

"I was thinking in terms of working with street kids," said Jones, "Community policing, contacting the parents, that sort of thing."

"Well we've got plenty of those," the commander sounded dubious; "I suppose something could be arranged, although it does seem rather a waste of your talents."

"It's what I want to do, sir," said Jones, "I learned a lot about it on the mainland."

The commander seemed surprised at that and sniffed noisily against the sound of the air-conditioning. "When would you like to start?" he asked finally.

"I'd like a bit of leave first, sir," Jones replied. "I need to catch up on some family business back at home."

"Of course, Jones, some rest and recreation, you deserve it," agreed the commander, "consider it done."

\*

# Epilogue

# Chapter 29.  The Funeral

It was a good turnout; he had to admit. Looked like half the town had showed. But then the old bastard had always been popular, the sort of bloke who volunteered for church functions and charities. The hole yawned deep and dark, a gaping wound or the earth's last swallow. Ma was sobbing openly beside him as they lowered the coffin. He put his arm around her and she cried into his shoulder. Gus was on the other side, looking confused and embarrassed. She pulled herself together as the sexton passed over the spade. Jones reached out but she shook her head and took it herself. The shovel of dirt dumped on the lid with the dull thud of a broken drum. She handed the spade to Jones and stood back. He did his duty mechanically: no sense, no feeling. Not relief, not even guilt. He was just filling in the corners of his life, burying the past.

When it was finally over he escorted her through the smother of sympathisers and unctuous platitudes and the relieved condolences of those who were only too glad that today did not belong to them. At the car she opened the door but would not get in.

"It's just that it was so sudden," she shook her head and looked back across the cemetery, "How could he have been so selfish?"

Jones could not answer her. Death by misadventure had been the verdict handed down by the coroner. The gun had gone off while he was cleaning it. The third commonest form of death by firearms, Jones had informed her, next to hunting accidents, and suicide. He glanced away.

"I had a talk to the DVA counsellor," she continued. "She said it might have been the arrival of the baby. Sometimes innocence triggers guilt."

Bloody idiot, thought Jones, why on earth couldn't the meddling cow have stuck to the official line? "Perhaps it's just time to let go?" he proffered.

She shook her head and lapsed into silence.

*

She spoke to him at the wake, sat in a corner out of the way of the eddying throng. He had never known her to drink, but she held a glass in her hand this day.

"He was a hard man," she said softly, her voice flat, empty and wrung out, "But a good one," she continued.

Of course he had not seen that. She, of course was biased.

"I know what you're thinking," she said, "Never speak ill of the dead?" She paused and stared off into space. "You realise don't you that I knew him before he won the lottery and got called up? He was never the same when he came back. He'd never talk about it either. But some of the other wives knew, and they talked. Some women and kids got killed; partly the Americans fault, partly ours. Of course it was war, but I don't think Clem could forgive himself. When he came back, he said he wanted kids, but I couldn't have any, or so we thought. So he said that's OK, we could give some kids a home that really needed one. It was his way of trying to make up for what happened over there, I suppose. He was willing to foster a whole bunch, but you were such hard work, it put me off!"

Jones was almost offended by this condemnation, but decided the occasion was not one that deserved retaliation.

"Do you remember anything, you know, before you came to us?" she asked out of the blue.

It was Jones's turn to stare off into space now. "I think I remember my mother," he hazarded, "asleep on the bed. But sometimes I wonder if it was just my imagination?"

"They said she'd been dead for two days when they found you," she stated bluntly, "You were curled up on the bed beside her." She stared straight at him. "There were some rumours of problems at the institute they sent you to. Do you remember anything from there?"

He shook his head deliberately. "Nothing. It's a complete blank," he muttered finally. "What do you mean, rumours?" There was something in her tone.

"There was some talk of abuse," she said matter of factly, almost a throwaway line, "Probably just nasty gossip. I had no time for it. It's all in the past now," she subsided into an angry silence.

"What did Dad think about it?" he wondered out loud.

"They couldn't place you, said you were too difficult," she avoided the question, "The superintendent didn't want to let you go, but Clem insisted. The super died soon after, and they closed the place down. So we couldn't have returned you even if we'd wanted!" Her tone was beginning to grate on him now.

"I used to wake up with him in the bed with me," he said, "I remember that!"

"Who, the super?" she asked, completely throwing him.

"No, Dad of course. But you knew that!" he accused her.

"You used to have nightmares, proper screaming fits," she retorted, "I couldn't handle it. I was working in those days.

But Dad used to climb in bed with you and cuddle you. You used to both cry yourselves to sleep."

"Both of us?" he asked in confusion.

She nodded into the distance, reliving old memories. "I asked him about it once. 'Tears for the dead' was all he'd say. It must have been bad, whatever it was he'd been involved in. He was not a man to show emotion."

No, thought Jones, he was surely not.

Tilly was on her way over, loaded down as usual.

"I just don't know what I'll do without him," Ma moaned softly, "We were together so long, he was my life."

She turned away and noticed the baby in her daughter-in-law's arms. Her face was suddenly wreathed in smiles.

"Here's my bonny boy," she crooned.

"Yep," said Jones, "and you can help him grow into a fine young man."

He looked out of the window to the skyline, and wondered if the stink of Mulligan's corruption had been discovered yet over the distant horizon. Even if it had, it would now doubtless only be buried along with Campbell, another fine officer killed in the line of duty. It had seemed the line of least resistance at the time, an explanation that satisfied everybody and offended none: none that mattered, that was. Here at least he could try to clear the air. The smell only lingered in the memory. Today could be a clean slate if only he could reconcile himself to the past.

It was good to be home free. Tomorrow could be the future's child, innocent once more. Only time would tell, and he had plenty of that. Although he had only just left it, he decided to visit his foster-father's grave on the way back.

He had finally realised something; he owed him an apology.

www.ingramcontent.com/pod-product-compliance
Lightning Source LLC
Chambersburg PA
CBHW021324250626
47155CB00002B/609